Chrissie Manby

three days in Florence

HODDER

First published in Great Britain in 2019 by Hodder & Stoughton
An Hachette UK company

1

Copyright © Chrissie Manby 2019

A CIP catalogue record for this title is available from the British
Library

Paperback ISBN 9781473682955
eBook ISBN 9781473682962

Typeset in Sabon MT by
Palimpsest Book Production Ltd, Falkirk, Stirlingshire

Printed and bound in Great Britain by Clays Ltd, Elcograf S.p.A.

Hodder & Stoughton policy is to use papers that are natural,
renewable and recyclable products and made from wood grown
in sustainable forests. The logging and manufacturing processes
are expected to conform to the environmental regulations
of the country of origin.

Hodder & Stoughton Ltd
Carmelite House
50 Victoria Embankment
London EC4Y 0DZ

www.hodder.co.uk

For Victoria Routledge

Chapter One

Italy was a place of legend for Kathy Courage. Her middle name was Florence: her mother had fallen in love with the Renaissance city, which she had visited with Kathy's father on their honeymoon, and insisted on naming their daughter in its honour.

As a child, Kathy had loved to hear her mother Clare's stories about that long-ago romantic holiday. Not so much about the fabulous architecture, the frescoes and statues back then, but about the ice creams as big as a baby's head – 'and so many flavours' – the endless spaghetti, and the glamorous Italian ladies who carried small fluffy dogs in their Ferragamo handbags. Often Kathy's mother would get out the honeymoon photograph album and together they would marvel at the joys of *la dolce vita*. So different from life in the Essex suburbs where Kathy had grown up.

Kathy's favourite photograph was one of her parents standing together beneath the giant replica statue of Michelangelo's *David* in the piazza della Signoria. Her mother, with her flicked-up hair-do – 'very fashionable then' – was wearing a red dress with white spots that showed off her tiny waist. Kathy's father, Eddie, sported a hat – a sharp-looking Panama that he'd bought from a street vendor. It was the only time Kathy had ever seen him in a hat other than the grey knitted beanie he sometimes wore for the office commute in winter.

Her parents looked so young and so happy that Kathy became convinced of the power of sunshine and good ice cream.

Kathy's mother always promised that one day she would take her to Italy – 'when you're old enough to appreciate it'. For various reasons that moment had never come and, somehow, Kathy had never found her way to Italy on her own. As an adult she could in theory have gone anywhere any time she wanted, but over the years Florence had grown to occupy such a special place in the Courage family mythology that it would not have seemed right for Kathy to go there for the first time alone. It was a city she wanted to share with someone special, just as her mum and dad had shared it on their honeymoon all those years ago.

So, when David, younger brother of Kathy's long-term boyfriend Neil, had announced that he and his fiancée Shelley were getting married in Tuscany, Kathy was over the moon. She might get to see Florence at last.

Shelley and Dave outlined the plan over Sunday lunch with his and Neil's mother, Margaret.

'We went for a destination wedding,' said Shelley, 'so that people can combine it with a holiday.'

'If they've got time for a holiday,' said Neil, who worked as a corporate lawyer.

'We chose the Thursday before the bank-holiday weekend for the wedding day itself so you wouldn't have to take many days off to make a whole week of it,' Shelley continued.

'It sounds wonderful,' said Kathy, who was very fond of Shelley and Dave.

'I'll have to see what's in my schedule,' Neil muttered.

'Neil,' Dave looked upset, 'you're my brother. You've got to be there. And so have the children. Shelley wants both my nieces as bridesmaids.'

Sophie and Amelie, Neil's teenage daughters, shared a not very subtle look of horror at the thought.

'And Oscar can be ring-bearer if he likes,' Shelley joked.

Oscar, Amelie's twin, did not look up from his phone.

Margaret said, to no one in particular, 'I don't know if Italian food agrees with me.'

'Italian food agrees with everyone,' Shelley insisted, by now on the verge of tears.

Kathy said what she knew Shelley needed to hear. 'It's going to be lovely. I've always dreamed of going to Italy – and for a wedding? How perfect.'

Shelley gave her a grateful smile.

On the way home, Neil and the children continued to come up with reasons why the wedding could only be a disaster.

'It's selfish,' Neil announced. 'And pretentious. Typical of my brother to expect people to fly out to Italy. To stay in a palazzo, for Heaven's sake. It's going to cost a fortune.'

He said this, though Dave had already assured him that he and Shelley would be paying for the whole family's accommodation.

'And it's the same weekend as the Jolly Farmer Festival,' Sophie complained. 'All my friends are going to that.'

Kathy didn't think that would sway Neil. The Jolly Farmer Festival was not, as it sounded, a weekend of agriculture-based activities but a music festival that should have been banned after three drug-taking teenagers had ended up in hospital the previous year.

Seventeen-year-old Amelie groaned. 'I can't believe she wants us to be bridesmaids. I'm not doing it unless I can choose my own dress.'

Oscar didn't look up from his phone.

Did Kathy *really* want to go to the wedding? Neil asked, as they got ready for bed that night. *Of course* she wanted to go. While Neil complained that flying out on the Tuesday to attend the pre-wedding festivities would mean four days away from the office and a lot of inconvenience and catching up for him, Kathy was already planning her mini-break wardrobe and imagining herself standing on the terrace of a Tuscan palazzo, overlooking a splendid garden scented with jasmine and roses.

'Ridiculous to choose a date right before the bank-holiday weekend,' Neil continued. 'The airports are bound to be chaos.'

'But it's perfect timing,' Kathy jumped in. 'If the wedding party officially ends on the Friday morning, we can have three more nights in Italy without you having to take any extra holiday. We could hire a car and go to Siena. Or Montepulciano. Or Pienza. Even better, if you don't feel like driving, we could just spend three days exploring Florence.'

As Kathy said the words, the city shimmered in her mind. At last, at last, she would be visiting her namesake. She and Neil could even recreate the photograph of her mum and dad in front of the statue of *David*. Neil would look good in a hat.

4

'I'm sure the children would enjoy it,' she added hopefully.

In her imagination, Kathy glossed over the fact that Sophie, Amelie and Oscar would be scowling on the sidelines of any photo. Whenever a camera was brandished in their direction, Neil's children conspired to look like three ghosts come to deliver terrible news.

'Oh, Chicken Licken,' Neil sighed, 'it all sounds like way too much bother to me.'

Kathy bristled.

The one downside about having Florence as a middle name was that it rendered Kathy's initials 'KFC'. It was Sophie who had first made the connection with the fried chicken chain and christened her 'Chicken Licken'. Kathy didn't like it – the insinuation that she was cowardly or flat-out stupid stung – but Neil and the three children thought it was all great fun and, alas, the nickname stuck.

'I'll have had four really tough days at the wedding,' Neil continued. 'It isn't going to be a holiday for me. You know what my family's like. My brother. My mother . . . Shelley's lot are even worse.'

'Then all the better reason to tag on three days of pure fun at the end,' said Kathy. 'We'll be in Tuscany anyway. All we have to do is find a nice hotel for three days of chilling out and doing some very gentle sightseeing but mostly eating pasta and *gelato* and drinking Aperol Spritzes in sunny piazzas . . .'

Neil patted his flat-as-an-ironing-board stomach. 'Pasta and *gelato*? I'm watching my weight.' Kathy was sure she caught his eyes flickering to her stomach, which was more waterbed than ironing board, as he said it. Though, technically, Neil had only commented on his own weight, the implication for hers was there in every syllable.

'Well, no pasta or *gelato*, then. Though that would be a pity. We could rack up plenty of steps exploring the city.'

There was nothing Neil liked more than busting through his daily target of twelve thousand steps on the Fitbit. Sometimes, if he was short of steps when he got home from work, he did circuits of the kitchen-diner, pumping his arms as he went. He was wearing a groove in the tiles.

But Neil didn't respond to the enticement of breaking a record. By this point, he was rearranging things in the dishwasher – nobody else in the house ever stacked it to his exacting standards – and Kathy sensed she was losing the argument. She needed to change tack. If she could just get Neil to an 'I'll think about it' rather than a flat 'No', she could do some proper research, find the perfect hotel and persuade him that three extra days in Italy would be a treat rather than a chore.

'You know I've always wanted to go to Florence.' Kathy tried one last time. 'Perhaps if we considered it an early birthday present for me . . .'

She thought that might swing it, offering Neil the chance not to have to think about what to do for her big birthday – she would be forty in a year. Surely that was a win-win. But no.

'I've already been to Florence,' Neil reminded her.

Twenty-five years ago. He'd spent a week in Italy as part of a month-long Interrailing tour of Europe in his gap year.

'And I really wasn't impressed. I don't know why people go on about it,' he continued. 'A few boring old buildings, some dull statues and a lot of overpriced ice cream. Plus, it's full of pickpockets.'

'Oh,' said Kathy.

'So I really don't need to go back. Especially after four stressful days doing Shelley's bidding. Why they can't just get married in Guildford like I did, I do not know.'

Possibly because that wedding in Guildford was an unmitigated disaster. The thought crossed Kathy's mind but she didn't say it out loud. Neil's defunct marriage was a minefield.

'All I'll want to do when this wedding is over is come home and get some decent rest in my own bed. I'll have Melanie book us all onto the last possible flight out and the first possible flight back, on Friday so I can minimise the time I have to spend out of the office and catching up afterwards. I'm dreading it already,' Neil added, as he closed the newly tidied dishwasher with a nod of satisfaction. And that was the end of the conversation.

Kathy didn't give up hope that Neil might be swayed, but the very next day he announced that his *über*-efficient PA Melanie had already executed his orders and got them on the last possible flight out to the wedding and the first flight home. They'd have to get up at six the day after the wedding to get to the airport. Kathy knew that Sophie in particular would not be happy about that.

Kathy was disappointed, of course, but she focused on the good news. She was still going to get three nights in Italy – her first ever trip to the country of her dreams. She would be staying in a grand palazzo with a view of the Tuscan hills – the photographs on the Palazzo Boldrini website were pure Instagrammable perfection.

There would be great food, music and dancing. There would be excursions to Tuscan villages to taste wine and watch artisans decorating ceramics. Kathy had always wanted one of those big painted fruit bowls. There would be lazy hours by the pool and *aperitivi* on a terrace overlooking an olive grove. There would be glorious sunshine. There would also be a whole bunch of Neil's relatives with whom to make painful small-talk but, in Kathy's fantasy, they were firmly out of the picture.

Chapter Two

Now, six months after Shelley and Dave had announced their wedding plans over Sunday lunch, Kathy and Neil were on their way to Tuscany.

Melanie had arranged a minibus for the trip to Gatwick (Kathy had long since given up being offended that Neil didn't seem to trust *her* with any travel plans). They swung by Neil's former family home – now his ex-wife Caroline's house – to pick up the children, who had refused to do anything so helpful as be at Neil's the night before they had to travel. As a result, though it was almost midday, none of them was ready to go when the minibus pulled up outside. Even before the holiday started, Neil and his teens were at daggers drawn.

'I don't even want to go to Italy anyway,' Amelie reminded them loudly.

'I can't believe I've got to miss a festival for this,' Sophie complained.

Oscar didn't look up from his phone. He didn't look up from his phone or say a single word until they were two minutes from Gatwick, at which point he announced, in a wavering voice, 'I think I'm about to be sick.'

Oscar was sick. Kathy had to give the minibus driver fifty quid to deal with it. Neil argued that a cleaning fee should be included in the original fare. It wasn't as though Oscar was drunk, he pointed out. He was *travel sick* and probably as a result of the cabbie's appalling driving. But Kathy knew that, as far as the driver was concerned, vomit was vomit, however it came about, and if she didn't pay up, they would never get into the terminal.

The terminal was where it could all go wrong. Mindful of past airport traumas, Kathy corralled Neil's children while Neil gave the minicab driver a piece of his mind through the dark tinted glass of the driver's window.

'I'll report you for that too!' Neil informed him. 'This glass is illegal. You're supposed to be able to see the driver of any vehicle.'

Kathy wasn't sure that was true but she stayed out of it. She looked at her watch. They still had two hours before the flight took off. That should be long enough to get through security with minimum stress. She scanned the horizon for signs that would lead them to the departures lounge. She speed-read a board full of flight numbers and had a route straight to the check-in desk worked out before Neil took the steering bar of the luggage trolley.

Kathy led her group through the terminal with the determination and expertise of a soldier ant, steering them past potential dangers such as slow-moving pensioners.

'Shouldn't be allowed to travel!' Neil tutted.

Or fast-moving toddlers.

'Ought to be on a lead.'

At security, Kathy made a lightning calculation as to which was the fastest-moving queue. She yanked Oscar into it before he blundered into a retractable barrier. His eyes were still on his phone. When Sophie went into a small meltdown over the prospect of verrucae, having been told to take off her enormous clunky trainers, Kathy handed over her own sandals so that she didn't have to walk barefoot over the sticky mat under the security arch.

'Have you got a verruca?' Sophie asked, in lieu of saying 'thank you'.

Then, when Amelie set off the X-ray machine with a belly-button piercing that her father didn't yet know about, Kathy told Neil, 'It's probably her bra,' and quickly ushered him forwards so that he couldn't see Amelie flashing her tum for the guards.

Over the next hour and a half in the departures lounge, while Neil scrolled through work emails (and watched reruns of great Fulham FC goals), Kathy dropped eighty pounds in Ted Baker and Accessorize. Not for herself but on Sophie and Amelie, who both insisted that the clothes they were wearing smelt of Oscar's puke. Oscar didn't seem to mind wearing his own puke-scented hoodie, thank goodness.

Then both the girls claimed to have forgotten their make-up.

'We need to get some here,' they told Kathy. 'We don't know what they'll have in Italy. It'll be the wrong colour.'

As far as Kathy could tell, Amelie and Sophie were always wearing the wrong make-up colours, but she couldn't be bothered to disagree. That was another forty quid down.

Then they started arguing about which of them actually owned the ridiculously expensive primer of which there had been just one tube left in the store.

'Can't you share it?' Kathy suggested.

They looked at her aghast.

Meanwhile, Oscar and Neil kept their eyes on their phones.

By the time Kathy heard the boarding announcement, she was beginning to wonder if she shouldn't try to sneak onto the flight to Málaga that was boarding from the adjacent gate.

'I shouldn't be here,' said a little voice in her mind.

She shook her head, which caused Sophie and Amelie to share one of their patent she's-gone-cuckoo looks. Ignoring them, Kathy promised herself this was the last time she would find herself in this situation. When they got back from Italy, she was going to address what had happened and make a plan for the future that took *her* feelings and dreams into account. For now, though, she had a wedding to attend.

'Are you all right?' Neil asked her.

'Yes,' she lied. 'And you?'

Chapter Three

The flight went reasonably well. Providence put them near the front of the plane so the chances of Neil being upset by someone taking too long to put something in an overhead locker were considerably reduced. The three children sat in one row. Neil and Kathy were across the aisle. Neil took the window seat while Kathy sat in the middle. Neil hated to have to sit next to someone he didn't know. He took one of Kathy's armrests. A portly male stranger took the other. Kathy kept herself small and concentrated on her book. It was only a short-haul flight, after all.

She had picked up *The Magic of Jasmine* back in March, when the thought of this trip still filled her with excitement. The paperback's summery cover seemed to embody everything she'd hoped for back then. Warmth, relaxation, romance. It was about a woman called Jane, who had given up her important job in finance to become a simple farmer in Tuscany.

'Nothing is impossible,' the book enthused. 'If you want something enough, you can make it happen. You can live your dream.'

Hmm, thought Kathy. If you don't give a toss about anyone else. Perhaps Jane the-financier-turned-farmer didn't have a mother, widowed for the past twenty years, who needed her within an hour's drive. Or a partner with an important job and three children firmly tying him to London. Kathy snuck a glance at Neil's profile. He was enjoying the view of southern England in the sunshine as they took off.

The flight landed on time and disembarked promptly. The Italian border guards waved Neil, Kathy and the twins through with a smile, though they lingered on Sophie's passport for far longer than necessary, Neil thought. Kathy assured him that it was random and not lecherous before he picked a fight.

Melanie had arranged for a fancy car to pick them up at the airport in Florence, of course. The only problem was that she had not told the taxi firm she needed a car big enough for five and the driver would only take four.

After much outrage on Neil's part – which did not increase the size of the vehicle – it was decided that Kathy should follow in an ordinary taxi. She didn't mind. The trip wasn't long and she relished having a moment to herself, without the girls fighting, Neil griping and Oscar moping. She needed a moment to prepare herself for walking into the Palazzo Boldrini, for acting suitably pleased for Shelley and Dave, for seeing Neil's mother . . . She was pleased for Shelley and Dave but she definitely needed time to prepare for meeting Neil's mum, whose past opening gambits had included such gems as 'You're looking tired' and 'I feel like I've seen that coat a few times now.'

In the back of the taxi, with no air-con, Kathy could relax. She wound down the window and enjoyed the warmth. If only she could ask the driver to stop at a bar where she might get a cold beer and listen to Italian rock music for half an hour. She knew, however, that

Neil would be checking every couple of minutes that the taxi was still behind the air-conditioned limo he was sharing with his kids. If she stopped, he would notice and come back for her.

He sent her a text message: *Are you safe?*

It was a little late for that. Kathy was tempted to text back, *I'm being abducted.* Instead she typed, *I'm safe. Still right behind you. See you at the hotel.* It wouldn't have been fair to tease when he was showing concern.

In the late afternoon the mini convoy arrived at the Renaissance palazzo turned hotel that Dave and Shelley had chosen for their wedding. As Kathy's driver swung his car between two huge stone gateposts topped with lions rampant, he announced their arrival: 'Welcome to the Palazzo Boldrini.'

Kathy gasped with delight at her first glimpse of the vast white building with crenellated towers, which was to be home for the next three nights. A flag, featuring lions to match the beasts on the gateposts, fluttered from one of the turrets. A slightly smaller flag, with the initials of the bride and groom, fluttered from another.

Neil and his children piled out of their car. Amelie looked as though she had been crying. Sophie was jabbing angrily at her phone. Oscar clearly hadn't looked up from his. He tumbled from the car and staggered straight to a flowerbed to throw up again. Neil went on ahead into the palazzo.

Leaving Neil's teens to bicker and puke – thinking, Not my circus, not my monkeys – Kathy walked from her taxi to the edge of the driveway, wanting to savour the view. The palazzo was right at the top of a hill. Below, the Tuscan countryside unrolled like a patchwork blanket of peaceful olive greens and lavender blues, embroidered here and there with imperial cypresses and umbrella pines. It was so perfect, so much like a photo on a postcard, that Kathy wanted to clap with delight.

'My village,' said the taxi driver, drawing Kathy's attention to a cluster of honey-coloured houses nestled in the valley, turning golden in the last of the sun.

'What a beautiful place to live.' Kathy sighed.

The driver beamed with pride.

When he left her alone again, Kathy gave herself a quick pep talk. 'I'm here for Shelley. I'm going to enjoy myself. I'm not even going to think about last week until I'm back in London. I'm just not.'

Having taken in the view and sucked in a lungful of clean Tuscan air, Kathy joined Neil and the children at Reception. He was leaning against the desk, tapping his foot on the polished tiled floor, while a young woman took their passport details. The children were given keys to their rooms in the modern annex. Sophie and Amelie would be sharing.

'How does that work?' Sophie complained. She jabbed a finger at Oscar. 'He's her twin.'

'You have a room in the old building,' the receptionist said to Kathy and Neil.

'I hope it's got decent plumbing,' said Neil. He tapped his foot a little faster while the woman searched out their key, which was a real old-fashioned key, not one of the modern cards she'd handed to the children. It had an enormous wooden fob to boot.

'You'll have to carry this,' said Neil, passing it straight to Kathy.

Kathy hoped that once they were inside the room Neil might finally begin to relax. In his professional life, he was renowned for being cool, calm and collected. Out of the office, when his perfectionist tendencies met with the incompetence – as he saw it – of the general public, he could be a pain in the arse. After five years, Kathy was used to it but she wished that, just for once, Neil could be a little more chilled out about travelling.

A porter carried their cases upstairs to the first floor – the *piano nobile* – where the palazzo's grandest rooms were situated. Hand-painted signs pointed to a library, a music room and two guest suites. Their bedroom was called the Dante Suite.

Kathy was thrilled by the suite, which had floor-to-ceiling windows looking out over the valley to the back of the building. It was one of the bedrooms she had admired on the website. One of the best in the place. Dave must really love his big brother to have allocated him such a good room.

'Look at the view,' she said. In the formal garden directly below, the roses were in full bloom. She couldn't wait to go outside and walk among them. She would have flung the windows wide, but they were a little stiff and took some effort to budge. And when she did manage it, Neil said, 'Don't open them now, Chicken Licken. This is exactly the time of day when mosquitoes come out. The last thing I want is to get bitten.'

Kathy agreed that would be 'sub-optimal', as Neil liked to say, so she wrestled the windows shut again, contenting herself with looking out through the glass, which was wavy and uneven with age.

Neil lay down on the neatly made bed, still wearing his shoes and tapping on his phone. Kathy kicked off hers to lie down beside him.

'Isn't this lovely?' she said. 'It's exactly as I imagined it would be. Look. There are swallows painted on the ceiling.'

Neil glanced up but then something else caught his eye. Something floating in the air between the painted ceiling and his face. He pulled off one of his shoes and made a swipe at it, almost rolling off the bed in the process.

'See? What did I tell you, Chicken? There's a mosquito in here already. For crying out loud!'

He got the Jungle Formula from his overnight bag and sprayed it so liberally that Kathy thought she might choke to death. The mosquito kept flying regardless.

Chapter Four

Within half an hour of arriving, Kathy, Neil and the children were expected on the palazzo's pool terrace for the first formal event of the wedding.

The pool was gorgeous. Long enough for proper laps and illuminated for the evening with underwater lights that changed colour to the music on the terrace speakers, it could not have looked more inviting.

While Neil scanned the crowd for his close relatives, Kathy took a glass of Prosecco from a silver tray. As she sipped, London seemed satisfactorily far away. Shame that the same couldn't have been said for Neil's mother. Kathy spotted Margaret on the other side of the pool, holding court from a sun lounger, regarding the comings and goings as though she'd smelt something bad.

'This is all a bit fancy, isn't it?' Neil said, as he rejoined Kathy at the pool's edge.

It really was. The terrace was decorated like a spread in a travel magazine. Shelley and Dave had hired a wedding planner who'd organised a roster of events worthy of a corporate retreat, let alone a small family marriage.

Kathy knew something of the timetable, having spoken to Shelley often over the past few months with regard to Sophie and Amelie's bridesmaid duties. Kathy had been cast in the role of *de facto* mother since

Caroline, Neil's ex, and his brother Dave did not speak. Caroline would not have lifted a manicured finger to help her ex-brother-in-law's wedding run smoothly.

It was Kathy who had had to drive the girls to and from various rendezvous at Bluewater, where Shelley cajoled them through a number of miserable trying-on sessions in various shops and department stores. Both Sophie and Amelie had very strong ideas about what they were willing to wear. It had to be from Pretty Little Thing. It had to be skin tight. And it had to be in 'nude pink' – a colour more like sticking plaster – which flattered no one unless they were perma-tanned. Fortunately, both Sophie and Amelie, though they were redheads with skin that was naturally the colour of milk, were fake-tanned to a shade of American walnut varnish at all times.

Poor Shelley had planned for her colour scheme to incorporate all the colours of a Tuscan spring, which would have looked lovely had the girls agreed to the flattering shade of pale green Shelley wanted them to wear. Their dogged insistence on dressing as though they were ballroom dancers who'd forgotten to put dresses over their body stockings had changed the plan somewhat.

On that first evening, Sophie and Amelie came down to the poolside dressed like . . . well . . .

'Hookers!' was the first thing Neil's ancient uncle Tony said upon seeing them. 'I thought Dave was supposed to have got that out of the way on his stag do.'

'These are your great-nieces, Uncle Tony,' Neil reminded him.

Uncle Tony's dementia had robbed him of his ability

to be appropriate, though Kathy suspected he'd never been all that appropriate to begin with. While Amelia and Sophie scowled and huffed, and Oscar kept his eyes on his phone, Kathy sought out the bride.

Shelley was crouching between Neil's mum and her own, on their sun loungers.

'Did you have a good journey?' Shelley asked.

'Yes,' Kathy said, before Neil could begin his litany of all the reasons why they hadn't. 'This place is beautiful,' she continued.

'I'm glad you think so.'

'It's like something out of a fairy tale. Thank you so much for inviting us.'

'I've been bitten,' Margaret announced, apropos nothing.

'It's a matter of time before I am,' said Neil.

Kathy greeted her. 'Hello, Margaret. How lovely to see you.'

'When did you buy that dress?' Margaret asked. 'Not recently by the look of things.'

Kathy was suddenly conscious that it was a little tight over the hips.

'It's a beautiful dress,' said Shelley's mother, Elaine.

'For someone younger, perhaps,' said Margaret, as though Kathy wasn't there.

Fortunately, before Margaret could say anything else, they were distracted by the sound of feedback from a microphone. Shelley joined her fiancé on a little stage to greet their guests officially. Dave wasn't used to public speaking and Margaret rolled her eyes at her younger son's ineptitude as he struggled to get the microphone to work. In the end, he gave up.

'Can you hear me?' he asked his audience.

Margaret shook her head and said, 'No,' although Kathy thought Dave was doing perfectly well. Margaret should turn up her hearing aid.

'On behalf of myself and my future wife . . .' Shelley beamed '. . . we'd like to thank you for coming all the way to Italy to celebrate our wedding.'

'I've been bitten again,' Margaret muttered close to Kathy's ear. 'I don't know what Shelley was thinking. A foreign wedding . . . Insects, strange food. I bet we're miles away from the nearest hospital if somebody's allergic . . . I know this wasn't my David's idea.'

'It means a great deal to us both to have all of you here together,' Dave continued on stage. 'All our favourite people in one place. We look forward to making some happy memories with you.'

Then he stepped back.

'Was that it?' Neil asked. 'Was that the whole speech?'

'I expect he's saving himself for the wedding day,' said Kathy.

'I hope he does better than that.'

Kathy smiled faintly. As an only child, she didn't always understand why Neil and Dave were such bitter rivals. She suspected that Margaret had played them off against each other since they were small. She certainly did now. Every Mother's Day, birthday and Christmas turned into a bitter competition. Which of her boys had sent the better card or the bigger bouquet? Although Margaret had expressed nothing but disapproval of this Italian wedding, Kathy knew that, once everyone was back in the UK, its extravagance would be held up as evidence of how well Dave – a tech geek, who developed trading software for financial institutions – was doing in comparison to Neil, plodding along as a partner at his medium-sized City law firm.

Now that the speech was over, waiting staff began to circle with canapés. Neil was soon deep in conversation with his mother. Kathy reintroduced herself to a couple of Neil's cousins, who called her by his ex's name. Caroline had studied to be a lawyer – she and Neil met when they were training – but had given up her career to have her children. When the children started school, she had retrained as an image consultant. Her skill at combining colours and fabrics was spoken of in terms of awe.

Kathy had been made redundant from her admin job in March and was still looking for something else to do – or, at least, something else to talk about. Not that she didn't have enough to fill her days, what with looking after Neil and, one week in every two, his children. Actually, his children seemed to be around more and more, since their mother had moved her new lover, a tennis coach, into the family home. Neil had commented that Caroline didn't need to shack up with anyone with a proper job since she'd taken more than half of Neil's money.

'How are you, Caroline?' one of Neil's aunts asked now. 'How's the fashion business?'

Kathy didn't correct her, knowing the aunt didn't care anyway. 'I'm very well,' she said. 'And the fashion business is absolutely fab.'

That evening's reception did not go late. Dinner – a buffet arrangement with freshly made pizza – was over by half past nine, ending with another short address by Dave, during which he asked 'the younger guests in particular' to refrain from skinny-dipping. The wedding party would be fined a hundred euros for anyone caught in the pool after 8 p.m. 'If you get caught,' he added, with a wink.

'Urgh!' Sophie and Amelie chimed. Oscar did not look up from his phone.

Neil was not in the mood for skinny-dipping.

Back in the bedroom, he filled Kathy in on the family politics that had passed her by. Shelley's half of the party was full of 'people who don't know how to behave'. Apparently Shelley's brother kept mentioning his new car. Shelley's younger sister claimed her necklace was worth five grand. Neil's own cousin, Jeff, had attracted his ire by pointing out that they were wearing the same watch, but since Jeff had bought his entry-level Rolex at Duty Free in Zürich, he'd saved enough on the retail price Neil had paid to get himself some matching cufflinks. Kathy didn't understand why Neil got so upset about the showing off. He was doing perfectly well and could have shown off with the best of them (indeed, probably did). It was touching, in some way, that he couldn't seem to let it wash over him. The little boy who'd grown up in a council house in Wolverhampton, determined to prove himself, was never far from the surface when his family was around.

Halfway through his diatribe, Neil leaped out of bed with such haste that Kathy wondered if he'd heard someone trying to break into their room. He snapped on the overhead light.

'There is a bloody mosquito in here!' he exclaimed.

He armed himself with one of Kathy's shoes and Kathy duly joined him in searching every inch of the room for the tiny critter. Even with four pairs of eyes on the job, they didn't find it. However, as soon as Neil decided they should go back to bed, the high pitched whining started anew. The light went back on. They got out of bed. The mosquito stayed out of sight. They went back to bed.

'Buzzzzz.'

Neil turned the light on. They got out of bed.

And it carried on like that until well after two in the morning.

Chapter Five

The next morning, Kathy and Neil joined the rest of the family for breakfast. A vast buffet had been laid out on the terrace. Piled high with fruit, charcuterie and cheese, the table was as beautiful as a still-life painting. Still Sophie complained that she could find nothing that fitted with her gluten-free vegan diet (apart from a chocolate croissant – she totally ignored the fruit). Then Amelie complained that Sophie had kept her awake all night, Skyping her boyfriend. He was at the festival and she needed to be in contact with him at all times to make sure he wasn't cheating on her, she explained. Oscar didn't look up from his phone as he mechanically stuffed three pastries into his mouth.

Shelley joined them, eager to talk about plans for the day ahead. That day – Wednesday or 'Wedding Eve' as Shelley called it – minibuses had been booked to take the guests on a couple of excursions. Dave was having a last-minute stag do for the male guests, with wine tasting following by paintballing in a nearby forest. The 'ladies' were invited to join a trip to the Mall – a nearby designer retail outlet, where all the big labels could be had for a song. Sophie and Amelie's eyes lit up while Kathy felt her credit-card wilt at the very idea. She knew that the girls saw her as an extension of their father's wallet.

'The outlet bus leaves in an hour,' Shelley said. 'Nine o'clock. Don't be late!'

There was no way Amelie and Sophie would be late to go shopping.

With an hour to kill, Kathy decided she'd spend half of it catching up on the sleep she'd missed, thanks to Neil's all-night battle with the mozzie. She'd dared not suggest that if you thought hard enough about mosquitoes you'd always hear one, even if you were in a hermetically sealed bunker three thousand miles from the nearest breeding ground.

Now, with Neil out of the way – the paintballing bus had already gone – Kathy turned off the air-conditioning and lay down on the bed. It didn't take long before the room started to warm to something approaching actual room temperature. She set the alarm on her phone for half an hour. Alas, she forgot to turn it on. When she woke up, it was already 9.05.

'Arse!'

Kathy grabbed her bag and her floppy sunhat and cantered down the stone staircase to the palazzo's lobby. It was ominously empty. She burst through the big doors into the sunlight. Likewise, no one was standing outside on the driveway from where the minibus to the outlet was due to depart.

Because it had already departed.

'They've gone,' said the hotel manager, who rushed out to join her on the gravel. 'I could arrange for a taxi to take you. You'll catch them up. I'll call right now.'

'No,' Kathy said at once. 'No. That would be far too much effort.'

'It would not be charged to the wedding,' the manager assured her.

'There really is no need.'

'I thought I'd made sure everyone was on the bus.' The manager seemed worried. 'I must sort this out.'

'Please don't,' Kathy insisted.

'But there's no one else here.'

No one? Really? Not even Margaret? She was a little miffed that none of the women in Neil's family had bothered to find out where she was before they'd set off on their shopping spree but Kathy felt a smile spread over her whole body. Apart from the staff, she had the palazzo entirely to herself.

'You don't want to be with your party?' the manager persisted.

Kathy reassured him: 'Absolutely not.'

Kathy spent the rest of the morning pleasing herself. After taking coffee in the rose garden, which was infinitely more pleasant without a soundtrack of Neil's relatives sniping about foreign food and blood-sucking insects, she had a swim in the pool. She would never have dared go near it if Sophie and Amelie were still around, but with no one to pass judgement on her ancient swimming cozzie, or the 'ancient' body inside it, she felt like the luckiest woman on earth.

She had a whole swimming pool to herself under the glorious heat of the Tuscan sun. She'd never had a pool to herself before. After three lengths – which felt like plenty – she leaned against the edge, with her forearms on the warm limestone flags and the rest of her body in the cool water. She listened to the hum of the industrious bees in the lavender planted all around.

Small white butterflies fluttered by, looking like rose petals making an escape on the wind. Swallows played above her head. Occasionally, one would dive-bomb the other end of the pool for a sip of the azure water or to scoop a hapless insect off its surface. Kathy could imagine nothing more perfect than that moment. This was *la dolce vita*. For a little while she could forget the sadness and anger – yes, anger – of the past seven days.

At lunchtime, the hotel manager had the kitchen staff lay a table for her in the garden, this time in the shade of a thousand-year-old olive tree. Kathy chose a melon, prosciutto and rocket salad. The bread that came with it was addictive, sticky with olive oil and wickedly salty. Kathy ate the lot. Then she had pasta – *pici*, the local speciality, a sort of chubby spaghetti – in tomato and basil sauce. She also had a cheeky glass of Chianti and a bitter black coffee with a butter-soft *gianduja* chocolate on the side.

After lunch, Kathy went back to the bedroom to change out of her swimming costume. She'd noticed that, in the short time she'd been out, she'd caught the sun on her shoulders so decided she'd best stay in the shade for a while. She considered a nap but didn't want to waste a minute of her glorious solitude.

There was plenty to explore indoors. On the first floor of the old building, at the opposite end of the corridor to the Dante Suite, a small library was lined with antique red leather-bound books. They were off limits, locked behind glass, but there was a selection of paperbacks left by previous guests, which gave a fairly accurate record of the bestsellers of the past two decades. There were six copies of *Fifty Shades of Grey* in four languages. *The Da Vinci Code* was still hanging in there, at least fifteen years after its publication.

Kathy sat down in a lumpy leather armchair and flicked through a Tuscan travel guide that was only two years out of date. She found the pages on Florence, turned over at the top corner so a traveller could easily find them. The text was underlined in places and someone had added notes. 'Best tagliata of my life!' was the comment beneath one restaurant. 'Don't miss the tiramisu here,' said the note beneath another.

Kathy sighed. She would be missing the *tagliata* and the tiramisu. She would also be missing the Pitti Palace. 'Great costume exhibition,' wrote the traveller who wasn't afraid of scribbling in books. And the natural history museum. 'Weird-shaped stuffed animals but Joshua loved it.'

'Lucky Joshua,' Kathy murmured.

The guidebook also contained photographs of the most popular paintings in the Uffizi Gallery. Kathy was familiar with most of them. Botticelli's *Primavera* and *Birth of Venus* featured, of course, but there was one painting Kathy didn't recognise.

It was called *Doni Tondo* and was by Michelangelo. The subject of the painting was the Madonna and Child, with Joseph, sitting in what looked like a Tuscan garden. The colours were as fresh and bright as if they had been painted the day before. Mary was in bright pink and blue robes, Joseph in blue and gold. The baby Jesus was pictured at about a year old with gorgeous brown curls. A crowd of cherubs looked on. The composition, in its round gold frame, was beautiful. But it was the face of the Madonna that really touched Kathy's heart.

Michelangelo's Madonna could not have been more

different from the stiff, flat-faced Madonnas Kathy had seen in the backgrounds of her parents' honeymoon photos. She was so very real. Her pose was so natural. She sat on the ground with a book open in her lap. Joseph leaned over her. The Madonna was turning towards the Child, whom Joseph held up over her shoulder. Her arms looked safe and strong.

'It's hard to tell whether Mary is giving Jesus back to Joseph or taking the baby from him,' said the accompanying text by an art expert. 'Looking at her face, which seems a bit annoyed to me, I like to think she's passing the baby Jesus to her husband so she can have some well-earned me-time.'

Catching snatches of their conversation over the past day, Kathy knew that 'me-time' was a preoccupation for many of the women at the wedding. None of them seemed to think they had enough.

Looking at the painting in the book, Kathy liked to think that the Madonna was taking the baby into her arms. His chubby little limbs were irresistible. A sharp prick of envy hurt Kathy's chest as she thought about it and she felt a familiar ache behind her eyes. 'Not now,' she chided herself, as she closed the book.

From the library, Kathy padded along the corridor to the other public room she had yet to see. The door was ajar. She leaned against the jamb and peered in. This was the music room.

In the centre of the parquet floor was a grand piano. Beside it stood a harp, draped in a white cotton sheet to keep off the dust. In front of it, a small collection of music stands stood in disarray, as though waiting for the return of a choir that had left in a hurry.

Kathy stepped inside. The piano was open. There was a music book already on the stand. It was a tattered old collection of Chopin's waltzes, carefully annotated with finger positions and other instructions in Italian and in English.

Kathy played a single note – middle C – then looked around as though expecting someone to tell her off. She'd had piano lessons as a child – at the behest of her father, who was self-taught – but she'd never played a grand before. And this one was a Bösendorfer. Thanks to her dad, Kathy knew it was an expensive instrument.

She made a calculation. There was no one in the palazzo but the people who worked there, which meant no one was around who knew or cared who Kathy was and might use her clunky playing to embarrass her later on. It had been a very long time since Kathy had sat at any piano and she wasn't sure she still remembered what to do but she settled on the worn dusty pink velvet stool and gently placed her hands on the keyboard. The white keys were yellowed and cracked with age but this was a piano that had been well loved. And was still well loved. As Kathy played a tentative scale, she could hear at once that the notes were perfectly in tune and true.

Kathy tried a little Chopin – the music book was open at a waltz she thought she knew – but she soon remembered why she'd found Chopin so difficult. Chopin had enormous hands that could span ten notes at a time. Kathy's were rather smaller. Instead she tried some tunes she knew she could play and was astonished to discover that the memories of all the pieces she'd learned as a child were still in the tips of her fingers.

Debussy's *Clair de lune* reminded her of her mother,

who always requested it. Erik Satie's *Gymnopédie* took her back to practising for her grade-four exam one long hot summer. Joplin's *The Entertainer* reminded her of her dad, who liked to play music to get the feet tapping and the heart singing along. She tried a few bars of that and could almost see her father standing at the end of the piano, nodding in approval.

While Kathy was playing, she lost track of time. The self-consciousness she'd felt as she played the first note soon melted away, and it wasn't long before she was humming to her own accompaniment. Then she was actually singing. She played songs she'd sung in the school choir. She'd loved to sing once upon a time. Still loved to, when no one was listening . . .

Chapter Six

Kathy did not know how long she had been playing when she was suddenly aware that someone was standing behind her.

'Don't stop,' he said, when she turned to see him – a dark-haired man, leaning against the doorframe, his arms folded.

Kathy immediately stopped halfway through a phrase and, her hands still hovering over the keys, started to apologise. 'I'm sorry. I'm probably not supposed to have touched this, am I? I didn't see a sign . . .'

'It's a piano,' the man said. 'It's meant to be played.' He unfolded his arms, which immediately made him look friendlier, and walked into the room. He was tall but obviously at ease with his long legs. He had a grace to him. In his loose white shirt and black trousers, he looked like he might break into flamenco.

The man was about Kathy's age. Late thirties or early forties. Though he looked thoroughly Italian, with his wild black hair and smooth olive skin, his English was perfectly accented. His name, too, was a portmanteau of the two cultures.

'Henry Innocenti,' he said, holding out his hand to her.

Kathy shook it. 'Kathy,' she said. 'Kathy Courage.'

'Pleased to meet you. So you're a pianist?'

'I'm out of practice,' she said automatically. She could only hope he hadn't heard her sing.

'It doesn't show.'

Kathy batted the compliment away. 'I've been making a lot of mistakes. It must be fifteen years since I last played.'

'When did you learn?'

'Oh, when I was really small. My father taught me when I was tiny and I had a few formal lessons at school.'

'Snap. My father taught me as well,' Henry said. 'I think if you learn early enough, you never really forget.'

Kathy nodded. She knew she would never forget the happiness she'd felt sitting on the piano stool with her dad while he guided her hands on the keys.

'I haven't seen you here before,' Henry added.

'I haven't been here before. I'm here for the wedding.'

'Ah! Are you the bride? Snatching your last few moments of freedom?'

'What? No,' said Kathy. 'No chance. Always the bridesmaid, me. Though I'm way too old for that this time.'

'Really? Is there a cut-off point?' Henry asked.

'Not exactly but . . .' She thought of Sophie and Amelie, slinking around the London living room in the awful dresses they had chosen for the wedding. She was glad she wouldn't have to stand alongside them.

'Well, I'm the resident minstrel,' Henry said. 'I'm playing at the wedding tomorrow.'

He gave Kathy an extravagant bow and flourished an invisible hat. She imagined it with a plume of feathers, like the hat in the portrait of the Laughing Cavalier.

'Will you be playing this piano?' Kathy asked.

'No, I'll be using an electric keyboard since we're

going to be outside. I'm here to check everything's in place ahead of the big day but I thought I should drop by and say hello to this grand old lady first. I always do. A piano can die from lack of love. I'm very glad to discover I'm not the only person to give her the attention she deserves.'

'She does have a beautiful sound.'

Henry came to stand beside the piano. He rested one hand gently on the polished black lid and looked into the strings. He blew away some dust. 'This piano is very special,' he said. 'It's good enough for a concert hall. It's a shame it's ended up hardly ever being played. That's why I try to play it whenever I have a gig here.'

Leaving the piano for a moment, he opened a painted cabinet in a corner of the room, as casually as if he were in his own house, and pulled out a sheaf of sheet music. Kathy watched as he flipped through it, setting aside a smaller pile of pieces he must have been interested in playing. His profile was serious but rather beautiful. It was a cliché to say it of an Italian, but there was a hint of Michelangelo's *David* in his straight nose and generous mouth.

'Do you ever duet?' he asked suddenly.

'I . . .' Kathy began. 'I mean, I haven't had the opportunity. Not since Dad . . .' The words tailed away.

'Would you like to duet now?'

'I'm not sure I'm good enough.'

'You're good enough. I've been listening to you play.' Henry pulled a book from the pile. 'This is easy enough on a first read-through. You probably know it already. It's one of the first I learned. You take the right hand and I'll take the left.'

Henry moved the Chopin waltzes from the music

stand and replaced them with Hungarian Rhapsody, No. 2 by Franz Liszt. Kathy gawped at the busy staves. If she did know this piece, she couldn't tell by looking.

Henry searched around for another stool or chair he could put at the keyboard. Finding none he said, 'Move up.'

Kathy hesitated.

'I can't play standing. Well, I could but . . .'

Kathy duly shuffled to the right-hand side of the stool. It wasn't a big stool. It would have been cosy for two friends. For two strangers, it was extremely intimate. Sensing Kathy's discomfort, Henry perched one buttock on the left-hand edge, so there was still a little gap between them. All the same, he was now close enough that Kathy could smell his aftershave, which had hints of sandalwood. Luckily she liked it.

'Comfortable?' he asked.

In all sorts of way, no, Kathy thought. Out loud she said, 'I think so.' When she shifted to give him a little more room, the sleeve of his white shirt touched her bare arm and brought her up in goose bumps.

This was all very strange. Was Henry paid to play piano with the guests? Was he the musical equivalent of a tennis pro or one of those chaps who lurk by the edge of the dance-floor, looking for lonely women to partner in a samba?

'Good,' said Henry. 'Your part goes like this.'

He reached across her to play the first few bars at her end of the keyboard. His hands were large – which fitted his height – but somehow still elegant, with long, strong fingers. His nails were neat and clean. The backs of his hands and his forearms were sun-kissed and lightly hairy.

'I think I do know it,' said Kathy, hugely relieved.

'Then have a go.'

'What? Now?'

Henry nodded. This was really happening.

Leaning close to the music, as though that would make it easier to understand, Kathy pecked out the notes that Henry had played with such ease.

'Perfect,' he said, though Kathy knew her rendition had been far from that.

'Now we'll try it together. We'll take it slow to begin with. One, two three . . .'

He counted them in, tapping his foot on the floor in lieu of a metronome.

They managed two whole staves before Kathy made a mistake.

'Sorry,' she said, stopping instantly.

'No need to stop when you make a mistake. Just carry on.'

They started again. This time, Kathy was slightly too slow and the side of her hand touched the side of Henry's as he played up the scale while she was playing down. Kathy whipped hers away.

'Sorry,' she said.

'From the top,' said Henry.

When it happened again, Kathy blushed magenta.

'It's OK,' Henry assured her. 'This is meant to be fun. If it isn't fun . . .'

'No, no, please,' said Kathy. 'It is fun. Let's carry on.'

Henry had Kathy play her own part alone so she could get past the phrase where she always seemed to stumble. His suggestions and instructions were expert. 'I sometimes teach piano to children,' he explained. 'I know what it's like when you keep making the same mistake. It feels like it becomes automatic – ingrained somehow – and then it's harder to fix than ever. So slowly now . . . You're going to get past that bit this time. Break the spell.'

Kathy tap-tapped her way through the sticky part.

"Excellent. Wrists a little higher,' Henry suggested. 'And keep breathing, please. Keep breathing all the time!'

Kathy laughed at that. 'What do you mean? I am breathing.'

'Really? You look still as a statue to me.'

He leaned back a little to get a better look at her. He seemed about to say something but decided against it. 'Take a deep breath,' he said instead. 'Relax, relax! Shake your arms out.'

Kathy wriggled her wrists.

'More vigorously,' Henry said. 'We'll do it together.'

They both stood up and shook out their arms.

'I can't believe we're doing this,' said Kathy.

'What? Playing the piano? Stranger things have happened,' Henry assured her.

They sat down again, carefully preserving the tiny distance between them.

'Good! From the top,' Henry said. 'Faster, this time. And louder. Come on. This bit is meant to be *forte*. *Fortissimo!* Louder! Loud!'

What am I doing? Kathy asked herself, as they played. Really, what am I doing? She was squished up on a piano stool with a man she didn't know. She felt hotter and hotter. She was sure her face must be bright red. She was making a fool of herself.

'I should leave you to play on your own,' she

managed to say, when they finished the piece for the second time.

'No way!' said Henry. 'Do you know how rarely I meet someone I can play with? You're staying here.'

'This is not how I expected to spend my afternoon.'

'It's better, though, isn't it?' he said.

Kathy gave a curt nod.

He was right.

They played the Liszt five or six times over before they got it absolutely spot on. When they did, Kathy assumed that would be the end of their duetting, but Henry said, 'I know exactly what we should play next.'

'No,' Kathy tried to say. 'I've taken up enough of your time.'

Ignoring her, Henry went back to the painted cabinet. 'You'll know this one.' He frisbeed the music across to her.

'"The Arrival of the Queen of Sheba"?'

'You can Handel it,' Henry punned. 'Ever played it?'

'I used to play it with my father.'

'Then this will be great.'

Henry sat back down and soon they were hammering on the keys again. Since this strange man was not going to let her off easily, Kathy decided she should just forget to be self-conscious and play. She should simply enjoy the ride. She'd forgotten the joy of playing with someone else. She'd forgotten the pleasure of those perfect moments when four hands were exactly in time. To be so in tune with someone she'd met only half an hour earlier was, in an odd way, exhilarating. It was like dancing. It was like running down a hill, holding hands. It was bonkers. It was the best fun she'd had in a long time.

When she'd played the last note on a perfect run-through, Kathy rocked back laughing with adrenalin and joy, her hands still on the keyboard. Henry carried on playing a jolly ad lib on the last phrase of the piece, then played his way right over Kathy's fingers to finish with a sonorous dong on the low C.

With their hands still in place, their wrists crossed on the keys, they looked at each other. They were both breathing hard. Henry's brown eyes were crinkled at the edges. Kathy nervously dropped her gaze.

'Well, that was fun,' she said eventually.

'Wasn't it?' said Henry. 'Excellently well played.'

When she looked up again, his eyes upon hers were so genuine and kind that Kathy allowed herself to be convinced he had enjoyed playing with her just as much as she'd enjoyed playing with him. Slowly, they took their hands from the keyboard. While they'd played, they'd moved closer together on the stool too, until their thighs were actually touching. Henry stood up, breaking the connection and the spell, and Kathy smoothed her crumpled linen skirt. Then they both went to speak at the same time.

'I should be getting ready for tonight,' said Kathy, just as Henry said, 'I should be going.'

'I'll leave you to play,' Henry continued. 'You can practise your part for next time.'

'I wish . . . I don't know when I'll next get the chance to play,' Kathy admitted.

'You should make it happen. Thank you. I enjoyed our duet.'

'As did I.'

'As did the piano,' said Henry.

Kathy laid her fingers on the keys again.

'I hope you enjoy the rest of your time here, Queen of Sheba. Remember to keep breathing.'

Henry gave the polished lid of the piano an affectionate pat and wandered off, humming. Kathy watched him go. What a strange but perfectly wonderful encounter.

If Kathy had wanted to carry on playing, it was too late. The clock on her phone said that she and Henry had been playing together for more than an hour and now it was six o'clock.

When she stood up, she saw from the music room's long windows that the coach carrying the stag party from their day of paintballing in the woods was already back. Soon she heard voices echoing round the hallway. They were loud and excited, lots of joshing going on. At any minute, people would come upstairs to their rooms to change for supper. Kathy didn't want any of them to catch her at the keyboard.

She slipped out of the music room and ran along the corridor to the suite she shared with Neil.

'What are you doing here?' Neil asked, when he found Kathy in their bedroom. She was sitting in the chair by the window pretending to read one of the hotel magazines and she knew as soon as she saw him that he was in a bad mood. 'I didn't think the women were back from the shops yet.'

'I don't think they are. I didn't go with them.'

'Why not?'

'I had a headache,' she lied.

'So you just hung around here all day? Chicken

Licken,' he sighed, 'people will wonder where you got to.'

'How was the paintballing?' Kathy asked, to change the subject.

'Bloody painful. I'm not sure paintballing should be called a bonding activity. Too many grudges get played out with what are frankly dangerous weapons. People kept going for the head. Jeff nearly had my eye out. There's no way that shot was an accident either. He was a clay-pigeon champion in his youth.'

Kathy was glad Neil wanted to talk about his day. It saved her having to talk about hers. She didn't think 'I played piano duets with a handsome Italian' would go down awfully well. She felt as shy about it as she might have done had she and Henry had actually spent their time dancing the tango and discovering that their bodies were a perfect fit. That there was a chemistry that might just quickstep off the dance floor . . .

Chapter Seven

The minibus from the outlet returned shortly afterwards. Amelie and Sophie were laden with bags and
hyper with excitement about the contents. Shelley, stepping off the bus right after them, looked haunted.

'We found these great dresses in Gucci,' said Sophie,
'that will look so much better with Shelley's wedding
dress than the things we got from Pretty Little Thing.'

Never mind the bride's plan.

'We'll make it work,' said Shelley.

That evening, dinner was another buffet on the terrace
but this time, instead of music from Dave's iPhone, the
guests were entertained by a proper DJ – a man in his
twenties, with long floppy hair and a multiple piercings.
That seemed to cheer the girls up. Maybe Tuscany
wasn't so boring, after all. In fact, Amelie and Sophie
started the dancing, vying for the handsome DJ's attention. Margaret, sitting with Neil and Kathy, complained
endlessly about the volume. Oscar kept his eyes on his
phone.

After a word from Neil about the age range of the
people present, the DJ put on some music more suitable
for the older crowd. Amelie and Sophie sat down in
disgust. Shelley and Dave took their place, dancing to
the eighties and nineties hits that never seemed to get
old. Kathy tapped her feet in time until she couldn't

bear to sit still any longer. When a song she loved –
Deee-lite's 'Groove Is In The Heart' – came on, she
reached for Neil's hand and asked him to join her in
a spin around the dance-floor. 'Show off your best dad
dancing,' she joked.

'Someone's got to stay with Mum,' he said, as though
getting up to dance would mean having to be a mile
away from his mother. Kathy recognised an excuse
when she heard one. Margaret would have been
perfectly happy to sit at the table with her grandchildren, pursing her lips as they played on their phones
and generally ignored her. It would give her something
else to complain about later.

But Neil still would not dance. Instead he got up to
fetch drinks for himself and his mother, and Kathy
went to dance alone. By the time she got onto the floor,
the song had changed. Now it was 'Tainted Love',
which seemed about right.

As she twirled around on her own, conscious of the
eyes of Sophie and Amelie upon her – critiquing her
style, no doubt – Kathy remembered a time when Neil
had danced because she wanted to and her wanting to
had been a good enough reason.

It was early on in their relationship, when they were
still 'courting', as Neil liked to call it. They'd gone to
a Spanish restaurant and drunk too much Rioja as they
gazed at one another across the table. A live guitarist
was playing. When several of the regulars got up to
dance, Kathy reached for Neil's hands and pulled him
up onto the makeshift dance-floor. He didn't protest.
He wasn't a natural dancer but right then he just wanted
to make her happy. He held her in a slightly awkward
pose and grinned over her head as they rocked from

side to side. But that was fine. Kathy was delighted to be in his arms.

Kathy's eyes prickled as she remembered the Kathy and Neil who had spun around to the music on that long-ago date. When was it? Only five years ago? It suddenly felt so much longer. He would have done anything to make her smile then.

When Neil got back to the table with drinks for himself and Margaret, Kathy caught his eye. She tried to persuade him to get up one more time, miming reeling him onto the floor, like a fisherman bringing in a salmon.

'If he gets up to dance,' Kathy said to herself, 'there is still a chance we can salvage this. We can still make it work. All relationships go through their challenging moments. . .'

But Neil shook his head and stayed resolutely seated.

Then Uncle Tony fell arse over tit into a rosebush and the dancing and the evening were brought to a close.

Chapter Eight

Neil was not Kathy's first, second or even seventeenth Internet date. Shortly before they met, she was beginning to lose hope. She had run into all the usual Internet romance problems. The men who lied about their age, their height, their being in gainful employment. Not to mention the men who lied about their marital status. She had come to recognise that when a man posted a picture of himself that had obviously been cropped, the missing section usually contained a girlfriend who wasn't quite an ex. If a man said he would rather exchange photos privately, that was an even worse sign. It was inevitably because he didn't want his wife's friends – or even his wife herself – to stumble on his secret dating profile.

The week Kathy met Neil, she'd already had a date with a man who claimed to have been single for three years but had a tell-tale indent on the ring finger of his left hand. Surely after three years of separation it should have gone. He also spent an inordinate amount of time in the loo. Probably calling his wife to say he would be 'late home from work'.

So when Neil turned out to be exactly as he had described himself – forty years old, properly divorced for two years already, in possession of all his own teeth and some hair – the first thing Kathy felt was relief. Here at last was someone nice and honest and normal.

He wasn't immediately her type. Raised on the Brontës and Jane Austen, Kathy would have said she liked her men to be artistic and dramatic. But Kathy's type had not got her very far. For a start, they were thin on the ground outside the literary world and it was time to get real. She had just turned thirty-five. Most of her friends were married. Many were starting families.

When Kathy first moved to London in her mid-twenties, there was always somebody to go out with on a Friday or Saturday night. Lately, she'd spent whole weekends alone, talking to no one but the chap in the corner shop or her mum on the phone.

So, Neil was not her type but maybe that was a good thing. Exciting was good but exciting couldn't keep you warm in front of *Strictly* on a Saturday night. And Kathy wanted that Saturday-night comfort now. She wanted to step off the merry-go-round of dating and join the contented, settled women who posted about their bliss on their contented, settled women's blogs. She wanted to be with someone with whom she could make plans. She wanted a family of her own. Most of all she wanted to feel safe. For all sorts of reasons, she wanted someone else to take charge of her life for a while.

'I think that went quite well,' said Neil, as their first date at a coffee shop near his office in the City drew to a close.

Kathy didn't know then that he wasn't leaving to go back to the office but was actually going on to date number three. 'Yes,' said Kathy. 'I think it did.'

'Perhaps we'll see each other again,' he said.

'I'd like that,' Kathy agreed.

But Neil didn't suggest another meeting straight away. Later, she would discover that he'd waited until he'd met all three women he was scheduled to see that day to decide which acquaintanceship to take forward. Kathy won. Neil was very honest about it. He told both the other women they hadn't got the position of probationary girlfriend the very next day by email. Then he quickly booked a second date with Kathy. This time it was a proper evening date. They went to a Chinese restaurant and Neil kissed her lightly on the lips as they said goodbye in the ticket hall at Embankment. It was a polite kiss. There was something old-fashioned and charming about the way Neil operated. Kathy found she was intrigued and excited about a third date.

There were no immediate fireworks, but after a month of seeing each other three times a week, Kathy felt something she thought might be better than wild passion: steadiness – Neil always did what he said he would – and growing warmth. Kathy's mum was pleased to hear it. She reassured Kathy that this slowly unfolding affection could be the most precious kind of love of all.

Neil said he wanted the same things Kathy did. He wanted stability, consistency and trust. He liked being in a relationship. A few weeks into their courtship, he admitted to Kathy that it was his ex-wife Caroline who had pushed for a divorce. Otherwise he might have stayed married. He *liked* being married. That was music to Kathy's ears.

'I don't know where I went wrong with my ex,' he said. 'I gave her everything she wanted.'

But not, it seemed, everything Caroline really *needed*.

She'd left him for another man who 'understood' her.

That arrangement hadn't lasted long and Neil said he would have taken her back – everyone is entitled to his or her moment of madness – but Caroline didn't come running back.

The first time she'd heard Neil explain how his marriage ended, Kathy couldn't believe that Caroline had been so hard to please. Caroline was crazy to think that the grass could be any greener elsewhere. Neil was so kind and so reliable. He was sweet and thoughtful. He wasn't the philandering kind. When he asked Kathy to move in with him, she was over the moon. She felt cherished and chosen. It wasn't a marriage proposal but it was a definite commitment.

On her first night as Neil's live-in girlfriend, Kathy could not have felt happier. Neil made dinner, which they ate cuddled up on the sofa. Knowing that she would not be going back to her singleton's flat when the weekend was over gave her an enormous sense of relief. Wrapped in his big arms, she was sure Neil gave her everything *she* needed.

Kathy thought about those lovely early days with Neil as she lay awake on their second night in the palazzo. She was mature enough to know that all relationships evolve over time and that the high romance inevitably fades to be replaced by comfortable love and companionship and other pragmatic considerations, but she missed it all the same. And if those other pragmatic considerations weren't being fulfilled either. Then what?

Kathy studied Neil's profile in the dark. He was fast asleep. Nothing troubling his brow. Not even a stray mosquito.

In order to ensure the rogue mozzie they'd failed to find the night before didn't bite him, he'd insisted they had the air-con on again. It was turned down to thirteen degrees, since Neil had read somewhere that mosquitoes couldn't function below fifteen. Kathy certainly couldn't function below fifteen.

After two hours of sleeplessness – during which Neil snored like a wild boar – Kathy got out of bed and put on jeans, socks and a sweater, then climbed back under the sheets. Only then was she warm enough to drop off.

Chapter Nine

At last, the day of Dave and Shelley's wedding dawned. The wedding planner cornered Kathy and the girls at breakfast to give them their bridesmaid instructions. She assumed that Kathy was their mother.

'Er, no,' said Sophie. 'I mean, we don't look anything like her.'

Kathy tried not to take the way Sophie had said that – complete with curled lip – as an insult.

The wedding would be taking place at four that afternoon. Sophie and Amelie needed to be ready to have their hair and make-up done at one o'clock sharp. Kathy promised she would make sure they were in the right place at the right time. Amelie rolled her eyes. 'We're not, like, children,' she said.

All the same, at five past one, Kathy found herself trawling the entire palazzo to track the girls down. They were flat out on a pair of sunbeds by the pool, topping up their fake tans. Of course they'd completely forgotten where they were supposed to be that lunchtime.

Kathy delivered the girls to Shelley's suite, where the hair and make-up team were waiting. She then went to their room to fetch their dresses, then back to her own room to fetch the shoes she had been planning to wear that evening: Sophie insisted that Kathy's shoes would look much better with the new Gucci bridesmaid dress than the pair Shelley had bought to go with the original dress from Pretty Little Thing.

'But what will you wear?' Shelley asked Kathy.

Kathy shrugged. She found she didn't care all that much. Sure, there would be photographs, but it was very unlikely Kathy would ever see a picture of herself wearing the wrong shoes on Margaret's mantelpiece. What mattered was that Sophie and Amelie made it through the ceremony without throwing a fit and making things difficult.

At three, Kathy left the bridal suite to go back to the Dante Suite. Neil was just about ready. 'I had to put in my own cufflinks,' he said.

That was something he often asked Kathy to help with.

The dress code for the wedding was black tie. Neil was furious about that. He hated to have to dress up 'like a penguin', as he put it, especially in the heat. No matter how many times Kathy told him he looked gorgeous in his black jacket and bow tie, Neil was determined to be grumpy about it.

But Neil had no choice about what to wear. That day he was one of the ushers. He wasn't the best man. That honour went to Dave's best friend Matthew from university. Neil wasn't happy about that, Kathy knew. All the same, at a quarter past three, he went to pose for pre-wedding pictures with the groom's party, leaving Kathy to get ready on her own.

Kathy was normally happy for any excuse to dress up. That particular afternoon, however, she wished her choice for the evening was as easy as Neil's black suit and a white shirt. Since she wasn't working, she'd had no budget for a new frock. Let alone a long frock she would have the opportunity to wear just a couple of times a year, if that. Instead she'd brought with her a maxi dress she'd had for a very long time. It was plain black, which she hoped hid the fact that it was not exactly new. She hoped it would also hide the fact that she hadn't held back on the pasta. She'd told herself it would be elevated by the addition of her new red sandals, but Sophie would be wearing those now.

On her feet Kathy wore a pair of sparkly flip-flops instead. No one would notice.

A slick of lipstick and Kathy was ready. She locked the door of the Dante Suite and hurried across the landing to the stairs, just as Henry Innocenti was walking out of the music room.

'Wow,' he said.

Kathy paused and looked behind her. Was that 'wow' meant for her?

'It's the Queen of Sheba.' Henry met her at the top of the big staircase that swept down to the lobby. He bowed. 'Your humble servant, Majesty.'

For a second, Kathy felt the free-fall top-of-the-rollercoaster sensation she hadn't experienced in a long time. Laughing a little nervously at Henry's dramatic greeting, she pushed back her hair. She hadn't forgotten that he would be at the wedding but equally she hadn't expected to see him except from a distance. She'd not expected to have a chance to speak to him again.

'Nice dress,' he commented.

'It's old,' she said.

'It's still nice. You're ready for the wedding, then?'

Kathy smoothed the front of her skirt. 'I think so.'

'It's going to be a lovely evening for it.'

'Yes. You're so lucky to live here. Tuscany's like Heaven.'

'On a day like this, I can't disagree.'

Through the large windows opposite the staircase, the valley looked more beautiful than ever.

'Are you playing for the ceremony?' Kathy asked.

'Yes.' He gestured with the sheaf of music he was carrying. 'And afterwards with the band. I'm here all evening.'

Kathy nodded. Tried not to seem too interested. 'What sort of music will you be playing?' she asked.

'For the ceremony, the old traditional stuff. In the evening, whatever you fancy. We take requests. Except Coldplay. There is a special place in Hell for people who request Coldplay.'

'OK. No Coldplay.'

'Or Ed Sheeran.'

'I think I've run out of ideas in that case,' said Kathy.

'You must have one song you'd like to hear,' Henry Innocenti said. 'Tell me. What's your favourite? Yours will be the very first request we play.'

He held her eyes, making Kathy feel warm in the cheeks again, as though they were flirting. Were they?

'I've got rather old-fashioned taste,' she said.

Henry raised his eyebrows. 'I'm intrigued.'

'How about "The Way You Look Tonight"?' Kathy suggested. 'Do you know it?'

'From *Swing Time*? Of course. That's a proper song. I'll put it on my list. Can I call on you to come and duet later on?'

'Oh, I don't think so.' Kathy batted the idea away.

'I enjoyed our piano session very much.' Henry hesitated for a second, then continued, 'I found myself smiling all the way back to Florence yesterday evening.'

'You live in Florence?'

'Born and bred.'

'It's my middle name. Though I've never been there.'

'Well, that's ridiculous. Are you interested in art as well as music?'

'Of course.'

'Then you must come. I'll show you around. Come tomorrow when the wedding's finished.'

Kathy knew she should say something then to make it clear that she wasn't in Italy alone. 'I've got an early flight,' she said, stopping short of saying 'we'.

'Now that is a shame,' said Henry. 'If you're ever back here then you must . . .'

Kathy was suddenly aware that Dave and his ushers, including Neil, were gathering at the bottom of the staircase for a group photograph. Neil looked up to where Kathy and Henry were standing. His eyes narrowed as he saw them. Kathy held her breath until he looked away.

'I've got to go,' she told Henry.

'I'll see you later,' said Henry, seeming oblivious to Neil's scowl.

As Kathy wove her way through the ushers, who were arrayed on the bottom two steps, Neil pretended he hadn't seen her. When he was forced to acknowledge her, he said, 'Everyone's outside already. You'll be late.'

Henry followed Kathy down the stairs. Deliberately or not, the ushers closed ranks so that he had to ask them to let him through. 'If I don't get to the terrace, the bride will be walking down the aisle to the sound of silence,' he said.

Glancing back, Kathy saw Neil move only very slightly so that Henry couldn't get by without brushing his shoulder.

Kathy kept her eyes front for the rest of the walk to the terrace. She found her seat in the second row, next to Neil's mother. Oscar, on the other side of his grandmother, did not look up from his phone.

'It's too hot,' Margaret said. 'I knew it would be too hot. I hope Shelley doesn't intend to compound the mistake of getting married outside in this ridiculous heat by being late for the ceremony. There's tradition and there's being selfish.'

Dave and his best friend Matthew walked down the aisle to find their places. Dave looked nervous but happily so, Kathy thought. A couple of minutes later, Neil slid into the row of seats next to Kathy. He squeezed her knee, which was as close as he ever got to a public display of affection.

'OK?' he asked her.

'Of course.'

'Dave's bricking himself,' Neil observed.

'Neil!' Margaret complained.

Kathy was grateful that now Neil was sitting down his mother could direct her criticisms at him. Kathy nodded from time to time but really she was only watching the stage at the front of the terrace, where the ceremony would take place and where Henry Innocenti was settling down at his keyboard. At three minutes past four – late but not too late – he began to play Bach's 'Sheep May Safely Graze' as the processional. Beautifully, of course. All eyes – except Oscar's – turned towards the palazzo, where the bride's party was gathering by the doors onto the terrace. Shelley stepped out into the sunshine on her father's arm. Sophie and Amelie slinked along behind, secretly enjoying their catwalk moment.

'They're both bright orange,' Margaret observed in a whisper. 'Did Shelley hire a professional make-up artist? They look ridiculous. Kathy, you should have told them.'

Like Kathy could have told Neil's daughters anything.

'They're glowing,' Kathy told Margaret. Radioactively, was the word she didn't add.

Kathy watched the bride. She smiled broadly and gave a little thumbs-up when Shelley caught her eye.

'Wedding dress looks a bit tight round the middle,' Margaret commented.

The ceremony was short but special. Both Dave and Shelley cried. Kathy, who had been expecting to blub, was surprised to find she didn't during the exchange of vows, though when Shelley's mother gave a reading about the newlyweds stepping into the future together, the tears came close. The celebrant gave a very funny speech about Italian wedding traditions and told the guests to shout, '*Auguri!*' when she pronounced the newlyweds man and wife.

Then it was time for Dave and Shelley to process back down the aisle as man and wife. To 'The Arrival of the Queen of Sheba'.

When Kathy caught Henry's eye, he grinned at her. She couldn't help smiling back.

'You look very happy,' said Margaret, as though it were inappropriate.

The wedding party gathered for drinks and photographs in the rose garden while the terrace was transformed for that evening's dinner. A harpist played as they sipped Prosecco and ate canapés.

At one point, Henry crossed the garden towards the house. Kathy pretended not to have noticed him but definitely felt herself grow warmer under the collar of her old black dress as he passed. Margaret looked at her strangely again. Neil was too busy talking to Shelley's brother about his new car to notice where his girlfriend was looking.

After a few minutes, Kathy excused herself and went back into the hotel and up to the room she was sharing with Neil. Alone again for a moment, she touched up her make-up, then sat and gazed at her reflection in the dressing-table mirror.

What did other people see when they looked at her, she wondered. Neil's children saw a woman on the verge of middle age, whose views on everything and anything were irrelevant. His mother saw a woman who didn't take enough care of her figure. Kathy's mother saw a child who still needed to be wrapped in cotton wool, though for the past two decades Kathy had been doing the caring in that relationship. Neil saw . . . What did Neil see? Kathy had thought he saw her as his partner and his equal. After the past seven days, she wasn't so sure.

What did Kathy see in herself?

She saw a woman who'd had plans and dreams and had put them all aside for other people. She saw a woman who had grown used to being largely over-looked. But did she see a woman who was willing to settle in order to be *settled*?

In six months' time she would be forty but she was still relatively young. She could still change her life for the better. She could still do everything she'd ever wanted to do. If, when she got back to London, the conversation she and Neil had to have panned out as she expected it would, it wouldn't be so bad. She just had to have courage. Like her surname. She'd been a braver person once.

For just a second, Kathy felt it was time to do something stupid. Something rash.

Not now. Kathy plastered on a smile to go back outside. Today was Shelley and Dave's day.

Chapter Ten

The terrace – already so beautiful – had been transformed. The rows of chairs for the wedding had been
rearranged around a number of large circular tables.
Each was laid with a sparkling white cloth. In the centre
of each was a display of olive branches studded with
roses. Kathy loved the contrast of the olive's silvery
leaves, which reminded her of old copper turned green,
with the delicate cream of the rose petals.

Up on stage, Henry Innocenti was at the keyboard
again. This time he was part of a four-piece band
that included a female singer. They were working
through the usual wedding classics. Unable – or
unwilling – to break into any of the conversational
groups that had formed among the guests, Kathy
stood at a little distance and watched the band for a
while.

Then someone rang a gong to let everyone know it
was time for the guests to sit down. Kathy already
knew where she and Neil were sitting. They were on
the same table as his auntie Judith and his cousin Jeff,
Judith's son.

Turning away from the stage and from Henry, Kathy
caught sight of Neil, who was staring in her direction
with a frown. He summoned her with an impatient
hand gesture. Kathy zigzagged her way through the
other tables to get to him.

'What were you doing?' he asked. 'You looked like you were in a trance over there.'

'I was just listening to the band.'

But Neil was already turning away from her to pull out a chair for Jeff's wife. Madeleine was not wearing an 'old thing' that evening. She was dressed in a floor-length burgundy silk dress that screamed 'expensive'. It fluttered around her long legs like the petals of a flower.

'One, two, one, two.' Matthew, the best man, was on stage, failing to get the microphone to work.

Henry Innocenti duly obliged.

'Thank you. OK, everybody. Ladies and gents, I hope you've found your places. We've kept it simple and put people on the same tables as their partners, rather than mixing you all up. I know some of you would rather not be next to the people you came with, but you can sort that out when it comes to the dancing. Now, if you'd all be upstanding for the bride and groom . . .'

Shelley and Dave entered the terrace and took their place at the top table, flanked by Shelley's parents, Margaret and the radioactively made-up bridesmaids, Sophie and Amelie. As soon as they were seated, the waiting staff moved into action and delivered the first course.

Neil was quickly deep in conversation with Madeleine. Kathy listened quietly while Jeff, on her left, and Judith, to the left of him, shared their views on the state of the United Kingdom. They agreed it 'was better in the old days'. Oscar, to Kathy's right, was deep in communion with his phone.

The conversation was dull but the food was delicious. The wine was wonderful. The evening was balmy and scented with jasmine, just as Kathy had imagined. And then there was the music.

Henry Innocenti and his band were a cut above. It was a shame there was so much other noise for them to compete with. The braying laughter. The shouts from one table to another. The increasingly heated debates about the future of the Conservative Party from Neil's relatives on Kathy's table.

A first course of pasta in sage butter was followed by steak – *tagliata* – with a rocket and tomato salad. White wine followed Prosecco. Red wine followed the white. Soon Kathy was getting tipsy. After the steak, came a palate-cleansing sorbet. Then tiramisu. You couldn't come to Italy and not have tiramisu, Neil announced across the table.

Madeleine agreed, though she took only the tiniest mouthful. Kathy, on the other hand, would have licked the dish clean if she could have been sure no one was watching.

It was then that she heard it. Kathy half turned in her chair as the song began. Those first few notes were unmistakable. She caught Henry's eye. He nodded and gave her a little salute. 'The Way You Look Tonight' had been Kathy's favourite song ever since she'd first heard it as a teenager, watching *Swing Time*, the old black-and-white Fred Astaire movie, with her mum and dad one Sunday afternoon. It was their song, they told her. The first song they'd danced to at their wedding. The tender, melancholy romance of the lyrics had touched Kathy's heart. She'd written them out in the back of her school notebook and prayed every night that one day she might find someone who felt that way about her.

It didn't happen while she was at school, where the boys largely ignored her. Long before she was Chicken Licken, Kathy had another nickname she hated. Born with a condition that caused her left eye to turn inwards, she'd been dubbed Cross-eyed Kathy by her peers. The nickname outlasted the condition – she'd had an operation to correct it when she was eight – and the self-consciousness she'd developed as a result had long outlasted the nickname.

At secondary school, the boys acted as though they thought her junior-school unpopularity might still be contagious so Kathy's teenage romantic life was confined to romance novels, black-and-white movies and old songs, and wishing that life would bring her a real-life hero. Of course, she grew up and realised that a good, solid man was preferable to a matinee idol but she still loved a song that could take her back to those earlier, less complicated times.

On stage, the band's female singer had stepped back so that Henry could take the vocal part. How Kathy wished that the whole terrace would fall silent so that she could hear every note of this special performance. Savour it. But the party continued. Madeleine was laughing like an actual donkey at something Neil had told her.

When the music stopped, Kathy was the only person to applaud. Neil looked at her. 'Did I miss something?' he asked.

'Just my favourite song,' she said.

'Oh, right,' said Neil. 'Didn't hear it. More wine, Madeleine?'

Looking across the terrace to the stage, where Henry was already playing something else, Kathy held the special moment close. From the way he had played that song for her, she felt understood. Maybe it *was* time to do something stupid.

Chapter Eleven

Then coffee and petit fours were on the table and Matthew the best man was heading back up to the stage, albeit a little less steadily than before. Once again, he tapped the microphone and addressed it, 'Testing, testing,' standing too close and making it shriek. Once again, Henry Innocenti got up to tweak the volume and to remind Matthew to stand a little further away if he didn't want to make the guests' ears bleed.

Kathy had her back towards the stage. She should probably have turned her seat so she could see Matthew properly but nobody else seemed to be bothering with that. Half the people on the adjoining tables were continuing their conversations, oblivious to the fact that the speeches were about to start.

Matthew introduced Shelley's father first. His pride in his daughter was clear as he spoke about her happy childhood and the woman she had become. Shelley sobbed happy tears throughout.

'Speeches are the worst part of any wedding,' said Jeff. 'They should just email what they want to say to the guests in advance so we can get on with eating and talking.'

Kathy disagreed. She envied Shelley the chance to hear her father make that speech.

Dave's speech, which came next, was almost as brief

as his speech on the first night of the wedding party. But it was full of a deep and quiet love. No one could doubt that Dave would honour his vows.

Then Matthew stood up again.

'I know this is the moment you've all been waiting for,' he said. His best man's speech was the usual mix of bad jokes and rambling anecdotes that were only funny if you'd been there. Kathy found herself zoning out. She tuned back in for the traditional toast to the bridesmaids, then zoned out again as Matthew rumbled on.

Soon Matthew's voice was just background noise. Kathy wanted to make the most of that last evening in Italy. Of the gentle scent of flowers and wood smoke on the night air. The sound of the cicadas. The soft light from the lanterns in the trees and the candles on the tables. The taste of the warm red wine. The memory of her song being played. As far as possible, she also wanted to pretend she was alone on that terrace – well, perhaps not entirely alone. She was so absorbed in taking in the atmosphere that she didn't even notice when Neil got up from the other side of the large round table at which they were seated to take over on the microphone. But then . . .

'Kathy! Kathy Courage! Come on up!'

'Go on!' Madeleine leaned over to shake Kathy back to attention. 'You're wanted on stage.'

'What?'

'Kathy!' Neil bellowed into the mic. Then he added, in an aside to his audience, 'See what I have to put up with, ladies and gents?'

Kathy rushed to the front of the terrace where Neil was waiting for her. She struggled to get up on the stage. She couldn't find the steps. She hadn't been watching closely enough to see where they were. Her long dress tangled around her legs as she tried to climb up the front. Behind her, there was laughter. Neil looked tense. Eventually, he grabbed her by the wrist and hauled her up, as if he was hauling her out of a roiling ocean.

Kathy smoothed her skirt, checked her bodice for crumbs and then grinned towards the darkness. The lights on the stage made the rest of the terrace invisible. She was painfully aware this meant she was absolutely in the spotlight and everybody could see her. Chicken Licken. Cross-eyed Kathy. She felt a little sick.

What was going on? Were she and Neil supposed to be giving their own toast to the bride and groom? Had she missed a vital instruction?

No.

Neil was getting to his knees, fishing in his jacket pocket and flipping open a small red-velvet-covered box.

It couldn't be . . .

Oh, God, it was.

Now? After everything . . .

'Kathy Courage,' Neil said, looking more nervous than she had ever seen him. 'Will you marry me?'

Their audience burst into applause before Kathy had even properly taken in the question. There was no need to wait for her answer. Of course there wasn't. What could she possibly say except 'yes'?

As it was, she didn't even have to say 'yes'. She blinked in shocked surprise and that seemed to be good enough. Neil stood up right away. He took Kathy's left hand, which was trembling, and slipped the ring onto her finger. Once the ring was in place, Neil lifted Kathy's arm above her head as though she had just been declared the winner of a boxing bout. Then he wrapped his arms around her waist and pulled her in for a kiss, which mostly landed on her nose.

Matthew came back onto the stage and patted Neil hard on the back.

'Congratulations, Neil and Kathy. Let's have three cheers for the happy couple, another Mr and Mrs Sherwin in the making . . . Hip hip . . .'

'Hooray!'

Neil continued to smooch Kathy's nose until she gently pushed herself backwards away from him. She couldn't breathe.

'Do you like the ring?' Neil asked. 'It's supposed to be like Meghan Markle's.'

'Is it?' Kathy's voice came out high and squeaky.

And then the band struck up 'Yellow' by Coldplay.

'I wanted you to have your first dance as my fiancée to your favourite song,' said Neil.

Her favourite song?

As Neil whirled her around as though they were teenagers at a drunken ceilidh, Kathy caught a glimpse of Henry Innocenti, playing the song he hated most and looking more than a little surprised. He wasn't the only one.

Chapter Twelve

Before Kathy and Neil had stepped down from the stage, Amelie had burst into tears and Sophie had flat-out fainted (or at least pretended to). Oscar didn't look up from his phone. While Shelley's sensible sister tried to persuade Amelie and Sophie that it wasn't the end of the world, other guests at the wedding rushed forward to congratulate the newly affianced.

Shelley confirmed to Kathy that she and Dave had known all along Neil was planning to propose. That was a small relief. The idea that Shelley might have thought Kathy wanted to upstage her at her wedding was particularly painful. Meanwhile, Margaret had not known the proposal was going to happen and she wanted to know why.

'You might have warned me,' she told Shelley.

Kathy heard Jeff, Neil's cousin, say, 'What do you want to get married again for, you idiot? The rest of us are still trying to unravel our first mistakes.'

Neil laughed heartily at that. 'Second time lucky,' he said.

'I thought the phrase was third time lucky,' said Jeff.

'Shoot me if I ever get to that stage,' said Neil.

Meanwhile, Kathy was gathering a crowd of her own, mostly women, who all wanted to see the ring. Some of them stared at it with such intensity that Kathy half expected someone to whip out a jeweller's eyeglass to check the diamonds for colour, cut and clarity. How much had Neil splashed out, was what they really wanted to know. Was there a whole month's salary on Kathy's finger? Kathy thought there might be. She couldn't believe what she had on her hand. The stones were so big and they glittered so brightly. They hardly looked quite real.

'Congratulations!' The word rang out again and again. Kathy accepted hugs and kisses, all the while feeling as if someone had shoved her into an industrial tumble-dryer and pressed 'on'. She didn't know where to look or what to say. 'You must be so happy!' people told her. Yet the proposal was genuinely the very last thing she'd been expecting.

As soon as she could, she escaped to the nearest ladies' loo, where she met Madeleine by the basins. Madeleine leaned over and took Kathy's hand to inspect the new bauble. 'Very nice,' she said. 'That's at least a carat and a half. I hope it's worth it.'

'Worth it?'

'Your part of the bargain. In my experience, matrimony is always a one-sided affair. One partner inevitably benefits much more than the other. My engagement ring was a consolation prize. Had I known . . .'

Kathy was too gob-smacked to respond to Madeleine's comments, which were worthy of the bad fairy at Sleeping Beauty's christening. Fortunately, she didn't have to. The wedding planner was looking for her. She dragged Kathy back onto the terrace to pose with Neil for the wedding's official photographer, who was going to take their portrait. Neil's children could not be persuaded to join them.

'They'll come round,' Neil said, when Kathy

expressed her concern. Amelie was bawling. Sophie was still feigning a coma. Kathy wasn't sure Oscar had even noticed what was going on yet.

'Don't worry,' Neil insisted. 'They'll be pleased when they think about it.'

The photographer had Kathy look up at Neil, with her hand on his chest to show off the ring. Like in a royal engagement portrait. Neil was looking straight ahead.

'I wish I'd known,' Kathy said.

'The photographer can probably do something about your hair with Photoshop,' said Neil, which wasn't quite the answer Kathy had expected.

It was getting late. When the photographer was sure he had the shot he needed – and Neil agreed with him – Neil suggested he and Kathy have one more dance to celebrate their newly engaged status.

The band was already packing up, leaving only Henry playing the electric keyboard.

'Oi, mate,' Neil called to him. 'Play "Yellow" again.'

With a raised eyebrow, Henry obliged.

Unable to look in Henry's direction as he struck up the first few chords, Kathy let Neil take her into his arms.

'How are you feeling, my darling?' he asked.

'This is all really, really . . .' She searched for the word. Sudden? Unexpected? A disaster?

'I can tell you're happy, Chicken Licken. You must be relieved. I knew I'd get round to asking you eventually but you must have started to wonder if it was ever going to happen.'

So many words bubbled in Kathy's brain but didn't quite reach her lips. Had this happened a year before, she would have been over the moon. To marry Neil had been all she ever wanted. But now? Madeleine's comment upon seeing the ring echoed in Kathy's mind. Consolation prize . . .

'And that's all we've got time for, ladies and gentlemen,' said Henry, at the end of his encore of 'Yellow'. 'We hope you've enjoyed your evening and of course we wish all the luck in the world to our newly-weds and the newly-soon-to-be-weds.'

The band paused in packing up to applaud.

While Neil and Kathy accepted more congratulations from their fellow guests, Henry disconnected the microphone with another ear-splitting shriek.

'Hang on a minute.' Neil turned to the stage and beckoned Henry to the edge of it. 'Here you are, mate. I want to give you something.'

Neil had a five-euro note curled in his hand. 'Thanks for playing our song.'

Henry glanced at the note then told Neil, 'Consider that rendition of "Yellow" my engagement gift to you.'

'No,' said Neil. 'I insist. I know you guys don't get paid much. Starving artists and all that.'

'Well, in that case,' said Henry, 'I'll take it for the band. Thank you very much.'

He reached to take the note but Neil whipped it away so that it was out of reach.

'It's not for the band. It's for you, mate. You person-ally.'

Instead of letting Henry take the note from his hand, Neil tucked it into the top pocket of Henry's shirt. It was a gesture intended to make a point and to establish some kind of pecking order. 'It's for you to buy yourself a decent shirt or get a haircut. Then you might be able to get yourself a fiancée as good as mine.'

Henry straightened up. Still standing on the stage, he towered above Neil but Neil had already turned away. He'd put his arm around Kathy again and was explaining to another cousin how Kathy had fallen for him. 'She's been dying for me to pop the question ever since she met me,' he assured his audience. 'Isn't that right?'

Kathy felt as though she was underwater and running out of breath. She looked back to catch Henry's eye. She wanted him to know she was sorry for what had just transpired between him and Neil. But Henry wouldn't look at her.

'Isn't that right, Chicken?' Neil asked again.

Chapter Thirteen

Now – less than eight hours after Neil's big surprise – they were on their way back to London. This time, they were in a luxurious car big enough to take five passengers. Kathy couldn't help thinking back wistfully to their outbound travel arrangements. None of Neil's children had addressed a word in her direction since the previous evening. The girls wouldn't even look at her. At least, not when she was looking at them. She felt them glaring daggers when she wasn't.

Kathy still had to tell her mother what had happened. She was surprised to hear Neil hadn't consulted Clare before he popped the question. She knew her dad would have liked to be asked, were he still alive. It was one of Kathy's big regrets that her father had never had the chance to meet her future husband.

'But why do we need to ask anybody?' Neil said. 'We're both adults.' He had a point. 'I asked. You said yes. Job done.'

Kathy still wondered whether she'd actually said yes. The whole proposal had come as such a shock that technically she'd just stood there and gulped, like a fish plucked from the water and plonked gasping on the bank.

In the back of the air-conditioned car, Kathy hugged herself for warmth. She was wearing a sleeveless blue linen shirt that was just right for the weather outside but not for an ice-chilled car. She had decided against asking if she could grab a cardigan from her suitcase. Neil was already stressing about the time it would take to get to the airport. He wasn't convinced Melanie had thought far enough ahead.

'The roads around here are terrible,' he said. 'It would take just one lot of unexpected road works for us to miss the flight.'

Before they had left the palazzo grounds, his attention was entirely concentrated on his phone. Though it was still only six in the morning back in London, the world of corporate law was already awake and sending emails.

'I can't be out of the office for even half a day without it all going tits up,' Neil said.

The children said nothing.

It was not how Kathy had expected the morning after her once longed-for engagement to be.

The car took the winding roads smoothly. The driver obviously knew them well. For the first several miles, their route was lined with tall dark pine trees, punctuated by the odd farmhouse. Kathy peered into the gloomy woods in the hope of seeing a wild boar or a deer. She'd heard some deer barking over the past few days but hadn't caught a glimpse. She'd also found porcupine spines on a walk around the palazzo's grounds. Until then, she'd had no idea there were porcupines anywhere in Europe.

The hill towns were still waking up. A group of elderly locals sitting at a bus stop watched them go by, following it with their heads as though they were in a luxury car advertisement. Occasionally the taxi shot through a tunnel. The driver kept his sunglasses on at all times, despite the sudden darkness. When they came out at the other end, Kathy struggled to see in the brightness of the sun.

Out of the woods, they passed bright green vineyards – the grapes still tiny and sour – and fields of silvery wheat peppered with blood-bright poppies. White climbing roses covered the wild banks at the side of the road, like snowflakes, while the flowers of sainfoin – the 'holy hay' – turned the meadows pink. Kathy didn't think she had ever seen anything so beautiful as the beginning of a Tuscan summer. It had all been so much lovelier than she'd imagined. If the trip hadn't exactly worked out as she'd hoped, she still wanted to remember this landscape for ever. The light, the colours, the smell of the air.

Then, twenty minutes into the journey, she saw the view she had waited to see for as long as she could remember, since she was a little girl looking through that photo album with her mum. As the taxi came out of another tunnel, it appeared in front of them, like a mirage. The skyline of Florence. It had to be. It could only be.

'Is that . . . ?' she started to ask the driver.

'Duomo?' He nodded. He must have been asked the question a thousand times.

'Really?' Kathy asked.

'*Vero*,' the driver confirmed.

The terracotta-red dome was much larger than Kathy had expected. It dominated the horizon, standing tall above the buildings around it. She shook Neil's arm to draw his attention to the marvel that was laid out before them.

'Look,' she said. 'Over there. It's Florence. There's

the cathedral. The Duomo . . .' She tried out the word for herself. 'You see that orange dome right there in the middle? That's it!'

Neil glanced up from his screen so briefly he couldn't possibly have focused on the view. His eyes went straight back to his emails, but he did take the time to say, 'So now you've seen Florence, you can stop going on about it.'

Kathy felt a small prickle of shame beneath her armpits. Had she been 'going on about it'? She turned to Neil to read his face for reassurance. His eyes flickered across the screen of his phone. He hadn't meant it nastily, she decided. He had a hangover. That was all.

Kathy turned her own eyes back to the horizon, to the unchanging skyline of the city that had inspired so many over the centuries. She wound down the car window so there was nothing between her and the view she had dreamed of. Soft warm air kissed her face and bare arms, smoothing away the goose bumps, like a tender caress.

After a moment or two, Neil put down his phone and turned to face her. Sensing him move, Kathy looked back towards him and smiled, eager to share her happiness at seeing at least the roof of the Duomo. Neil took her hand – the one wearing the engagement ring – and for a second or two she thought he was going to kiss her and make the moment perfect. But he was unsmiling as he said, 'Chicken Licken, when the window's open, the air-conditioning doesn't work.'

Chapter Fourteen

The taxi pulled up outside the door to Departures. Neil jumped out and immediately went to stand by the boot of the car to make sure no one was able to swipe their luggage. Sophie, Amelie and Oscar tumbled out after him, all glued to their phones. Kathy fished about in her bag and found a five-euro note for the driver.

Neil walked ahead into the terminal, pushing all their luggage on a single trolley. His children followed without ever looking up from their screens. Kathy hurried to catch up with them, desperately scanning the signage as she did so. By the time Neil had reached the bottom of the escalator that would take them to the check-in desks, she'd already worked out exactly where they needed to go. She'd also, in record speed, scanned the departures board to ensure their flight was not delayed or cancelled. Navigating an airport with Neil was a matter of pre-empting what could go wrong. That morning, Neil tutted at the dawdlers who crossed their paths but, thanks to Kathy's speedy airport navigation skills, they made it to the desk without him swearing at anyone in particular.

So far, so good. Kathy handed her passport to Neil so he could present all five to the woman on the desk. She accepted them with a smile. '*Grazie.*' She held the passports open as she copied their names into her system. She waited for the computer to give her the boarding details. Then the check-in assistant's lip-sticked smile folded into a frown.

'Is there a problem?' Neil asked.

Please, God, don't let there be a problem, Kathy said to herself.

'Perhaps,' said the check-in attendant, whose badge said she was called Sabina. 'Miss Courage, is it possible you have been booked onto the flight under a different name?'

'Of course not,' said Neil, answering for her.

'Only I can't find you on the list of passengers.'

'Did you type her name in correctly?' Neil asked.

'I can do it again,' Sabina said. 'Just in case.'

Sabina mouthed the letters of Kathy's name as she typed them, to give Neil the reassurance he needed that she was spelling it properly. She waited a moment for the computer to react.

'No,' she said. 'Miss Courage, I'm afraid you are not on this flight.'

'What do you mean, she's not on this flight?' Neil was still speaking for her.

'Her name is not listed on the passenger manifest. Mr Sherwin, you are here. And the three other Sherwins. Your children? They are all here. I can print off your boarding passes.'

'What good's that to me?'

'So four of you can get on the plane.'

'I can't fly without my fiancée.'

'Miss Courage is not booked on this flight.'

'Well, that's ridiculous.' Neil pulled out his iPhone and began scrolling through emails. 'Of course she's on this flight. And if she isn't, then you need to put her on. As per this confirmation email right here.'

Neil pushed the phone under Sabina's nose.

'May I?' she asked, before delicately opening the email attachment with a beautifully manicured finger. She read the details.

'Aaaah,' she said. 'I see what has gone wrong. Mr Sherwin, four of you are on this flight today but Miss Courage is not booked to fly back until next Monday. It's the same flight but a different day,' Sabina clarified. 'Look. Here. Your flight is today. Miss Courage's flight is on the twenty-seventh.'

Neil gave the screen a cursory glance. 'Well, obviously you need to change it.'

'I wish I could,' said Sabina.

Kathy fervently wished she could too.

Standing behind Neil right then, Kathy felt like a small creature living on the side of a volcano that senses the eruption long before it happens. Like a small creature, she wished she could just disappear into a hole packed with nice warm straw and sit the whole thing out. On her own. Sophie and Amelie were glaring at her, as though it was Kathy's fault they were being kept from the retail opportunities beyond security.

'If you don't put my fiancée on the same flight as the rest of us, then you'd better have a bloody good reason.' Neil had gone from nought to swearing in fifteen seconds.

Sabina addressed her response to Kathy: 'I can't put you on the flight using this system. It won't allow me. This terminal is for check-in only. The only thing I can suggest, Miss Courage, is that you go to the ticketing desk and see if they can sell you a new seat. I think there is some space.'

'OK,' said Kathy. 'I'll try that.'

'You will not,' Neil insisted.

'I can't help you any further.' Sabina shrugged.

'Then heads will roll,' said Neil. 'I hope you've got plenty of hobbies, Miss Italia, because you're going to have a lot of time off when you lose your job.'

Sabina maintained her best customer-service smile.

'Let's do what she suggests,' Kathy pleaded. 'There's no queue at the ticket desk. If I hurry, I'll be able to catch you up. It's obviously a mistake at our end.'

Kathy laid her hand on Neil's arm. Behind them, a long queue was building. She was pretty sure that the children wouldn't care too much if she was left behind anyway.

'Leave this to me, Chicken Licken,' Neil said.

Her nickname did not sound friendly this time. It sounded like he wanted her to know she was letting him down by living up to it in yet another situation where only aggression would win the day.

'Who's your supervisor?' Neil asked the long-suffering Sabina.

Sabina's supervisor was duly called but the supervisor only confirmed what Sabina had said. It was not possible to change Kathy's booked flight at the check-in desk. For now, the best solution was for her to buy another ticket and sort out any mistake when they were back in London. There was a long queue behind them. The flight would begin boarding in forty-five minutes. Other people needed to be checked in.

'Sir, if you and your family don't go through security in the next five minutes, you'll be unable to board the flight, as will these people behind you. We will look after Miss Courage.'

Kathy crossed her fingers and closed her eyes.

'I'm not happy about this,' said Neil. 'I'm not happy at all.'

But at last he moved away from the desk.

Chapter Fifteen

It had taken almost fifteen minutes, but felt much longer, for Neil to be persuaded that nothing more could be achieved by invoking international consumer rights. The girls, Oscar and he would go through to board the flight, leaving Kathy to queue for a new ticket. He kissed her forehead and said, 'Don't take no for an answer, Chicken.'

Sabina's supervisor smiled tightly.

Neil headed for the security gates. Kathy waited to say goodbye one more time but he didn't turn round to see her wave. The girls hadn't said goodbye at all. It was as though she didn't exist to them. At least Oscar had muttered, 'Later.'

'Are you OK?' the supervisor asked, once Neil was gone.

'Of course,' said Kathy, feeling guilty relief flood her body now she could sort things out in her own way. 'I'm sorry for the way my fiancé reacted. He gets tense when we're travelling. He's a nice man, I promise you. He doesn't mean to be rude.'

'We're used to it,' the supervisor said.

All the while, the queue at the ticketing desk had grown from two to ten. Kathy joined the back, knowing time was of the essence but worrying that people would take offence if she asked whether she might go ahead. Everyone at an airport was in some sort of hurry, weren't they? She could only cross her fingers and hope the queue moved quickly.

And it did move quickly to begin with. There were two women on the desk and they both worked steadily, issuing customers with new tickets and oversized-baggage tags at a reassuring pace. But then, when there were just three people left in front of Kathy, one of the ticket-desk attendants suddenly put a little sign on the counter in front of her – *chiuso* – got up, shrugged on her jacket and disappeared. From the mime she gave her colleague – which was of someone knocking back an espresso – it was time for her coffee break.

Her colleague continued to work through the queue. She issued two more people with tickets. She was fast and efficient. There was only one person in front of Kathy now. Final boarding had already been called for the flight Kathy hoped to get on, but the woman standing behind her – who was also British – explained they always called boarding early for UK flights because of passport control at the gate.

Kathy tried to be reassured by the observation. Nevertheless, as the next customer stepped up to the desk, Kathy muttered a silent prayer. Please let this customer's request be an easy one.

Alas, the customer ahead of Kathy did not want to buy a new ticket. He wanted to know why his old ticket did not come with a sufficient luggage allowance for the two enormous cases – big enough to hide all the bodies – that he'd dragged up to the desk.

The woman behind the counter responded to each and every one of the man's utterances with a shake of the head. The customer got louder. The ticket vendor continued to shake her head. He gesticulated. She merely shook her head again.

As the minutes ticked down, Kathy felt like a desert traveller seeing an oasis when the woman who had taken a coffee break returned to her counter. However, she didn't sit down and take the next in line. Instead, she – rightly – joined forces with her colleague to deal with the increasingly angry man with too much luggage. Kathy couldn't follow the Italian but could see from the hand gestures that it was not going well. The *chiuso* sign remained on the other desk and it wasn't long before a security guard was called to take the unhappy traveller away.

By which time, all hope Kathy had of being on the same flight as Neil was absolutely *finito*.

When the coffee-break woman finally sat down at her desk and greeted Kathy with a beaming smile, she seemed astonished that Kathy had ever dreamed of getting back to London that day.

'There is nothing until tomorrow and even then, you know, I'm not so sure. French air-traffic control . . .' She shrugged as though a French air-traffic-control strike was as much a part of the annual cycle as the return of the migratory birds.

'Why don't you keep your flight on Monday?' she asked. 'I can't get you back more quickly. Unless you want to take a train to Rome or Milan or Genoa and catch a plane from there.'

A train? An Italian train? Kathy's face betrayed her consternation. She could almost hear Neil's voice asking, in a Greek chorus with her mother's, 'How will you know what ticket to ask for? How will you make sure you get off at the right station? How will you get out of the station without being robbed?'

The woman at the counter waited for Kathy to make up her mind. While Kathy pondered the alternatives, the woman behind her in the queue piped up, 'If you don't have to be home for anything in particular, you should just stay here and enjoy yourself. Eat lots of *gelato* for me!'

Staying in Florence for another three days might have sounded like the best outcome to Kathy's queue mate but Kathy's queue mate didn't have to deal with Neil. While Kathy had been trying to get a new ticket, Neil had texted five times to ask, *What the hell is going on?* As soon as Kathy stepped away from the ticket desk, she dialled him. Though he was almost certainly on the plane by now, with luck he would still have his phone on.

He picked up at once.

'Where are you?'

'Still by the check-in desks.'

'What? Why aren't you through security? The flight's closing.'

'I couldn't get a ticket,' said Kathy. 'The queue was long and it took ages for me to get to the front.'

'Why didn't you tell the people in the queue it was urgent? Why didn't you say you had to be somewhere fast?'

'Everybody in the queue had to be somewhere fast.'

'For heaven's sake, Chicken. You didn't even try, did you? And now I've got to fly back to London with the children on my own.'

'What should I do now?' Kathy asked. 'Should I keep the ticket I've got? The Monday flight?'

'I can't have you stuck out there until Monday! The kids are at our place all weekend. I suppose I'm going to have to sort this out myself.' Neil sighed. 'There's another BA flight at nine o'clock this evening.'

'It's full,' said Kathy. 'The woman on the ticketing desk said there's no space on any direct flight to London today.'

'Of course it's not full. There's always a spare seat on those planes for a VIP and I'm a VIP.'

'But you're already on a plane.'

'I mean, because I'm a VIP, they'll put you on it. As soon as I get to London, I'll have Melanie call BA and sort it out using my executive club details. Just stay exactly where you are and try not to get yourself into any more trouble.'

Trouble? Kathy wanted to tell Neil that it wasn't her fault she hadn't been booked onto the flight but he carried on talking over her.

'Stay in the airport and wait for me to call. This is an absolute shambles. Heads will roll over this. Starting with that girl on the check-in desk and ending with the CEO of British Airways.'

'Sir, you'll need to turn your telephone off now, please.' One of the cabin crew on board Neil's flight cut the conversation short.

'Just stay where you are and keep that engagement ring hidden,' Neil instructed Kathy. 'I'll call you as soon as I land.'

'Safe flight,' said Kathy. 'I love you,' she added. But Neil had already hung up.

Chapter Sixteen

Dragging her wheelie case behind her, Kathy trundled across to a bank of seats and sat down heavily.

What a disaster. She'd had to get up too early (as far as she was concerned – Neil was a natural lark) and she hadn't had any breakfast. The drive to Peretola airport had been icy on all fronts and now she was facing a day at the terminal. She realised then that she didn't even have any euros to buy a cup of coffee since she'd given the cabbie her last fiver. So she was facing a day with no coffee and no food, drinking out of the tap in the loos. Kathy had not been especially excited about going back to London but it would have been infinitely better than the day she was looking forward to now.

She idly pressed the on button of her phone and scrolled through the photographs she'd taken over the last three days. As she sat on the hard plastic seat, it was difficult to imagine that just a few hours earlier she'd been in such a beautiful place as the Palazzo Boldrini. She was wistful as she scrolled through a series of spectacular views and a close-up of an enormous peach-pink rose that had reminded of her childhood copy of *Beauty and the Beast*.

A few pictures further on, she came upon a shot of the music room, of the beautiful Bösendorfer piano and the stool she had shared with Henry Innocenti. It was a memory she'd hoped to cherish but it was over-laid now with that awful moment when Neil had shoved the five-euro note into Henry's pocket after making him play 'Yellow' at the wedding dinner. Kathy cringed at the memory.

She scrolled forward through the photos again until she got to a picture someone had taken of her and Neil, seconds after their engagement. She looked red, flustered. Had she known what was coming, she would definitely not have had so much wine. But then had she really known what was coming, she might have swerved the wedding altogether. She now understood why a public proposal was far from romantic, giving the person on the receiving end no real opportunity to answer freely or to ask questions of their own. It was an ambush.

Kathy closed the photo app. But it had reminded her that she had yet to call her mother and tell her the 'good news'.

Clare answered her phone at once. Kathy wondered if her mother carried the landline receiver around the house in a pocket. She never let it ring more than twice.

'Are you OK?' was always her first question.

'Of course,' Kathy assured her.

'You're flying back this morning, aren't you? I won't be able to relax until I know you've landed so make sure you text when you do.'

'I may be a while yet.' Kathy explained the problem.

'Neil left you at the airport? On your own?'

'Mum, I told him to. No point in us all being stuck here. Besides, Neil probably needs a little time alone with the children. He had some big news for them last night and they're still digesting it.'

'What is it? He's not ill, is he?'

'No, Mum. It's good news. We're engaged.'

'What?'

'It happened at the wedding. After the speeches. Neil asked me to marry him in front of everybody. The ring is . . . Well, you'll see it.'

Kathy looked at it on her finger. How would she describe it? Big? Flashy? A consolation prize?

At the other end, Clare seemed lost for words. 'Oh, my darling,' she said eventually. 'I'm so happy for you both.'

'Thank you, Mum.'

'Have you set a date?'

'Not yet. I was surprised he asked. I had no idea.'

'You must have had some inkling he was going to propose?'

'No,' said Kathy. That much was true. Kathy did not think the thought of marriage had ever crossed Neil's mind. Especially not after . . . No, she wasn't going to tell her mother about that. Not now. 'We hadn't spoken about it, that's all.'

'I suppose a divorce like Neil had would make any man shy of standing at the altar again. But I was beginning to worry about you. There's no reason why you shouldn't have everything you want out of life because his first wife was unfaithful and ended up with half his money.'

'More than half.' Kathy heard Neil's voice in her head.

'I wonder what changed his mind?' Clare mused.

Kathy had an idea but she said, 'Perhaps he just fancies a big party like his brother's.'

'How did the children react?'

'They seemed pleased,' Kathy lied. 'I expect they're glad I'm going to be around to look after him in his old age.'

'You do look after him very well,' Clare said.

'He looks after me too,' Kathy said. It felt like the right thing to say.

'It's a huge weight off my mind. Oh, Kathy, your father would have been so pleased. One of the things that upset him most about the cancer was that he knew he'd never be able to walk you down the aisle. But he wrote a speech,' Clare told her then, 'so he could be there in spirit whatever happened. I've kept it safe for exactly this moment. Oh, your dad loved you so much. I can't believe he's missing out on this. You were the apple of his eye.'

'Mum, stop it,' said Kathy. 'You're going to make me cry in the airport.'

'I'm making myself cry here,' said Clare.

'Getting engaged is a happy event.'

Clare gave an anguished sniff.

'I should have waited to tell you in person,' Kathy said. 'Then I could be giving you a hug.'

'That would have been nice,' said Clare. 'Will you be able to come and see me soon? Both of you?'

'Well, I will, definitely,' said Kathy. She knew that Neil might have more important things to do. He usually did.

'There'll be so much to talk about. Do you think you'll have the wedding near you? Or near me?'

By 'near me', Clare meant at St George's, the church where she and Eddie had married. The church where they'd met, in fact, as members of the choir.

'We probably won't go for a big white wedding,

Mum,' said Kathy. 'Seems a bit over the top, given Neil's been married before and I'm hardly twenty-one. But,' she added quickly, 'I promise you'll be involved in every aspect of the planning. There's no way I could do it without you. You'll come dress shopping, of course.'

'Try and stop me. Will you have bridesmaids? Sophie and Amelie will want to be bridesmaids, I expect.'

Kathy doubted it. 'Look, Mum. I've got to go. I don't have much battery left on the phone. Neil's taken the charger.'

'Get home safely, won't you? I hope you don't have to stay in Florence for three nights. I don't like to think of you being there on your own.'

'I thought it was your favourite city.'

'It was,' said Clare. 'But that was because I had your dad by my side.'

Once again, Eddie's absence opened up between them, like a crack in the earth. Clare wasn't the only one who'd felt safer while Eddie was alive but Kathy had to be strong. 'I'll take care, Mum. Chances are I won't get any further than the airport. Neil is going to sort out a new ticket as soon as he lands. He thinks he can get me on a BA flight tonight. The last thing he wants is to have to look after the children on his own all weekend.'

'Your future stepchildren,' Clare observed. 'You're going to be a mother at last.'

'Yes,' said Kathy. 'After a fashion. Look, I've got to go.'

'OK, love,' said Clare. 'Have a safe trip home. I love you!'

'I love you too.'

Kathy had lied about her phone. It had plenty of

battery life and she had the charger in her handbag. Neil would be upset when he got back to London to discover that was the case. But Kathy didn't want to talk to her mother any longer that day. She was glad she'd been able to call Clare with the 'good news', but the fact was that if she'd continued to talk about it, she would almost certainly have given voice to the thoughts that had been eating her up over the last week. Since V-Day, as she called it in her head.

A coffee would have made things feel a good deal better. Kathy pulled her purse out of her bag and checked – knowing all the while it was hopeless – that she hadn't kept a couple of notes from their last trip to the Eurozone. No such luck. She checked the pockets in her handbag. She even felt around to see if a couple of coins might have slipped through to the lining. Nothing. She did have her cards, though. She could get some money out of a cashpoint. The exchange rate wouldn't be great. Neil always made sure to order their holiday cash months in advance to ensure the best deal. But this was an emergency. Would he really expect her to go the whole day with nothing but water?

'Probably,' said a little voice in Kathy's head.

'Sod it,' she said out loud.

Kathy did a few quick sums in her head and decided she should take out two hundred euros. What she didn't spend – and she would spend as little as she could, of course – she and Neil could take on their next trip abroad. She imagined justifying the decision and was satisfied that Neil would agree.

With the crisp new euro notes in her hand, Kathy went straight to the coffee counter. She ordered an espresso. Then changed her order to a double. And a pastry. One of the type filled with chocolate spread that she hadn't been able to eat at the palazzo for fear of Neil's or Margaret's or Sophie's disapproval. The barista rewarded the upgrade with a nod. Kathy stood at a high table to knock back the coffee and eat the delicate little pastry that was gone in a couple of seconds. She used her finger to pick up the last of the crumbs and savoured their buttery taste. She felt immediately more human as the coffee went straight into her veins.

As she finished, she watched the people coming and going. She glanced at the clock on her phone. It was still only nine. Even if Neil could get her on that evening's BA flight by pulling rank as a frequent flyer, Kathy still had ten hours to go before she would need to be at the check-in desk again.

Outside, the summer sun warmed the pavements. It was shaping up to be another glorious day. A quick look at the weather app on her phone had already told Kathy that Neil would be flying back into chilly London rain. She should at least stand outside the terminal, find a spot away from the smokers, where she could feel the sun on her face, and snatch her last chance of a tan.

Kathy walked out through the big automatic doors and wandered the length of the terminal. From the far end, she could see the Tuscan hills. She gazed enviously at a white house set in a coppice high above the airport. What were the people who lived in that house doing now? Drinking their morning coffee with a view over the valley? Could they see the Duomo from there?

Kathy sat on her suitcase and looked at the view

until a smoker in search of solitude also found her secret spot.

Smoked out, she abandoned her place and dragged her case back towards the terminal entrance. She headed for the row of seats where she'd been sitting earlier. They were all full. There was nowhere else to sit down. A school group had colonised every chair. Even the stools at the bar were full.

Kathy drifted around the polished halls with her suitcase. This was going to be a long day. Unless . . .

The centre of Florence was perhaps half an hour's cab ride away. Kathy knew from her research – back when she'd still thought Neil might agree to tag on a few days in the city after the wedding – that the price of a cab from the airport to the centre was fixed at about twenty-five euros. She had in her handbag 195 euros after her morning snack. It was more than enough to pay for a cab to the city and back and have lunch at a café in between.

Kathy felt her heart quicken as she considered her plan. She'd never been abroad alone before, had always travelled with her family or a boyfriend. These days she relied on Neil to tell her whether or not her plans were sensible. He was big on travelling safely. He had told her to stay put in the airport but it was a glorious day and Kathy was just half an hour away from the city she'd dreamed of since she was a child. It was crazy to come this far only to spend ten hours sitting in a plastic seat at an airport – assuming she could even find a plastic seat to sit on – when she could be strolling the streets of Firenze. It would be a criminal waste of a perfect opportunity.

'But you've got all your worldly belongings with you,'

Neil's voice said. 'You can't drag them around all day.'

Actually, Kathy could drag them around. She'd packed especially lightly – cabin baggage only – because Neil hated to wait at luggage carousels. She had just a small wheelie case and her 'travelling handbag' with all the zip-up pockets. She'd manage. All over the world every day, women had far bigger adventures in more dangerous places. They crossed deserts. They circumnavigated the globe. If Victorian women had climbed mountains in their petticoats, Kathy Courage could manage a single day alone in Florence.

She followed the sign to the taxi queue.

She was going in.

Chapter Seventeen

Sitting in the back of a taxi, Kathy's courage wavered. Neil had been quite firm about it. She should stay in the airport terminal. And the taxi could not have been more different from the car she and Neil had travelled in earlier that morning. The fake leather seats in the back were held together with duct tape that scratched Kathy's bare arms. There was no air-conditioning. The driver instead had rolled down all the windows. He was smoking out of his and every time the taxi paused at a light, the smoke would snake back into the car through the window next to Kathy.

But even the fug of cigarette smoke and the cloying scent of one of those horrible air-fresheners could not dampen Kathy's excitement. She kept an eye on the journey's progress via the map on her phone, as Neil often did to make sure a cabbie wasn't ripping him off. The names of the streets were musical, even if, for the moment, the buildings were not. Along one road, there seemed to be an inordinate number of petrol stations.

Then, as if a mirage had appeared, they were driving up to a medieval arch. The taxi driver bullied his way through, squeezing his car under at the same time as two scooters, whose riders beeped their disapproval. And on the other side, everything changed. It was as though the arch was a portal to another time. The streets suddenly narrowed. Pedestrians had to squeeze themselves into doorways to let the taxi pass as it slowed to walking pace, beeping to let them know it was coming.

They crawled on into the city. A horse might have been faster. Kathy felt like a child again as she peered out of the window, feeling transported back to the Florence of Dante and Galileo. Of Michelangelo and the Medicis. Of her parents when they were young.

And there was the Arno!

Sluggish and brown, it did not look like the river immortalised in literature and opera but Kathy was still enchanted. Especially when she looked up to her right to see what was arguably the most famous bridge in the world. The Ponte Vecchio, the Old Bridge, lined all the way across with buildings. Higgledy-piggledy, in a dozen different colours and distinctly ramshackle, they looked ready to fall into the water.

I'm going to walk across the Ponte Vecchio at last, Kathy thought, as she saw it. Excitement bubbled in her stomach and her heart. She was really in Florence now!

She asked the driver to take her as near to the Duomo as possible. He dropped her off at the piazza Santa Maria Novella, opposite the main railway station. She counted out four notes to pay him and he got out of the car to help her unload her luggage after she told him to keep the change.

The piazza Santa Maria Novella was not Florence's most Instagrammable location but to Kathy, who had never before stood in a piazza in a proper Italian city, it was magical enough. The church of Santa Maria Novella dominated one end of the square, splendid in black and white marble, facing a grand obelisk in the middle of an ornamental lawn. She had been dropped off right in the middle of Florentine life. Elegantly suited men and women on their way to work crossed the piazza as though they were in a catwalk show. Dodging out of the way of the scooters and the taxis, Kathy sheltered in the shade of a colonnade as she took in the spectacle. She felt a little underdressed in her linen shirt and Marks & Spencer chinos, but she was there to see things, not to be seen.

The Duomo was signposted, of course. Kathy pulled her case, rattling, across the square and joined a throng of human traffic heading in the right direction. At a crossroads she had to wait as a procession passed. A group of men dressed in Renaissance costume paraded slowly along the street to the beat of a single drum. At the front of the procession a horse wore matching Renaissance livery. The men walking behind it each carried flags. As they drew level with Kathy they stopped and tossed them high into the air, catching them with the skill and precision of a band of manly majorettes.

Kathy was immediately enchanted. It was as though the show had been put on especially for her. As the members of a German tour group that had somehow surrounded her tried to catch a frame of the flags unfurled in mid-air, she watched the spectacle hungrily, wishing she knew what the procession meant and where it was going. She snapped some photos of her own to show Neil.

Once the parade had moved on, Kathy continued on her path to the cathedral, keeping her eye on the signs that seemed sometimes to be leading her in a circle. She followed a rat-run of ever-decreasing alleyways

– *vicoli* – until she saw sharp sunlight on the cobbles to the end of one, and there, the vista suddenly opened up again.

At last, Kathy stood in the shadow of the world-famous Duomo. It was all she could do not to cry out in happiness. She had made it to Florence and she had made it to the Duomo. The Cathedral of Santa Maria del Fiore. What was more, she'd made it there by herself. She felt like a medieval pilgrim, though her journey had been considerably less arduous.

The black, white and green marble-striped walls of the cathedral were exactly as she had imagined them. The doors, so intricately carved, begged to be inspected more closely. And that huge dome, orange terracotta striped with white tiles, was a true feat of engineering. In front of the Duomo was the Baptistery, itself bigger than the average church back home. And there was the Campanile – the cathedral's bell-tower – even taller than the dome. Kathy's parents had climbed that tower many years before.

Though it was still relatively early, the enormous piazza del Duomo was thronged and the queue to go inside the cathedral snaked already almost all the way around the building. While sparrows strutted their stuff across the flagstones, swallows wheeled overhead. A cluster of young soldiers leaned against an armoured car, while young female tourists (and some older ones) queued to be pictured alongside them. Street sellers tried with their brightly coloured tat to catch the attention and pester power of bored children. A group of nuns in sober grey and black hurried by, like busy pigeons, and were ushered ahead of the queue into the nave.

Of course Kathy wanted to look inside the cathedral but the signs all around made it clear that she wouldn't be allowed in with her suitcase. She'd have to save making a proper visit for another trip. There would be another. She was sure about that. For now, it was just enough to stand in the cathedral's shadow and listen to the great bells in its campanile sound the hour. One, two, three . . . Eleven o'clock.

'I will be back,' she promised herself, snapping a couple of pictures. Perhaps even on honeymoon.

As she thought that, Kathy looked at her ring. She gave it a quick polish on the leg of her chinos. Then she turned it so that the stones faced into the palm of her hand, where they would be hidden from unfriendly eyes. Yes, she decided. She would tell Neil that she wanted to honeymoon in Italy. If he really wanted to marry her, if they were really going to get married, he couldn't deny her that. Not after everything else.

For now, with the Duomo in front of her and a whole day ahead of her, Kathy was sure that coming into Florence was the best idea she'd had in a long time.

There was so much to see and Kathy wanted to see it all. The taxi driver had given her a paper map from the wodge he carried in his glove compartment. She unfolded it now. She was aware as she did so that she was drawing dangerous attention to herself, marking herself out as someone who wasn't a local, but she figured her bright blue wheelie case and the fact she kept taking photos were already doing that.

With her finger, she worked out a route from the Duomo to the piazza della Signoria. Not that she really needed to do so. All the tour groups were heading in the same direction, like vast shoals of exotic migrating fish in brightly coloured shorts and backpacks. It wasn't long before Kathy caught up with the snap-happy Germans, who were pausing in a narrow street to admire – and take pictures of – a nondescript-looking window, while their guide chattered an explanation Kathy wished she understood. She took a mental note of the name of the street and promised herself she'd look it up later.

The narrow streets on all sides of the piazza del Duomo were clogged with slow-moving tourists, who parted with the leisurely bemusement of cows in a British country lane when a scooter or a taxi made an effort to get through. Kathy had no hope of making the crowd part for her, so she joined the flow and followed at a pilgrim's pace, clinging tight to the handle of her wheelie case. Her handbag was safely strapped across her body. Her passport was tucked into the breast pocket of her shirt. Her engagement ring was still turned inwards so that it looked like a very ordinary silver band. There were plenty of tourists an enterprising thief would target before he targeted her, Kathy thought.

The crowds slowed again to pass a roadblock caused by a man who had set up a portable card table and gathered a group of American tourists to watch the classic three-card trick. How did anyone not know that was a scam? Had Neil been there, Kathy was sure he would have told the gullible crowd that, while they were concentrating on the unwinnable game, the card sharp's accomplices were probably going through their bags.

A trinket seller waved an armful of colourful

necklaces in Kathy's face. 'Necklace? Sunglass? Umbrella?' he asked.

There was definitely no need for an umbrella in Florence that day unless you were a tour guide.

Kathy shook her head and didn't make eye contact. The trinket seller moved on to a more likely customer. Kathy could hear Neil's voice in her head as the man walked off: 'You feel sorry for those guys but if you give them any money for that crap, which isn't even made in Africa, all you're doing is supporting the drug trade.'

Kathy did not want to support the drug trade. All she wanted right then was to sit down and have a drink. After the excitement of seeing the Duomo, she was beginning to feel a little dizzy. The caffeine and sugar high she'd got from the espresso and pastry at the airport had long since worn off and she was tired and hot. A late night and an early start were catching up with her.

Kathy promised herself she would sit down outside a café at the very next opportunity, so she was delighted when the stream of tourists and traders turned a corner and the vista suddenly opened up again.

'La piazza della Signoria,' the German tour guide announced, with a flourish of her brolly. While the guide's followers went into a frenzy of photography, Kathy slipped around them and headed straight for the centre of Florence's most famous square.

And there he was. The enormous white marble replica of Michelangelo's *David* looked out over the tourists, implacable and timeless. Kathy drew breath. Though the piazza was heaving with visitors, she could imagine her parents in front of the statue. Her mother posing for a photograph. Her smiling face as she waited for her new husband to take the picture. She could imagine her father doing his best to get the perfect shot, then asking a passing stranger to take a picture of the pair of them. How happy the newly-weds had been.

But though *David* drew the eye like nothing else, everywhere Kathy looked there was something to catch her attention. She did a slow circuit of the whole L-shaped piazza, dragging her bag behind her. Behind *David* was the red-brick Palazzo Vecchio, with its distinctive tower. Eyeing Michelangelo's best boy from the corner of the palazzo was the equally impressively muscled *Neptune*, standing four metres high atop Bandinelli's fountain. Beneath a colonnade opposite *Neptune* and *David* – the Loggia dei Lanzi – were yet more replica statues. Cellini's *Perseus* held aloft the head of Medusa. The Sabines gracefully suffered their fate.

So much art and beauty! And how lightly the city wore its treasures, Kathy thought. She really couldn't see how Neil had failed to be moved, though plenty of the city's visitors that day seemed similarly unexcited, casually eating sandwiches with their backs to the statue of Judith finishing off Holofernes with a slash of her flashing sword.

Perhaps they weren't seeing it for the first time, as Kathy was. She couldn't quite take in the magnificence of it all. Was this what they called 'Florence syndrome' or 'Stendhal syndrome', after the nineteenth-century French author who'd had a funny turn when he visited the city? There were no words to describe how she felt. In that piazza, in the city she had wanted to visit for so long, she felt breathless with happiness. Overwhelmed with joy and – if she was honest – pride that she'd actually made it.

She was in Florence at last.

Chapter Eighteen

As in the other piazzas, the cafés in the piazza della Signoria were busy already. Kathy knew that, in the very heart of tourist Florence, the cafés would not be the best value, or even the best at anything, but she decided she would choose one all the same. There was safety in numbers. Neil would be happy with that. And this had to be the very best place in Florence to watch the world go by. Quite literally, the whole world. Kathy heard snippets of every language she knew and a great many she didn't. She felt she had at last scored an invitation to a party that had been going on without her for too long.

A waiter caught Kathy's eye and gestured with a flourish to an empty table right on the front of his terrace, which was opposite the Palazzo Vecchio. It was a great table. A couple making a beeline for it were clearly disappointed when Kathy was given preference. She let the waiter pull out a chair for her, and settled down with her wheelie case alongside her. She took off her cross-body bag and placed it on the table, where she could keep a close eye on it. From time to time, a system of pipes attached to the café's canopy puffed out a cooling mist. Kathy let it settle over her face, which she was sure must be as red as a tomato after the morning she'd had.

The waiter brought Kathy's water and some

breadsticks with the menu. When he asked her if she would like something else, she surprised herself by asking for a glass of wine. Pinot Grigio. It was the only Italian wine she could think of right then. The waiter smiled.

This was perfection. Well, it would have been perfection if Neil were there too, Kathy thought. Though, honestly, if he had been, he would have complained about the noisy American family on the table to the right. And the noisy Spanish family on the table to the left. And the noisy English family who were settling at the table behind, the mother assuring the children that there would be pizza with ham but none of that funny foreign ham they'd been so upset about the day before. If they ate their pizza, of course there would be *gelato*. Of course.

Kathy smiled to herself, reminded of previous holidays with Neil's children, who were very fussy eaters. Oscar wouldn't eat fruit. Amelie wouldn't eat vegetables. Sophie was a 'vegan'. Except when she got in late from the pub and the only thing she could find in the fridge was the Waitrose pepperoni pizza that Neil liked as a weekend treat. The rest of the week, Neil wanted plain grilled fish and vegetables. Food for him was about nutrition. That was all.

Kathy thought that good food nourished the eyes as much as the stomach. The beauty of that moment in Florence wasn't limited to the high art that dotted the piazza as casually as recycling bins dotted the high street back home. When the waiter returned with her glass of wine, he brought with him a little wooden tray, which was loaded with miniature snacks. A tiny golden breadstick wrapped in a curl of prosciutto as fine as silk. A lump of Parmesan, with the crumbly grainy texture that you never found in the plastic-wrapped Parmesan bought from British supermarkets. An oval slice of crisp bread topped with a delicious concoction of delicately chopped tomatoes and olives, mixed with fragrant herbs. It looked like enough to make a whole lunch but by the time Kathy had finished the little platter, she was hungry for more. Which was the idea, she supposed.

Could she have another glass of wine? Should she? And a bowl of pasta? She knew what Neil would do. He would say that one glass was enough and she should buy a sandwich from a supermarket rather than waste more money at such an overpriced spot. The prices on the café's menu were pretty hefty – that was true – but Kathy watched with envy as the waiter brought out the food the Spanish family had ordered. It looked delicious. They looked delighted. She ordered a small dish of pasta and a side salad. And another glass of the pale yellow Pinot Grigio, which tasted as innocuous as water flavoured with white petals.

If this was to be the only day she spent in Florence for a while, she was going to make the most of it.

Kathy had just finished the pasta when her phone rang. It was Neil. Kathy rushed to pick up the call before it clicked through to voicemail. Neil went straight into a rant.

'We circled over the airport for half an hour. It was an absolute shambles. I shall be writing to the head of British Airways. What's happening with your flight? Have you managed to get yourself on one today?'

'No,' said Kathy cautiously. 'I thought you were going to get Melanie to do it.'

'I still expected you to be trying in the meantime.

Tell me you did try. You didn't let yourself get fobbed off again, did you?'

'No—' Kathy began to protest.

'You can't let your fear of confrontation hold you back, Chicken.'

'It's just sometimes there doesn't seem to be any point in getting confrontational. You know the people who work on the desks at the airport can very rarely do anything.'

'That's what they'd like you to think. They want you to think they can't do anything so you'll go away and end up being someone else's problem. Chicken Licken, you've got to stop being such a pushover. Do you want to have to stay in Florence until Monday?'

Kathy declined to answer that. Because, really, would it be such a bad thing to have three days in this town? Looking out over the piazza della Signoria towards the statue of *David*, dazzling white in the sunshine, she thought she would have been perfectly happy to stay for the rest of the year.

'Where are you now?' Neil asked. 'Go back to the ticket desk and hand them the phone so I can talk to them and tell them what you need.'

'I can't.'

'Why not?'

'Because I took a taxi into the centre of Florence. I'm in the piazza della Signoria. I'm just looking at the statue of *David* and—'

'Wait. You're telling me you're not at the airport?'

'No. Because when I thought about it, it just seemed silly to sit there in the terminal all day. And I've always wanted to see Florence, as you know.'

'But now? Seriously, Chicken? Now? While we're

supposed to be trying to get you back to London? I asked you to stay where you were for a reason. Get another taxi back to the airport as soon as you can. Melanie will get you onto the BA flight this evening.'

'What time does the flight go?' Kathy asked, heart sinking just a little.

'Nine o'clock, but the sooner you're at the airport the better. Melanie may be able to get you onto something earlier going via Hamburg or Amsterdam.' Neil continued to tell Kathy about all the things he had planned to do that were going to be compromised or made impossible by the fact she had been stranded in Florence. Kathy listened and made the appropriate noises of contrition.

While Kathy was on the phone the waiter brought her a little glass of limoncello on the house. She sipped it surreptitiously, as though Neil would be able to tell she wasn't drinking water.

'I do not have time to deal with flight cock-ups. . .'

As Neil detailed exactly why he didn't even have time for this particular conversation, Kathy fiddled with the ring on her left hand. They would have to get it made smaller or she would lose it. Even with the heat, which was making her sandals feel tight, the ring twirled freely. As Neil spoke about the inconvenience of having to spend the weekend without her, Kathy decided she should probably take the ring off before it came to any harm. Still making the appropriate noises, she tucked the phone under her chin and slipped the ring into one of the zip-up pockets in her handbag – an interior one. Now there was no danger that it would fall off her finger and be lost in the cobbled streets. That would be a disaster.

'So get a taxi straight to the airport and wait for Melanie to call you with further details,' Neil concluded. 'Try not to get lost.'

Neil hung up, leaving Kathy feeling thoroughly told off. She could understand, though. She was in a sunny piazza, having just had a pretty wonderful lunch. He was on the Gatwick Express with three sulking teenagers, drinking too-hot tea from a plastic cup. And he was worried about Kathy being on her own in a foreign city. Of course he was. When Neil was worried, he often came across as brusque. Kathy didn't suppose his hangover was better yet either.

It was time to say what she hoped was a temporary *addio* to her Italian dream. Resignedly, Kathy put her phone into her handbag and turned in her chair to signal to the waiter that she was ready for her bill. And it was in that exact moment that the thief who had been lurking nearby saw his moment to strike. By the time Kathy had caught the waiter's eye, the thief had snatched Kathy's bag and made a run for it.

Chapter Nineteen

'Help!' Kathy leaped to her feet. 'Help! My bag! Stop thief! Help!'

She attempted to give chase but was hampered by the café tables, which had been packed in more tightly than tuna fillet in a tin, and though the other customers were interested in the commotion, no one seemed to understand that they needed to get out of the way.

'Someone took my bag,' Kathy explained, as she stumbled over chair legs, actual legs and other people's luggage. By the time she got out of the café terrace confines into the piazza itself, the thief was well on his way.

Though on some level she already knew she'd never catch him, Kathy ran in the direction he'd taken. The crowds didn't help. The thief seemed to have a magical ability to slip through the unrelenting sea of people that poured into the piazza from every corner. He was well camouflaged too. Kathy was only able to keep track of him at all because her bag was a particularly bright shade of purple.

Her heart pounded as she ran, from exertion and adrenalin. She found uncharacteristic brusqueness as she dealt with the tourists who milled about so aimlessly – though she did manage to say, 'Excuse me,' every time she gently encouraged someone out of her way.

When she wasn't saying, 'Excuse me', she was yelling,

'Thief!' but while that certainly made people turn to look, it didn't encourage anyone to stop the little bugger for her. His ability to part the people ahead of him was like some kind of magic trick. Without questioning why he was in such a hurry, the tourists moved aside, only to close up again, like water, when Kathy tried to follow.

Though she and the thief must have passed hundreds of people, only one other person reacted in any helpful sort of way. It was a woman. She must have heard Kathy shout and put two and two together with the young man who was moving against the human tide, carrying a purple bag that wasn't an obvious accessory for a bloke otherwise dressed in scruffy camouflage pants and a filthy black T-shirt.

'Thief!' the woman called in Italian. 'Stop that man!'

She even made a swipe at the thief's stomach with her own bag but it didn't slow him down for a second. Still the brave Samaritan took up the chase while, finally running out of energy, Kathy stumbled, having failed to see a gap in the uneven paving stones. She landed badly, skinning the heels of her hands on the pavement, having stuck them out to try to break her fall. With her hands stinging and her head ringing from the jolt, Kathy pushed herself up and collapsed against a wall, chest heaving. The thief and the Good Samaritan finally disappeared into the distance. It was time to give up.

Kathy swore extravagantly. Her bag, her phone, her wallet. All gone.

Unable to hold back her tears, Kathy stumbled on to the piazza del Duomo – the direction in which the thief and the Samaritan had run – and sank to the ground in the shade of the cathedral, with her back against a wall. She could not have felt more differently from when she'd arrived full of wonder just a couple of hours before. Now she sat with her hands covering her eyes as she caught her breath. If anyone had seen the chase, no one but the Good Samaritan seemed to care. The tourists carried on around her. Most were utterly oblivious. Those who saw her gave her a wide berth in case she asked them for money or help. Kathy certainly looked like she needed help. Her hands were filthy from where she'd planted them on the cobbles as she fell. The knees of her chinos were dirty too. One was actually ripped open, showing a nasty graze. She could not believe her bad luck.

After a couple of minutes, a passing *carabiniere* in shiny black boots tapped the side of Kathy's shoe with his toecap and told her she couldn't sit there. She was making the Duomo look untidy. 'Is not allowed,' he said.

Kathy struggled to get up. The combination of the race to catch the thief and the heat of the Florentine afternoon had left her feeling quite weak. She wasn't sure she could stand up without leaning against something. The *carabiniere* looked on impassively but suddenly Kathy felt a hand on her elbow as someone finally stepped in to help her find her feet. It was a woman, around Kathy's age. As she helped her upright, the woman was simultaneously upbraiding the police officer in angry Italian. The officer shrugged and walked off.

Kathy's new friend made a lewd gesture at his back. '*Stronzo!*' she added, for good measure. Then she turned back to Kathy. '*Inglese?*' she asked.

'Yes,' said Kathy. 'How can you tell?'

The woman shrugged. 'An instinct.'

She meant Kathy's outfit, Kathy was sure.

'Are you OK? Do you need to sit down again? Here, let me help you to a bench. That arsehole policeman won't bother you any more. I told him you'd just been robbed and if he was doing his job properly, instead of bothering tourists who aren't doing anyone any harm, he'd be running after the thief who took your bag. He could do with the exercise. I ran after that guy as far as I could,' the woman continued, 'but at the top of the road over there he had a mate with a moped waiting for him and they were gone in a flash.'

'You were the one who ran after him?'

'Yes. I was in the alleyway when he came flying through with you in hot pursuit. I knew at once what had happened. That wasn't his bag, I said to myself.'

'You tried to stop him with your own.'

The woman nodded. 'I'm sorry that didn't work. I should have swung at him harder. I wish I had. I'm Carla, by the way.' She offered Kathy her hand.

'Kathy.'

Kathy winced as they shook on their new acquaintance.

'Did he hurt you?' Carla asked. 'The thief?'

'No. But I fell over just after you joined the chase. I landed on my hands and knees. And I'm winded from all the running.'

Carla took both Kathy's hands in hers and turned them over so that she could see the damage. 'Ouch. We need to get you cleaned up.'

'It looks worse than it is,' said Kathy.

'All the same . . .' Carla fished in her bag for some wet wipes. 'Where were you when your bag was taken?'

'In the piazza della Signoria. I was sitting outside a café. One of the big ones opposite the Palazzo Vecchio. My bag was on the table.'

Carla shook her head and tutted. 'They watch for that. You think your bag is safe because it's in front of you where you can see it but, *pouf*, if anything, when it's up high like that it's easier to snatch. I expect he was watching you, waiting for the exact moment your attention was elsewhere.'

Kathy shivered at the thought. She'd been so happy outside that café. So utterly oblivious. The idea that someone had been watching her, like a sparrow hawk watching a mouse in the grass, was most upsetting.

'Was it an expensive bag? Did you have much in it?' Carla asked.

'My purse. My phone . . .'

'Your passport?'

'No, thank goodness, that's . . .' Kathy patted her breast pocket a little anxiously. 'Yes, that's still here. My fiancé is always telling me you should keep your passport separate from everything else for exactly this kind of eventuality. He was right.'

'Well, that is good news at least. Credit cards and phones are easy enough to replace. A passport is a whole different matter. I don't think you can even do that in Florence any more. Anything else in your bag? Anything important?'

'I don't think so. Just some make-up. Some loyalty cards.' But then she remembered. She covered her eyes with her hands again. 'Oh, my God. And my engagement ring!'

'Your engagement ring?'

'Yes. It's brand new. I only got engaged yesterday.'

Carla didn't ask why the engagement ring was in Kathy's bag and not on her finger. Instead, she nodded grimly and said, 'Don't worry. We'll sort it out.' She pulled a bottle of water from her bag and waited while Kathy drank some. 'You'll need to cancel your credit cards and I'll take you to the nearest police station. There's no point talking to any of the muppets patrolling round here but you'll need a case number for your insurance. You do have travel insurance, I hope?'

Kathy was sure Neil must have arranged that, though whether it covered her belongings if he wasn't with her, she had no idea. And would it cover a brand new diamond ring that should have been on her hand?

'It will be OK,' Carla reassured her again. 'At the end of the day, it's only stuff. All of it. Even the ring. Your fiancé will just be glad you're safe.'

Kathy hoped Neil would see it like that.

Chapter Twenty

While Carla walked with Kathy back to the piazza della Signoria to find the wheelie case she'd left behind – which the Americans on the next table had taken into their care – she asked if there was someone Kathy wanted to call.

'Your fiancé, of course,' she said. 'But perhaps you ought to wait to call him when we've finished at the police station. There's no point unduly worrying him. Once we've seen the police, you'll feel better.'

That seemed like a solid plan. Though, as it was, Kathy couldn't remember Neil's mobile number, only the number for their home landline, which no one ever picked up because the only people who called it were salesmen or Neil's mother. Neither Neil nor his children seemed to want to talk to Granny Margaret.

The waiter at the café told Kathy that the Americans had not only looked after her bag, they'd paid her bill.

Then it was off to the police station where they joined a queue of unhappy tourists all waiting to report similar incidents. While Kathy used Carla's phone to call her bank and stop the stolen cards, Carla took control of reporting the theft, going straight to the desk and asking for the relevant forms in a way that suggested it wasn't the first time she'd had to do this. When an officer finally appeared, Carla chivvied him into getting the forms stamped *'pronto'*.

Kathy was profusely grateful. Grateful but slightly confused. She'd heard of the kindness of strangers but never before had she actually experienced it. This wonderful bilingual woman didn't know her at all yet she'd gone out of her way when she'd tried to catch the thief. Perhaps even put herself in danger. She must have better things to do than help a British woman she'd never met before.

'Why are you helping me?' Kathy asked, as they filled in the forms together.

'Why wouldn't I?' Carla said, looking surprised. 'Actually, think of it as a case of what goes around . . . When I was a student in London, people were kind to me in the same way.'

'They were?'

'I was at art college and worked as a waitress in the evenings. I lived way out at the end of the Piccadilly Line. One night I fell asleep on the way home, and when I woke up as the train reached its destination, I realised all my bags were gone. My handbag. My bag with my clothes in it. I was still wearing my TGI Friday uniform. They even took the big folder I used to carry my artwork around. All of it was gone. I had nothing. I didn't even have my keys to get back into my flat and my flatmate was away for the weekend.

'Two old ladies came to my rescue. Proper old Londoners, sisters, on their way home from the pub. They took me to the station and made sure the police treated me properly. Then, when I'd made my report, they took me back to their flat and made me tea and spaghetti hoops on toast. Because that was the only Italian food they had, they said.' She smiled at the memory. 'And the next day they clubbed together to give me fifty quid to keep me going until I could get my bank cards sorted out. That's the sort of kindness you don't forget. Think of this as me paying it forward.'

'Then I'm very grateful to those Londoners,' Kathy said.

'Where are you staying?' Carla asked. 'When we finish here I'll walk you there.'

'I don't have a hotel,' said Kathy. 'I was supposed to be flying back to London this evening.'

'Then what time is your flight? We can get you a car to the airport.'

'I don't know. I don't even know if I'm on it. I mean, it wasn't confirmed.' Kathy explained the situation.

'Then you had better come with me,' said Carla.

'Where?'

'Back to my family's place.'

'I don't want to impose. It's one thing you helping me file a police report, it's another taking me back to your home.'

'You would not be imposing. We're used to having guests. We run a hotel.'

'But I can't pay. I've only got . . .' Kathy pulled out the euros she had folded into her passport. That was another of Neil's travel tips. Don't keep all your cash in one place. '. . . Fifty euros to my name. That's not enough for a hotel room. Is it?'

'Stop it,' said Carla. 'You don't need money to stay at the Casa Innocenti. I'll text Mamma to say we're on our way.'

And that was that. Since Neil had not yet returned the call Kathy had made from Carla's mobile while they were in the police station – she'd had to leave a message on the landline – she wasn't sure what choice she had but to follow this Italian stranger home. She couldn't just go to the airport and sit there, could she? Neil would have no way of getting in touch with her. She very much doubted she'd be allowed to sleep in the airport departure lounge until her Monday flight.

Besides, there was something about Carla that made Kathy feel she could trust her. Something about her eyes and her smile as she'd talked about the old ladies in London who had helped her in her own moment of need. That sounded like a genuine story. Then there was something about her face, which was as warm and open as the face of a Renaissance Madonna and which seemed somehow familiar, like the face of someone she already knew and liked.

'But how can I repay you?' Kathy tried one more time.

Carla laughed. 'Believe me, Kathy, everyone at the Casa Innocenti ends up singing for their supper.'

Carla insisted on taking Kathy's suitcase for her. She said it was no problem because she was used to carrying heavy bags, thanks to growing up in a hotel. Kathy was grateful. It was hard enough to navigate the uneven pavements without the case and she was suddenly so very tired.

'It's nice to find someone I can bore with my memories of London,' said Carla. 'I was at St Martin's College. Do you know it?'

'Doesn't everyone?' Kathy asked.

'No. I studied fashion. Like in the song. You know, the Pulp song? Except I was living like the common people in London because I had to, not because I wanted to. Which is why what those two old ladies did when they took me under their wing that night was life-saving. I think I would have given up and gone home to Italy without them. They gave me the strength to stay.'

As they walked, Carla talked about her home city. The Casa Innocenti – 'It sounds far grander than it really is' – was on the Oltrarno, she explained, the opposite side of the river from most of the big tourist spots. 'Though I won't take you over the Ponte Vecchio,' Carla said. 'Have you been across it yet?'

'No,' Kathy admitted. 'It was on my plan for today.'

'Well, now is definitely not the moment to try. It will be full of international fashion bloggers taking wistful selfies. It was always bad enough with the tourists but now everyone is a blogger and they all have to take a hundred shots then look through them, then shoot them again, and then look through them, and start again with a different lipstick on. Then they add so many filters, you can't tell what they're standing in front of anyway. So many tourists, it's a wonder the bridge doesn't fall down. The Ponte Vecchio is like a Brueghel painting of Hell in the summertime. That's what my brother says. You'll meet him later on.'

A brother? Kathy felt a small wave of weariness at the thought of meeting more new people.

'You'll like him.' Carla was sure.

They paused on a bridge upstream from the Ponte Vecchio – the Ponte alle Grazie – to look back at the iconic bridge that had come to symbolise the city almost as much as *David* and the Duomo.

'You can take a selfie from here if you like,' said Carla. 'I won't mind.'

'I don't have my phone,' Kathy reminded her.

'Of course! I'm sorry. I should check mine. See if your fiancé has called while we've been walking.'

He still hadn't. There was nothing. How long would it take him to wonder why he hadn't had a text from Kathy in a while?

Seeing Kathy's frown, Carla assured her, 'He will call soon.'

Neil would pick up the voice message, wouldn't he? When he hadn't heard from her for a few hours, he would start to worry. Or was he sending messages to her mobile and assuming she was getting them? He wouldn't automatically check the answer-machine at home.

'You can try to reach him again from the house,' said Carla, reading her mind. 'Don't look so worried. He'll be pleased you're safe.'

Am I safe? Kathy wondered.

As Carla had explained, the other side of the river was quite different from the Florence most people who visited for just a few days got to know. Only a couple of streets back from the riverside, the crowds had largely disappeared. The streets were labyrinthine there, the houses tall and close together. The further they got from the river, the quieter the streets became.

They were oddly anonymous. Kathy didn't know how she would ever find her way back if she had to. Though she wanted to trust Carla absolutely, and their conversation about London and Florence and all the differences between the two cities was comforting, a sense of unease was creeping in. The dark, shuttered windows of the houses to either side seemed ready to turn a blind eye. Although the sun was still high in the sky, the height of the buildings made the narrow streets dark and gloomy and, in places, actually dank.

They seemed to walk for ages but, at last, they arrived at a plain blue gate in a plain grey wall. In the gate, which was faded and peeling from years of Italian sun, there was a small door that could be opened if you weren't planning on bringing anything bigger than a person through. It wasn't obviously a hotel, though a smudged brass plaque announced that this was the Casa Innocenti and visitors should ring the bell to be admitted. Carla searched through her bag for a moment or two, using her phone to see better into its depths, before she found a suitably ancient-looking key. 'Here it is.'

'It looks like the key to a castle,' said Kathy. Yet the door looked like it went straight into a dungeon.

'Oh, once upon a time this *was* the key to a castle. Or at least to a palazzo.' Carla struggled with the lock. 'This door needs to be rehung,' she complained. 'The lock is always tricky.' At last it worked. 'Mind your head as you come in. The people who made this gate weren't as tall as we are today. And watch your step on the other side too. The floor's a bit uneven. We were going to get it sorted out for the beginning of the tourist season but I suppose now we're waiting for the end. We're always waiting for something!'

Carla pushed open the door, making a bell ring somewhere deep in the house, and ushered Kathy inside.

'Welcome to the Casa Innocenti.'

Chapter Twenty-one

If the key had looked like the key to a fairy-tale castle, then the view beyond the door did not disappoint. In true fantasy style, the plain grey wall and the sad blue gate in desperate need of a lick of fresh paint opened onto a most unexpected and wonderful view. Kathy stepped over the threshold into a sort of cloister, which she would come to know was a loggia, that was open to a garden beyond. The loggia was high-ceilinged with huge stone slabs on the floor. They were uneven from wear, as Carla had warned. An enormous brass carriage lamp hung from the ceiling. It was garlanded with cobwebs.

From the loggia Kathy could see a vast, sweeping lawn that led down to a line of cypresses and umbrella pines. Though it had been dark in the narrow street outside, the sun still bathed the enormous garden. The heady scent of lavender drifted across the grass. It was planted in huge swathes in the flowerbeds. Meanwhile roses grew everywhere, like weeds, winding up the loggia's arches, like the briars around Sleeping Beauty's castle. There was even a campanile, a folly, Carla would explain, which was shaped like a twist of brick-built barley sugar.

'You live here?' Kathy asked.

'I live *here*,' said Carla, jerking her thumb upstairs from the loggia. 'All that beyond the wall used to belong to my family, too, but, well, now most of it belongs to a Silicon Valley billionaire. Who never visits, I should add. Beyond those trees is the Palazzo Innocenti. Home of my forefathers and -mothers. We've just about hung on to this bit – the Casa Innocenti – which is a very grand name for the gatehouse. We live on this side of the arch. The hotel guest rooms are on the other.'

Someone upstairs must have heard them come in because as Carla opened another door, which led into the building, a small dog rushed out, all fur and ferocity. He barrelled straight for Kathy's shins. Had he not been so tiny, he would have been frightening. As it was, the little beast was merely comical as he danced like a boxer around Kathy's shins barking his I'm-a-bigger-dog-than-you-think-I-am message.

'Faustino, sssh,' said Carla. 'Be nice to our guest. Faustino is my mother's dog, though he loves my brother best. Forget all bark and no bite. He's all fluff and farts. Aren't you, Fausty?'

'Is he a Shih Tzu?' Kathy asked.

'Depends who you're talking to,' said Carla, gently moving Faustino along with the tip of her toe. 'He's a Pomeranian. And I can see he's had a wash today. Probably with my hair conditioner.'

Faustino continued to bark at the stranger in his domain until Carla picked him up and held him so he could inspect Kathy more closely. His legs wheeled furiously in the air. He clearly did not appreciate having been lifted straight off his feet. It was undignified. Carla sniffed the top of his head. 'Definitely washed with my conditioner. See? See, you evil fluffball?' She held the dog towards Kathy. 'Nothing to bark at. Be kind.'

Carla put Faustino back on the floor, whereupon he promptly peed on a nearby flowerpot to underline his frustration at having been humiliated when he was merely trying to defend the family home.

Satisfied that he'd made his point, Faustino was soon leading the way back up the stairs, like an enchanted pom-pom escaped from someone's winter hat.

The staircase was very grand for a 'gatehouse', as Carla had put it. The polished wooden balustrades were carved with all manner of creatures, some recognisable, others not. Meanwhile the ceiling of the stairwell was painted with fantastical scenes to complement the extravagant stairs.

'In their defence, my ancestors had only ever seen a stuffed elephant,' Carla explained, as she pointed out something that Kathy had assumed was a grey cat with a trunk. It had big ears but it also had whiskers. 'If you visit the stuffed animals in the natural history museum here you'll understand.'

Kathy remembered the comment in the guidebook she'd found at the wedding hotel. 'It's still amazing to me. All the work that must have gone into it . . .'

'This is just the fourteenth-century equivalent of Ikea,' said Carla. 'Lots of the houses round here are painted with the most incredible stuff. I'll show you more later. Come on. Mamma will be waiting for us.'

Indeed there she was, at the top of the stairs.

Kathy looked up to see a woman who seemed to have come straight from Central Casting for 'Italian mother, early seventies, glamorous'. She was standing with her arms open in a theatrical gesture of welcome. She was wearing a floral silk day dress with pleated skirt and padded shoulders, and a pair of neat gold-coloured Ferragamo pumps. Over her shoulders, she had draped a cardigan that picked out the bright pink in the flowers on her frock. Her hair was neatly waved. She wore a pair of rhinestone spectacles that gave her the look of a punked-up owl. She might have been Gina Lollobrigida's even more glamorous sister and yet, when she opened her mouth, to say, 'Kathy! You poor little thing. I am glad you're here,' the voice that came out was pure Essex.

Here was the reason why Carla's English was so good, above and beyond her years in London.

'My mother Roberta,' Carla said.

'I'm from Brentwood,' said Roberta, reading the surprise on Kathy's face. She was an Essex girl, just as Kathy was. 'Come in, come in. Let's get you sorted out.'

Kathy was ushered further into the house to a sitting room on the *piano nobile*, as Roberta called it, which had a surfeit of furniture that spoke of better days and much bigger drawing rooms. Though this room was big enough . . . There were three sofas facing a fireplace, in addition to several chairs and at least half a dozen occasional tables that seemed to have proliferated like mushrooms. An old mahogany upright piano stood next to a cabinet stuffed with beautiful porcelain. The walls were hung with a jumble of paintings. Landscapes, portraits and lurid scenes from Greek and Roman mythology jostled for space and attention.

A boy, aged around eight, sat on one of the brocade-covered sofas, scuffing his feet against the polished floor as he played a game on a tablet.

'My son,' Carla explained. She didn't need to. He was her mini-me in boy form. He had a younger version of that same friendly face.

'Oi! Manu,' said Roberta. 'Please put that down and say hello to our guest. Now, my little dumpling, please.'

Manu stood to go through the formalities.

'This is Emanuele . . .'

'Pleased to meet you,' Manu said.

Faustino, the Pomeranian, seeing his chance, quickly nipped into the cherished sofa spot the boy had vacated. Manu was outraged at the takeover and a tussle ensued over the most comfortable cushion.

Kathy was duly seated in a rather grand high-backed chair that seemed to force her to sit up properly.

'You need a drink,' Roberta announced. 'And something more than tea, I'm guessing.'

Carla was dispatched to find a bottle of Prosecco. Prodded by his grandmother, Manu followed Carla and carried back a tray of delicate snacks. More curls of prosciutto and slivers of cheese were served with tiny pristine white cocktail napkins.

'Not for the dog,' Roberta warned her grandson, as he dangled a piece of ham over Faustino's nose. Carla put a glass into Kathy's hand and poured out a generous slug of fizz.

'Now tell me exactly what happened, dear,' Roberta said, after they'd toasted Kathy's safe arrival at the house. She nodded along as Kathy replayed the tale of the piazza della Signoria, with Carla adding details about the dénouement of the chase and the subsequent trip to the police station.

'The little sod,' Roberta said. 'It's such a big problem in the summer. Wherever you get that many tourists in one place, you get people waiting to take advantage. But don't you worry, my love. Florence isn't all bad and we're going to make sure you know it.'

Roberta, Carla and Manu – if not Faustino – had given Kathy such a warm welcome that she was soon decided. She would stay in their hotel, no matter what it cost. She told Roberta, 'If you have a room here, at your hotel, I can arrange for my fiancé to call you with a credit-card number.'

'Well, I'm afraid the hotel is full, dear,' said Roberta.

Kathy's face fell.

'But we've always got room for a little one. Carla, shall we put Kathy in the attic?'

'Not like a mad woman. It's my brother's room,' Carla quickly reassured her.

'But where will Uncle H go?' Manu asked.

'He'll have to sleep down here on the sofa,' said Roberta. 'With the dog.'

'Oh, no,' said Kathy. 'I won't put anyone out of a bed. I wouldn't dream of it.'

'On a Friday evening, my son doesn't always make it up the stairs,' Roberta assured her. 'He won't mind a couple of nights down here.'

'He will,' muttered Manu. 'He definitely will. Don't you remember when—'

Roberta and Carla both shot the boy a shut-up-sweetheart look.

'Your uncle will sleep down here,' Roberta told Manu. 'I'll text to let him know not to go up to his room when he gets in tonight. Now, Carla, will you find fresh linen for the bed?'

'Of course.'

'Manu, you can take Kathy's suitcase up the stairs.'

Manu's mouth dropped open. 'But, Nonna—'

'And then we'll forget all about what I heard you say earlier,' Roberta added. Whatever he had said, Manu clearly didn't want his mother to hear it. He disappeared with the case forthwith.

To Kathy, Roberta said, 'You will stay here for as long as you need to. Our house is your house, as they say around these parts. You're at the Casa Innocenti now. Nothing bad can happen here.'

Looking at the kind face of her new Italian-British friend, Kathy began to believe it.

Chapter Twenty-two

When the room was ready, Kathy followed Manu up the stairs, which grew narrower with every flight, so that by the time they reached the top, she felt like Alice after she'd eaten the cake that made her bigger. The door to the attic room was, like the door in the gate, built for a much shorter person. Kathy ducked her head but not quite enough the first time.

Manu said, 'Nonna says that banging his head on the door is what must have knocked the sense out of my uncle.'

Kathy pressed her hand to the top of her head until the sharp pain of the knock subsided to a throb.

'Did you really chase a robber?' Manu asked, as he manoeuvred Kathy's bag into a corner by the wardrobe.

'Yes. And your mum helped.'

'Cool,' said Manu. 'But what if he'd had a knife? It's probably a good job you didn't catch him.'

'Manu.' Carla was at the low door now. 'There was no knife. Now, please leave our guest to relax for a little while. She's had a very difficult day.'

Suddenly Kathy knew she was on the verge of tears. She felt the old ache around her eye-sockets. Maybe it was only from having knocked her head on the door-jamb, but this kindness, from total strangers, it was more than she had ever imagined or expected. She didn't know quite what to make of it. Seeing the tell-tale glitter in her eyes, Carla patted her arm and handed her her mobile phone.

'Call your fiancé again and tell him you're safe.'

Once Manu and Carla had left her in peace, Kathy was able to take in her new surroundings. The attic room was small. There was really only space for a single bed but a double had been wedged in. Apart from that, there was an old wardrobe, with a badly foxed full-length mirror on the door. A small desk with a spindly chair was positioned beneath the window. It was covered with sheet music that Carla had hastily shuffled into piles to give Kathy somewhere to put her belongings. Seeing that, Kathy felt doubly guilty for having turfed Carla's brother out of his room. He'd doubtless left the house that morning expecting to come back to find everything exactly as he'd left it. Kathy hoped there wasn't some sort of method to the mess that Carla had destroyed when she'd piled the music willy-nilly.

The single window to the bedroom had the green-painted wooden shutters that were typical of the region. Kathy leaned across the desk – doing her best not to disturb anything more – to see that the window looked out onto the street and a row of other houses. Not the beautiful garden, as Kathy had hoped, but just as lovely right then. On one of the terracotta-tiled sills across from the Casa Innocenti, someone was growing pots of herbs and a bright red geranium that seemed to have been planted purely for the purpose of making a perfect picture. It seemed to glow in the late-afternoon light that had turned the yellow-painted walls behind it the deep rich gold of egg yolk and late buttercups.

Looking up and beyond the buildings immediately opposite, she could see the bell-tower of a church and the crest of an umbrella pine. There were no modern buildings to spoil the view. Was there no corner of Florence that wasn't photogenic? Certainly not that Kathy could see from where she stood now.

She stepped back from the window and looked at the paintings hanging on the walls inside. Like the sitting room, this attic bedroom contained far too many pictures for such a small space. Kathy supposed they, too, must have come from the palazzo Carla had talked about. Remnants of those bigger rooms again.

Above the bed was a view of the city from the hills. That oil painting was flanked by two white ceramic cherubs, wings tipped in gold, which must once have held candles in their chubby little hands. From one cherub's hands hung three festival passes. Kathy took a closer look. The passes – each from a few years before – said their holder was a performer with 'Access all areas'.

Having examined all the passes, Kathy unzipped her suitcase. She pulled out a white linen dress she hadn't worn at the wedding because in the bright Italian sun it had looked too old and too scruffy. It was now the only clean thing she had left. She shook it vigorously but it still looked like a rag. Opening the wardrobe for a hanger, she found photographs and pictures cut from magazines pinned to the inside of the wardrobe door, like in a teenager's room. They were of musicians. Not rock musicians but jazz musicians. Pianists especially. Kathy recognised Nat King Cole and Ray Charles.

Despite his love of older music, Carla's brother must

have been a teenager at around the same time as Kathy, guessing from the haircuts and clothes of the young people in the photos. They were frozen in the late 1990s. Kathy leaned in close to a picture of six kids posing by the fountain of *Neptune* to study their faces. She spotted Carla. Another had one of those crazy round-the-head tooth-braces. While she was gawping at the photos, Kathy suddenly felt self-conscious. She would have hated a stranger to see her childhood pictures. She closed the wardrobe and hung her linen dress from the hook on the back of the door to the room instead. It felt a little less presumptuous.

With her bag unpacked, Kathy was about to dial the landline in London when Neil called Carla's mobile. Kathy answered instantly.

'Chicken? Is that you?' he asked. 'What's going on? Why am I ringing an Italian number? Where the hell are you now?'

He didn't draw breath between questions.

'It is me,' said Kathy, when at last he could hear her. 'I'm OK. I'm being looked after. Everything is fine.'

'But what happened? Why are you on an Italian phone?'

Kathy took a deep breath. 'Someone stole my bag.'

'What?' Neil spluttered. 'Where from?'

'From the café table. It happened right after I finished speaking to you.'

'Chicken! Did they hurt you?'

'No.' Kathy elected not to mention the chase and her fall.

'Are you sure?'

'Yes, I'm sure.'

'Then what on earth happened?'

136

'A kid just snatched my stuff. I'd just put my phone in the bag and—'

'For Heaven's sake.' Now that he knew Kathy hadn't been injured in the incident, Neil's tone of concern was immediately replaced by irritation. 'That phone is only covered for accidental damage, not theft. You're not supposed to go anywhere it can get stolen. It'll cost a fortune to get it replaced.'

'I'm sorry.'

'I told you to keep an eye on your bag. In fact, I told you to stay at the airport, where you would have been safe. Do you think I say these things for the sake of hearing my own voice?'

It was a phrase he often used on the children.

And because she had heard him use it on the children, Kathy knew Neil wasn't in the mood to hear of any mitigating circumstances. Still, hoping he would be mollified to hear she'd done everything right since then, she told him about Carla and the police station. And the Casa Innocenti. She thought he would be pleased to know she was somewhere safe, awaiting further instructions.

'You're telling me you followed some random woman back to her house? Are you drunk? Was that what you were doing at that café? Drinking wine all afternoon?'

'No. No,' Kathy insisted. 'Well, maybe one glass but I certainly wasn't drunk.'

'Who is this woman?'

'She seems nice. Her mother is English. She's from Brentwood.'

'What? In Essex? Is that supposed to be a recommendation?'

Neil was often rude about Kathy's home county.

'Chicken, you are too trusting. Why didn't you just do as I asked?'

'I was going to. I was calling for the bill when the thief struck. I was going to go straight back to the airport. Have I missed a flight?'

'No.' Neil sighed. 'No, you haven't. Melanie didn't manage to get you onto the late flight. I shall be writing to British Airways on that matter after the bank holiday. For now, you're still on the flight back on Monday.'

'Then it's a good job I didn't go to the airport.'

'Except that this whole handbag-snatching thing might have been avoided if you hadn't left the airport to begin with. You'd be safe in a hotel there by now.'

'I'm safe here.'

'What's the name of the hotel again?'

'Casa Innocenti.' She began to spell it.

'I can spell it,' said Neil. 'And it doesn't have a website. What a surprise. You've let yourself get picked up by some scammer. I'll have to sort this out—'

'Did you spell it with two *n*s?'

'Of course, I— Ah. It does have a website. It looks like an old people's home.'

'It's very comfortable.'

'We have to find you somewhere closer to the centre. A proper chain hotel. If I pay from here, all you need to do is turn up. If you can manage not to get lost on the way.' Neil continued to chat as though he were only talking to himself, thinking out loud. 'As if I don't have enough to think about without having to worry about you. There was nothing in the fridge when I got back.'

'I was planning to go to Waitrose. Did you—' Before she asked the question, Kathy heard a sound that answered it. It was the sound of the fridge door being slammed, followed by the voice of Sophie complaining, 'There is *literally* nothing to eat in here. I'm starving. Doesn't she normally get Waitrose to deliver on a Friday?'

She? Charming, thought Kathy.

'Tell Sophie there's a lasagne in the freezer,' said Kathy. 'It's vegetarian. It will only take about forty-five minutes in the oven.'

'I had that for lunch,' said Neil.

'Really?' That lasagne was big enough for six. In Kathy's mind, at least. She'd certainly intended it to be big enough for six. It was meant to be a dinner for Neil, his children and herself, with just a little bit left over in case any of them particularly liked it. Which, if they did, they never admitted.

Pre-empting Kathy's dismay, Neil said, 'I was hungry. I had to skip breakfast. And as I was so late getting through security because of your plane ticket, I didn't have time to get anything at the airport and they don't give you anything on the flight any more. The standards on BA these days . . . Might as well be flying Ryanair.'

'OK,' said Kathy, mentally going through the freezer drawers for a Plan B. 'There should be some soya Bolognese sauce in the bottom drawer. If you put it into the microwave on defrost for five minutes . . .'

Before she'd even finished the instructions, Kathy knew it was going to be too much bother for Neil or any of his children. Though Sophie was nineteen and the twins would be turning eighteen later that year, they all needed spoon-feeding.

'I suppose I'll have to fork out for a takeaway,' Neil

concluded. 'Which will be another out-of-pocket expense, thanks to your flight cock-up.'

I didn't book the flights, Kathy silently reminded him. Out loud, she said, 'I could try to arrange an Ocado drop-off from here. I'll ask if I can borrow a computer.'

She waited for Neil to say it would be quicker and easier to go to Waitrose himself. He didn't. 'OK,' she said. 'Text me a list of the things you and the children want.'

'That's too much faff,' Neil decided.

'You're probably right,' said Kathy, with relief. 'I doubt I'd be able to get a delivery slot before Tuesday now anyway. I forgot to mention, I did tell Mum about the proposal. Before I lost my phone.'

'And what did she have to say?'

'She was pleased.'

'Of course she was. She's offloaded you at last,' Neil chuckled.

'She sends her love. She hopes we can visit soon.'

'With my workload? Not likely. I've already lost three days' holiday. Look I've got to go,' he said then. 'This call must be costing a fortune from the landline. Call me when you've found a proper hotel.'

'Neil,' said Kathy, 'before you go . . .' She needed to know what he wanted her to do next, with regard to getting home. Did Melanie's failure to get her on a flight that evening mean that Kathy really would have to stay in Italy until Monday?

'I suppose it does mean that,' said Neil, annoyance prickling his voice.

'Well, just let me know if anything changes . . .'

'Nothing is going to change unless I make it happen,

obviously, now that Melanie has left the office for the weekend. I've got to go. Someone has to feed the children.'

'Have a good evening,' Kathy told the dead air.

Kathy was glad she hadn't told him about the ring. She really didn't feel like dealing with that just yet. After five years with Neil, Kathy knew there were some things that had to be approached delicately. He could overreact from time to time.

But he was a good man. The robbery had shaken Kathy and, having been angry with Neil for the past week, Kathy found that now all she wanted was to be close to him again. He was dependable. He was her rock. He was always there for her. He did what he said he was going to do. Sometimes he was brusque but that was only because he was too intelligent to suffer fools lightly. He could occasionally be tactless, too, but, really, what man couldn't? What did it matter if he didn't notice a new haircut but always seemed to notice an extra couple of pounds? Neil looked out for Kathy's welfare in everything. Her physical and fiscal health. If he got frustrated it was only ever because she was letting herself down.

And now they were getting married, which must mean he had taken something of Kathy's wishes on board since the dreadful day that Kathy didn't want to think about. When she next spoke to him on the phone, she was sure he would be warmer. When he wasn't feeling so tired, when he wasn't hungry, when the children weren't complaining about something or other, Neil would be kinder. He'd just had a very long day.

As had Kathy, and perhaps she was seeing the glass half empty again as a result. Wasn't that what Neil had told her before? When he sang 'Always Look On The Bright Side Of Life' and told her not to be such a baby. Her life was good. Their life was good.

Deep breath, Kathy.

Chapter Twenty-three

Once she'd finished talking to Neil, Kathy showered quickly in the bathroom closest to the attic room. Since she didn't have any toiletries with her – she hadn't bothered to bring shampoo or shower gel on the trip, knowing they would be provided at the palazzo, and her make-up had been inside the stolen bag – she had to use a little of what was there. There were two bottles in the shower. She poured a tiny dollop of the shampoo into her hand and held it up to her nose. It had a masculine smell. Quite familiar. Very nice. She checked the bottle. Sandalo from Santa Maria Novella, the famous Florentine perfumery. That was one of the places she'd hoped to visit, back when she'd planned her fantasy Florence day trip.

As she was towel-drying her hair back in the attic room, Manu came to the bottom of the stairs and gleefully rang a bell to announce that dinner was served. No hotel residents were dining that night, Roberta had already explained, because she had a deal with a local restaurant to send them all over there for dinner on a Friday. Fridays were for family, as they had always been in the Innocenti household, and Kathy was the family's guest. Kathy quickly pulled on the white dress, which seemed to look more like a rag than ever, and hurried downstairs.

Carla and Roberta were already in the sitting room,

waiting with *aperitivi*. Manu was teaching the dog a new trick. Faustino was playing the situation for maximum prosciutto points, acting far dumber than he looked to encourage more encouragement.

'Were you able to speak to your fiancé?' Roberta asked, as Kathy sat down. 'He must be very worried about you. I hope you put his mind at rest.'

'I think so,' said Kathy.

'It must be very hard for you for this to have happened so early in your engagement. You just want to be together at such an exciting time for you both. But I hope you'll be able to relax at last.' Roberta pressed a glass of wine into Kathy's hand. 'Here's to your stay at the Casa Innocenti.'

Kathy toasted her hosts in return.

Roberta had claimed that supper would be a 'simple' affair but to Kathy it was anything but. Unless by 'simple' Roberta had meant that everyone would be eating the same thing. Even Manu. Back at home, when Kathy was cooking for the whole gang, she was used to having to provide several options to accommodate that week's dietary preferences. One memorable Friday night, Kathy had made dinner to accommodate a vegan, a gluten-free vegan and a raw food diet, only to have everyone decide at the last minute that they were going to eat the meat-laden lasagne she'd made for Neil. It looked nicer.

Manu helped his mother carry the food out from the kitchen to the dining room. He did so with the ease of someone who had been waiting tables since he was old enough to walk, which, as it turned out, was pretty much the case. Roberta proudly told Kathy how her grandson helped in the hotel restaurant during peak times.

As they ate, Roberta asked Kathy about the places in Essex she remembered from her youth. 'I haven't been back in a long time,' she said, 'but it sounds as though I'm about your mother's age. I wonder if I'd recognise her.'

Then she told Kathy some more about the house she would be staying in. She confirmed Carla's explanation that the house, which seemed grand enough to Kathy, was just the gatehouse of a far larger palazzo that lay beyond the line of trees in the garden.

'The Palazzo Innocenti is enormous,' Roberta said. 'When I first saw it, I thought it was like Blenheim Palace.'

'It's not quite that big,' said Carla.

'Well, I was just a young girl from Essex back then. It looked pretty impressive to me.'

Roberta gave Kathy a potted history of the family home. The first Innocenti to live on the land was Carlo – a lowly foot soldier – who saved the life of a great general on a battlefield. 'Carlo didn't know he was helping a general,' Roberta explained. 'He thought he was just another infantryman. And that was why the general was so impressed. That Carlo would have risked his life for someone who couldn't obviously help him in return seemed to speak of great goodness so he gave him this land as a reward.'

Back then it was just farmland, which lay outside the city. Two generations later, Carlo's grandson Aurelio had the ear of the pope and a fortune to match. He had built the palazzo, basing the plans for the house on Tiberius's palace on Capri. 'His wife reined in some of the wilder excesses,' said Roberta.

She gestured to the portrait that hung above the

impressive marble mantelpiece. It was hard to believe that that mantelpiece was built above the fire at which stable-hands and grooms had warmed themselves, but Roberta insisted it was true. 'In the main house, all the wooden carving was covered with gold, and the paintings you see on the ceilings here are clearly the work of apprentices let loose with a paintbrush for the first time.'

Kathy had already spotted another cat-faced elephant on the ceiling.

'The paintings on the ceiling in the palazzo, ah, they're something else.' Roberta went back to the portrait above the fireplace, which depicted a rather dour-looking woman, hair severely scraped back from her face and hidden beneath a bejewelled wimple arrangement. 'That painting used to hang in the main house. It's Francesca Innocenti,' said Roberta. 'She was considered a great beauty in her time. There are some who believe she may have been the model for La Gioconda.'

'Mona Lisa?' asked Kathy.

'That's right.'

'I can see it about the eyes,' Kathy said. But the smile. The smile was definitely not quite the same. Whereas La Gioconda looks as though she is suppressing the urge to laugh, Francesca Innocenti looked as though she had never laughed. Perhaps she didn't have much reason to, with her husband being such a big fan of Caligula.

'She scares me,' said Manu. 'When I was little, I used to have bad dreams about her.'

I can see that, Kathy thought.

But it turned out that while Francesca Innocenti

looked as hard as nails, she was a woman of true heart, treating the servants of her household with great benevolence. She also created an orphanage in the family's name, establishing the family's reputation for kindness as well as opulence. And that was where it all began.

'The Casa Innocenti has a long history of providing refuge,' said Roberta. 'The Innocenti Orphanage endured through centuries. The family employed the children who grew up there in the house and on their farms. It was such a good arrangement that some desperate parents left their children outside the orphanage on purpose, in the hope that they would get to live here. It carried on like that for years. During the Second World War, when the Fascists were all over Florence, my husband's parents hid a Jewish couple and their child in the secret room at the top of the campanile.'

'On a dark night you can hear them wailing,' said Manu.

Roberta frowned at him. 'You cannot hear anybody wailing. Kathy, they survived the war and moved to New York. Members of their family still visit from time to time. In fact, the couple's great-grandson will be coming to Florence next month to see where his great-grandparents and grandfather hid.'

'What a lovely thing to be able to do.'

'We have eight rooms in the hotel,' Roberta continued, 'but only six are ever available to paying guests. The other two are used by people who need somewhere to stay. One of those rooms, alas, is unusable at the moment, thanks to a small flood from the bathroom above it, or you would be in there. In the other we have Mr Caligari, who was my husband's schoolfriend. After his wife died, he really couldn't look after himself. Ugo would visit him at home and come back to tell me what a terrible state the poor man was in. He had no family of his own. Of course we took him in and he's welcome for as long as he needs to be here. It's as my husband wanted it to be.'

'And when one waif moves out, another moves in,' said Carla.

'There's never any shortage of people who need help,' said Roberta, in an admonishing tone. 'And that is why we stick by the Innocenti motto.'

Carla and Manu, who had obviously heard this speech several times before, laid down their cutlery, put their right hands over their hearts and chanted in unison, '*Deus ope, manus mea.*' They finished with a conspiratorial giggle.

'That means "God's help by my hands",' said Manu, for Kathy's benefit.

Roberta beamed at him proudly.

'A lovely motto to live by,' Kathy agreed. 'How lucky I am to have met Carla and now the pair of you, and to have benefited from that wisdom.'

'We love it when we can live by the motto. We actually have a scoreboard in the kitchen to show which of us has been the kindest this week,' Carla joked. 'I'm winning. More wine?'

After dinner, Roberta insisted that Kathy would not be helping with the washing-up.

'After the day you've had? Not a chance, dear. Sit and enjoy your coffee outside.'

A terrace ran all the way along the back of the house, over the top of the loggia. The family had reserved a piece of it for themselves, separated from part of the terrace the hotel guests used by a trellis thickly covered with jasmine.

Faustino and Manu accompanied Kathy out into the evening air. Manu had Faustino demonstrate his best tricks. Inevitably, the dog would respond to the command before the one he was given. So he stood there, tongue lolling and tail wagging when Manu asked him to sit. Then he sat when Manu asked him to lie down. When Manu asked Faustino to shake a paw, Faustino lay down on his belly and refused to let Manu get anywhere near his doggy feet.

'He needs some practice,' said Manu.

'I had a dog when I was your age,' said Kathy. 'And he wouldn't do any tricks at all unless he was bribed. Though he did know how to open the back gate and was always escaping.'

'Have you got a dog now? In London?'

'No,' said Kathy.

'Why not?'

'It's hard to have a dog in the city.'

'This is a city.'

'Then I don't know why I don't have a dog.'

But she did know why. It was because Neil didn't want one. Too messy. Too much of a responsibility. They'd never be able to go on holiday again without having to find a dog-sitter. They were all sound reasons. Still, Kathy would have loved to have a dog. Having established that Kathy was welcome in his family home, Faustino was utterly charming. If a little smelly, as Carla had warned. The one trick Faustino could seem to do was fart to order.

'Nonna sometimes calls him Foulstino,' Manu

explained. 'But it isn't always his fault. Sometimes Ernesto, the chef, drops a silent but deadly and blames it on the dog.'

'What are you talking about?' asked Carla, who had come to join them.

'You know he does it. Sometimes you do it too.'

Not too long after that, it was time for Manu to go to bed.

'Without your tablet,' Carla insisted. 'Come on.'

Roberta was the last to say goodnight.

'I hope you'll be comfortable in the attic,' she told Kathy. 'It's a long way up but my son has always loved the room. It was his when he was a teenager and he insisted on taking it again when he came back from New York three years ago.'

'I'm sure I'll be very comfortable,' said Kathy. 'Thank you. Thank you to you and to Carla and Manu for taking such good care of me today. I don't know what I did to deserve to meet such lovely people. I'm quite overwhelmed.'

'I know you'll pass it on, dear.' Roberta patted Kathy gently on the cheek. 'I can tell.'

Leaving Faustino alone in the sitting room to stand guard over his sleeping clan, and repel intruders with the occasional burst of toxic gas, Kathy climbed the stairs to the attic room and pushed open the creaky door. This time she remembered to duck. The warm golden light was gone now but in the glow of a single lamp the room looked cosy and the bed was inviting. She sat down on the edge of the white-sheet-covered mattress and slipped off her sandals. The terracotta floor tiles were cool beneath her feet, which rejoiced at being bare and free again.

Outside, the bells of the city tolled eleven. Just one day had passed since she and Neil had become engaged. Only twelve hours had passed since she'd stood in the shadow of the Duomo's campanile. But how much had changed in such a short time!

I could be happy here. The thought came to Kathy unbidden. I could be really happy here.

As a teenager, Kathy had dreamed of moving overseas. France, Italy, America, she wasn't fussy where she ended up so long as it wasn't Essex. Or even London. She just knew that she wanted her life to be bigger and better than the life her parents lived. They were content, so far as she could tell, to live in the town where they had both grown up but Kathy couldn't wait to get away. She wanted to experience everything the world had to offer. She wanted to go to university, then set off on a lifelong adventure. She pictured herself with a Frenchwoman's chic, an Italian's passion, an American's can-do attitude . . . She was going places.

When she left school, everything was on track. She had a place at university. Moving to Sussex for her studies, she was able to leave behind Cross-eyed Kathy at last, and reinvent herself as the confident young woman her dad Eddie had always told her she should be. Then, during Kathy's first year, Eddie was diagnosed with cancer and then he died and then everything changed.

Kathy finished her degree and moved back home. Her mother needed her. It would have been wrong to push ahead with her dreams when Clare was in pieces. Kathy thought it would be for a few months, a year at most, but the second year without her dad seemed worse than the first. The third year was worse than the second. And the fourth. And so on. Clare's grief never seemed to ease. At the same time, she grew increasingly fearful of losing Kathy, too. Her fear was infectious somehow. Kathy downgraded her plans. Even moving to London felt like an enormous step as the world with which her mum seemed willing to engage shrank ever more.

Soon Kathy resigned herself to letting go of her plans. She got herself a boring job, a little flat, settled into a smaller life. It was OK, she told herself. It was better than nothing.

But that night in Florence, it was the old Kathy who looked out of the bedroom window and felt her heart briefly soar again.

Chapter Twenty-four

Kathy slept more deeply than she had done in a long while. Possibly because of the delicious red wine with which Carla and Roberta had plied her at dinner. Possibly because she didn't have to listen to the squeaks and whirs of an unfamiliar air-conditioning unit or keep getting up to look for imaginary mosquitoes. If Roberta's son, Carla's brother, had come into the house late, she hadn't heard him.

Now, upon waking, Kathy realised the world was full of noise. Outside the window, which she had left open overnight, the swallows were finding breakfast, squealing through the sky, like feathered fighter pilots, as they plucked their desire from a buffet of unlucky flying critters. Meanwhile the city's hundreds of bells announced that it was seven in the morning, and in the street below, a lorry full of what must have been empty bottles from the nearby bars and restaurants clattered over the uneven paving. Friends greeted one another loudly. A dog barked its own hello. Somewhere nearby, someone sang a snatch of opera in an impressive tenor voice. Was that really 'Nessun Dorma'? It was like the soundtrack to a Hollywood movie version of Italy.

Kathy went to the window and looked out at the view. The sky, which was striped vanilla-ice-cream yellow and baby blue, promised another glorious day ahead. And she would be spending it in Florence. Her heart gave an involuntary skip at the thought. Then she searched about for her phone, thinking, as she always did whenever they were apart, that she had better check Neil had everything he needed before she started her own day. Only then she remembered that she didn't have her phone. Or her bag. Or her purse. Or her engagement ring.

'Ugh.'

That remembrance punctured the Florence feeling somewhat.

But she couldn't dwell on it. She wouldn't. There was still a chance that the police would catch the bag thief. Carla had said she would phone the station first thing to ask for a progress report. Somebody might have tried to sell Kathy's things on to an undercover officer. Or the bag might have been discarded and handed in. Often thieves just took what they could use immediately – like cash or credit cards – and chucked the rest. They might not even have noticed the ring tucked deep inside a pocket. . .

Kathy crept to the bathroom. Though it was already noisy outside, she wasn't sure if everyone in the house was up and she didn't want to interrupt anyone's dreams. But the taps in the basin came to life with an almighty clanking. No chance in this house that anyone would stumble in on someone else in the bathroom. The plumbing practically sang that it was in use.

She splashed water on her face and did her best to tame her hair, which had fluffed up with the borrowed shampoo. Of all the things she had lost in her handbag, she would soon be missing her make-up the most. She had to make do instead with pinching her cheeks and nibbling at her lips, like some 1920s heroine.

And of course she wasn't the first to be up in this house of hoteliers. Roberta was already fully dressed, beautifully coiffed and in the kitchen, issuing instructions to an elderly man, bent almost double with age, who seemed utterly oblivious to everything she said as he went about his business.

'Kathy, this is Ernesto, our venerable chef,' Roberta said, then introduced Kathy to him in Italian. Ernesto did not turn round but merely nodded and continued to crack eggs into a frying pan. Roberta rolled her eyes at Kathy over Ernesto's head.

Carla was also up and dressed, running plates to and from the terrace where the hotel's paying guests were making the most of the early sun. Manu was at the kitchen table, taking bites from a pastry between vanquishing more monsters on his tablet. Faustino was at his feet, waiting for the inevitable crumbs to fall. Faustino tore his eyes away from Manu for approximately three seconds, to check whether Kathy was carrying food as well. When he saw she wasn't, he gave her a perfunctory wag of his pom-pom tail.

Beyond the kitchen, the sitting room, where Kathy had met the family the previous evening, was still dark but Kathy could just make out a lumpen shape on the sofa. That must be Carla's brother beneath a pile of blankets. So he had come home, after all. A large pair of brown shoes, kicked off just inside the front door, confirmed it. They were very big shoes. Their owner was either very tall or he looked like a kangaroo.

Roberta handed Kathy a coffee cup and a plate.

'Help yourself,' she said. Then, 'Manu, go and wake your uncle, please. He's making the place look untidy.'

'In a minute.' Manu had to make sure the monsters were absolutely dead first. Then he would do his grandmother's bidding.

'In the traditional way?' Roberta suggested.

The grin on Manu's face lit the room.

'*Uno, due, tre* . . .' Manu counted, as he posed in the manner of all small boys about to start a running race, arms and legs ready to pump all the way to victory. He set off across the floor at speed, darting through the door and skidding across the polished boards of the sitting room, coming to a halt only as he leaped on top of the body on the sofa.

From the body on the sofa came a surprised 'Ooof' as Manu landed, then from Manu a squeal of delight as his victim came to life and rolled him off the sofa to the floor for a tickle fight.

'You little—' Admirably, Manu's uncle managed not to swear.

'Nonna made me do it!' Manu protested. 'Help! Help! He's tickling me!'

Manu wriggled free, leaving his uncle sitting on the floor, still wrapped in a blanket but now entirely awake. Manu was a very effective alarm clock. His uncle got to his feet, made a fruitless attempt to flatten down his wayward hair, and wandered to the kitchen door.

He stood in the frame, observing the scene inside with a faint and bleary smile. He took in the faces of the people there, his eyes finally alighting on Kathy, who was sitting at the table with a pastry and coffee in front of her. He continued to smile at her familiar face, because her face was familiar to him, it seemed.

'Henry,' said Roberta. 'This is Kathy Courage.'

Kathy got up and stuck out her hand towards him. The realisation had hit her just moments before. How had she not put two and two together? The family name? The piles of sheet music in the attic room? The backstage passes and the montage dedicated to famous pianists on the back of the wardrobe door? Even the smell of his shower gel. 'We've already met,' she said.

She was sure Henry's smile stiffened just a little as he said, 'Indeed, we have. Hello again.'

Chapter Twenty-five

Kathy gabbled an explanation to Roberta of how she had already met her son. Roberta seemed most interested to hear that Kathy played the piano.

'Well, you must feel free to play ours,' she said. 'We love music in this house.'

'I'm not sure I want to inflict my playing on you,' Kathy said.

Henry didn't leap in to say that she was being too modest about her ability this time, which was a disappointment.

'And I played for her fiancé's proposal,' he said in turn. 'Your favourite song. "Yellow" by Coldplay, wasn't it?'

Carla was passing with some plates to be returned to the kitchen. When she heard Henry mention Coldplay, her eyes widened, as though she had just heard him mutter an ancient curse, which it clearly was to him.

'Yes,' said Kathy. 'Though that's more Neil's favourite song than mine,' she added quietly.

'What a lovely coincidence,' said Roberta, oblivious to the peculiar tension between her son and her guest. 'It feels more than ever like Fate that you came to our house, Kathy dear.'

'Doesn't it?' said Henry.

While Henry helped himself to coffee, which he

drank in two swift gulps, then refilled his cup, Kathy ate the pastry she had been so looking forward to with a little less relish than she might otherwise have done.

Henry leaned against the sink for a while, giving Kathy the side-eye, she felt – she didn't dare look at him. Then he left the kitchen and his mother followed him into the sitting room, to stand over him as he tidied the blankets he had slept in. Although they were trying to keep their voices down, Kathy couldn't help but tune in to the conversation that was, of course, about her.

'What is the matter with you?' Roberta asked. 'Why are you being so prickly?'

'I'm not being prickly.'

'Henry Innocenti, you are. Do you have a headache by any chance?'

'I'm not hung-over, if that's what you're asking. I thought I'd been relegated to the sofa for someone who really needed a bed for the night. Some poor backpacker who'd been ripped off and only had the clothes she was standing up in. Kathy's new fiancé could probably afford to buy this place ten times over. Why didn't he arrange for her to stay somewhere in the centre?'

'As it happened, he did suggest she find somewhere else to stay and he would call through with his credit-card number. But how could I possibly agree to that?' Roberta hissed. 'The poor woman had just been robbed. She's all alone here. I couldn't send her out again into the city on her own. It's not about money, Henry. It's about making a woman feel safe. You'd have wanted someone to do the same for your sister.'

'If I had the money, I would have arranged for my sister to take a taxi straight to the Four Seasons. As her fiancé should have done. Instead, I had to sleep on the sofa with Faustino farting in my face all night. What have you been feeding him?'

Roberta broke off chiding her son to chide the dog. 'Faustino, you know you're not allowed on the sofa. Did you let him get onto the sofa, Henry?'

'Like you never do.'

'Only if he's very, very tired,' said Roberta.

'That's beside the point. Mother, it's just not right that I should be kicked out of my bed for yet another of your waifs and strays who isn't actually a waif and stray at all. I have to work. I need my sleep. No wonder this hotel is on the verge of ruin. Less than half the guests ever pay! We're not running a charity mission, Mamma. I thought we agreed that things had to change around here.'

'You know it is the family tradition that we help people whenever we can,' said Roberta.

'*Deus ope, manus mea*. I know. And that's how we've ended up living in the gatehouse instead of the palazzo,' said Henry. 'Do you suppose I'm allowed into my bedroom to fetch a change of clothes? Or has the poor waif with the millionaire fiancé had my stuff put out onto the landing?'

'Henry, please don't be unkind to our new guest. She's suffered enough unkindness in this city already.'

'When's she going?' Henry asked.

Roberta hesitated, 'On Monday, I think.'

'What? That's ridiculous!' said Henry.

'Just two more nights.'

'That I have to spend bunking with the dog on the lumpiest sofa in Italy.'

'Henry . . .'

'All right,' he said. 'All right. It's the code of the Innocenti, I know.'

'You should always be kind, because you never know when a stranger may be your saviour.' Roberta reminded him of Carlo Innocenti's lucky break when he helped the army general. The story that had started the Innocenti legend.

Henry sighed heavily enough for Kathy to hear.

Moments later, he and Roberta were back in the kitchen, both smiling broadly and looking as though they'd been having a conversation about the weather. Roberta reminded Manu that Faustino was not to be fed from the table. Manu slipped Faustino a piece of pastry the moment Roberta's back was turned. Henry asked Kathy if she would like some more coffee. To anyone who hadn't eavesdropped on the conversation he'd just had with his mother, he would have seemed perfectly pleasant.

'It's going to be a beautiful day,' he said. 'You don't know Florence, do you, Kathy?'

'Not at all,' she said.

'Then you must make sure to see all the sights. The Uffizi. The Accademia. The Ponte Vecchio.'

Thanks to Carla, Kathy already knew Henry wouldn't wish a visit to the Ponte Vecchio in the middle of summer on his very worst enemy. But she told him she was grateful for the suggestions. 'Actually,' she said, 'I was thinking I should spend this morning looking for somewhere else to stay. It isn't fair of me to take anybody's bed. I was very glad of your company yesterday evening,' she looked to Roberta and Carla, 'but I do feel much better after a good night's sleep. I've lived in London for years so I'm pretty streetwise.

I'm sure I can find somewhere I feel perfectly safe. Anywhere but by the main station, right?'

As she spoke, Kathy thought she could see some genuine warmth returning to Henry's face. Or relief, maybe. But—

'No!' Carla and Roberta chorused at once.

'We wouldn't hear of it,' said Roberta.

'It will be very difficult to find anything decent on a Saturday night at this time of year,' Carla added.

'Anyway, it's been decided,' Roberta insisted. 'Henry says he's perfectly happy to sleep on the sofa for a few nights. It will do his back the world of good. He's always complaining that the mattress in his room is too soft.'

'Am I?'

'You are,' his mother and sister said together.

'Well, you must let me pay to stay here,' Kathy tried. 'I'll get Neil to call with his card later on. Or do a bank transfer.'

'Good idea,' said Henry, even as his mother and sister shook their heads.

'And in the meantime, I'd like to help in any way I can. Perhaps I could do the washing-up.'

'That's an excellent thought,' said Henry.

Roberta disagreed. 'It's kind of you to offer but Ernesto has a system in the kitchen, which is why the washing-up is best left to one of us. It will only upset him if he has to tell someone new what needs to be done.'

Kathy thought she saw Henry roll his eyes. It was hard to believe this was the same person she'd played duets with just a couple of days before. Neil's crass move with the tip had clearly made a more lasting impression than their time together at the piano keys.

'There must be something else,' Kathy persisted.

'She could go to the market with Manu,' Henry suggested.

'Who's "she"?' Roberta asked. 'The cat's mother? Kathy is sitting at the table, Henry.'

Kathy dropped her eyes.

'Kathy. You,' Henry addressed her directly, 'could go to the market with Manu.'

'But I always go with you, Uncle H,' Manu protested.

'Then it will be a nice change for you to go with someone else.'

'Awwww,' Manu complained. 'But we always get *gelato*.'

'I like *gelato*,' said Kathy. 'You could show me the best place to buy some.'

'See?' said Henry. 'Sorted. Kathy will take Manu to the market and I will—'

'Do the washing-up, then fix that dripping tap in the bathroom of room six,' said Roberta. 'Perfect. I'll get the shopping list from Ernesto. Manu, will you take Faustino with you? He needs a walk.'

'Didn't I tell you you'd sing for your supper?' said Carla to Kathy then.

Chapter Twenty-six

Kathy was only too glad to have something to do that would take her out of the house and away from Henry Innocenti's obvious disapproval. Having convinced herself otherwise the previous evening, now she found herself agreeing with Neil that it was not a good idea to stay at the Casa Innocenti any longer than she had to. Henry was right. Neil could pay for her to stay just about anywhere in the city for two nights.

But of all the people who could have turned out to be Roberta's son . . .

Kathy was deeply hurt to think that when Henry looked at her he was not remembering their shared moment of enthusiasm over the lovely old piano at the palazzo. He could only associate her with Coldplay's 'Yellow', Neil's very public proposal and the way he had stuffed that five-euro note into Henry's shirt pocket afterwards. 'Get yourself a new shirt.' Kathy's cheeks flushed as she remembered it. It didn't matter that she hadn't been the one to say it. Henry must have thought Neil was a real prat and her association with him had tarnished her. No man liked to have another man take the mick out of him like that.

On the other hand, what right had a thirty-something bloke who still lived with his mother to act like such a git? Kathy had heard that Italian men took a long time to leave home, and this was a beautiful home, but what kind of man was content with a poky attic room when he should have had a house of his own? He didn't have the right to be so proud of himself or to be so judgemental of her. Kathy told herself she didn't have to take any notice of his opinion.

'Take Faustino!' Roberta called, as Manu and Kathy were heading out. 'Walking helps with his digestion.'

While Manu was looking for Faustino, who was snuffling around on the terrace, looking for anything the official guests might have dropped over breakfast, Henry met Kathy in the hallway.

'I'm sorry,' he said unexpectedly, 'if I seem a little . . . a little grumpy this morning. I had a hard night.'

'On the sofa, of course. I'm sorry. I could sleep on the sofa instead.'

'Absolutely not,' Henry said. 'My mother would never have it. But I also wanted to apologise for Thursday evening.'

'Why?'

'I didn't mean to embarrass you in any way. When I played "The Way You Look Tonight" I had no idea that you were . . .'

He didn't need to finish the sentence. He'd had no idea Kathy was at the wedding with a boyfriend. Because she hadn't told him.

'I should probably be apologising to you,' said Kathy.

If the implication was that they had indeed been flirting?

'I didn't say—'

'I didn't ask—'

Henry gave her a brisk smile. 'Anyway, here's Manu.

And the farting fluffball. Enjoy your trip to the market. And your *gelato*. A taste of the real Florence. See you later.'

'You can hold the dog if you like,' Manu said to Kathy, once they were out on the street.

'If you're sure?'

'Course.'

Kathy soon found out why Manu wasn't keen to hang on to Faustino's lead. Though the dog was only the size of a large hedgehog, he pulled on the lead with the strength of a wild boar and he had obviously never been taught to walk to heel. Manu shouted instructions at him all the time but was absolutely ignored – just as when he tried to teach Faustino tricks. It was fortunate that Faustino was just as keen to go to the market as they were.

'He wants to go to the salumeria,' said Manu. 'He's like this every Saturday.'

'Your English is very good, Manu,' Kathy observed then.

'Oh. That's because I lived in London until I was nearly six. When I came here, I could speak English better than Italian. Now I'm about the same in both.'

'I wish I could speak Italian.'

'I could teach you some if you like.'

'I would.'

'Do you know anything in Italian at all? I mean, can you say "hello" and "please" and "thank you"?'

'I think so. I know *ciao* and *buon giorno*. I know *grazie*. I don't know how to say "please", though.'

'*Per favore*,' said Manu. 'Practise it.'

'*Per favore*.'

'Excellent. Now I'll teach you how to say your name. *Mi chiamo Kathy. . .*'

'*Mi chiamo Kathy.*'

'Well done.' Manu gave her a thumbs-up.

He kept up the Italian lesson all the way to the market, which was set up in front of an austere white church on a nearby piazza, in the shade of some enormous umbrella pines. There were fruit stalls and flower stalls and stalls selling cheese. With Faustino at the end of his lead, Kathy was automatically an insider. The stallholders recognised the dog and, of course, Manu. They called out to him as he passed.

In turn, Manu greeted them all by name.

Kathy couldn't help but be struck by how polite he was. Neil's children never spoke to anyone over thirty unless they had to, or they wanted something. Manu actually passed the time of day with the stallholders who called out to him. Perhaps he, too, would retreat into sullen silence once hormones took hold.

Most of the stallholders asked Manu where his uncle was that morning. The woman who ran the vegetable stall in particular looked disappointed when Manu said that he was at home in the hotel.

'He's not unwell, I hope,' she said. 'If he is, then these will cheer him up.' She handed Manu a punnet of strawberries. 'I won't put them on the bill. Don't forget to tell him Gina sent them,' she added.

'All the women here want to marry my uncle,' said Manu, as he slipped the free strawberries into the basket.

He must usually be more personable on a Saturday morning, Kathy thought.

'But he's told me he'd rather be a monk.'

'Oh.'

Manu handed a slip of paper to the cheese seller, who parcelled up the hotel's order with the care of someone preparing a birthday gift. She, too, asked Manu to remember her to his uncle. At the salumeria, the owner cut fifty slices of mortadella. Fifty for the hotel and one for Faustino. Faustino's eyes were wide and wild with delight as the man dangled the extra slice above the little dog's head. Snap, snap. It was gone in two bites.

'I could have a sausage for you if you come back later,' the butcher told Kathy.

As Manu translated, Kathy did a double-take. The butcher grinned. Kathy told herself this wasn't the UK. That wasn't a double-entendre. Though it almost certainly was. She wasn't sure whether to be flattered.

The olive-oil vendor saw Manu coming and had two bottles ready for him.

'Where's your uncle?' she asked. 'I put my lipstick on specially.'

Manu, who was still translating everything for Kathy's benefit, said afterwards, 'She wanted to know who you were. She thought you might be my uncle's new girlfriend.'

Kathy had to laugh at that. She didn't think she'd seen anyone look at her with less romantic intention than Henry had that morning. Indeed, Manu confirmed, 'He's never going to have a new girlfriend. He said he'd rather have a pet crocodile. I'd definitely rather have a crocodile.'

'I see. What's next on the list?' Kathy asked.

'We've got everything,' said Manu. 'And when we've finished shopping, we always have *gelato*.'

'Then we must do exactly the same today,' said Kathy.

Manu led the way to a café on the edge of the market piazza. The tables outside were already full of people enjoying a morning coffee with a little ice cream on the side. Elevenses with ice cream seemed like a perfectly wonderful idea.

'What's the best flavour?' Kathy asked.

'They're all good,' said Manu. 'And it's hard to choose, which is why I normally have a large cone.'

'What? With five flavours? Before lunch? Are you sure?'

'I'm still growing,' said Manu.

'Fair enough. Though I think I'll stick with two. Will you order?'

Kathy chose the *cremino* and a dark chocolate *fondente*. Manu chose five flavours and insisted they should be topped off with nuts and a swirl of squirty cream. By the time the vendor had loaded all of Manu's choices onto a double-headed cone, Kathy could believe her mother's old tale that in Florence the ice creams were as big as baby's heads. Manu's confection certainly was. Kathy's choice looked rather mean alongside it, which was perhaps why the vendor topped hers with a complimentary strawberry.

The *cremino* was delicious. Basically, it was vanilla ice cream with chocolate spread, Kathy found out, but there was nothing wrong with that. There were few things in life that couldn't be improved with chocolate spread. Manu insisted she try a spoonful of each of his flavours. In turn he helped himself to about a quarter of each of the flavours Kathy had.

'And you do this every week?' Kathy asked.

'Every week,' said Manu. 'My nonna's favourite is

stracciatella. Mamma's is mint with chocolate chips. Uncle Henry prefers to eat *sorbetto*.'

Sour, thought Kathy. That figured.

'Or he just has a coffee if he's in a very bad mood.'

As he had been that morning.

'I can teach you some more Italian, if you like,' Manu said then.

'That would be very kind of you.'

Manu shrugged. 'It's no problem. I know I'm lucky to speak two languages.'

'So where should I start? How do I say, "This ice-cream is completely delicious"? I'd like to thank the ice-cream seller.'

Manu gave the question some consideration. He smiled into his ice cream. Then he said, 'You should say, "*Sei un grosso culo peloso*." Try it.'

Kathy repeated the words as she thought she'd heard them.

'Close,' said Manu. 'But not perfect. Try them again.'

Kathy tried again.

'Maybe if you do it like this.' Manu demonstrated the sentence with a theatrical hand gesture.

Kathy didn't notice the two grandmotherly women on the next table raising their eyebrows and sharing a look of consternation.

'Good,' said Manu. 'You're getting there.'

Kathy said the sentence one more time. With the accompanying hand gesture. 'What exactly does it mean?' she asked.

'Oh. It just means, "That was delicious,"' said Manu, taking another bite of his ice cream.

Kathy didn't notice the glint in the little boy's eyes. 'It seems like a long sentence.'

'To say something in Italian takes more words than in English. That's all.'

Soon – all too soon – the *gelato* was gone. Manu saved a tiny bit from the bottom of his cone. As soon as he glanced at Faustino, who had been sitting at his master's feet doing frantic puppy eyes, the little dog leaped up. This was what he had been waiting for.

'Watch this,' Manu said to Kathy. 'I've been teaching him a trick.'

It wasn't much of a trick.

Manu tossed the end of the ice-cream cone into the air above Faustino's foxy little head. Faustino made a valiant effort to catch it before it hit the ground, but he was too slow, or he snapped in the wrong direction. Whatever, the wafer ended up on the tarmac and he had to race a sparrow to get to it.

'Hmm. He needs more practice,' said Manu.

'As do I,' said Kathy. 'Could you say that phrase for me one more time?'

Manu obliged with a grin.

'You're a very good teacher,' Kathy said. 'I'm going to try it out right now.'

As they got up to leave the table, the ice-cream vendor was delivering a couple of enormous sundaes to some Swedish tourists. When he turned to go back to the counter, Kathy caught his eye and trotted out the phrase Manu had taught her.

'*Sei un grosso culo peloso*,' she said, with an enthusiastic smile.

For a moment, the vendor looked at her in confusion. He shook his head as though trying to clear his ears. Kathy tried it once more. This time the vendor's mouth dropped open in shock.

'*Mi dispiace*,' Kathy said. She at least knew that phrase – I'm sorry. 'My Italian isn't very good,' she said in English, since most of the Italians she'd met so far seemed to speak some. 'I just wanted to say how much I loved the ice-cream.'

The vendor nodded slowly but still looked more baffled than pleased. Kathy looked around to find Manu. He and Faustino had already skipped ahead and were waiting in the shadow of the church.

'That didn't go as well as I'd hoped,' Kathy told her new young friend. 'He didn't seem to understand what I was saying at all.'

'Must be because of your accent,' said Manu.

Chapter Twenty-seven

Kathy let Manu hold Faustino's lead on the walk back to the Casa Innocenti. He accepted with good grace, seeming impressed that she'd cottoned on to the fact it was neither an honour nor a treat to wrangle the small but solid dog. She preferred to carry the heavy basket.

They took a different route back, past a row of small shops, which included the boutique where Carla worked when she wasn't at the hotel. Carla waved as they passed. Manu had the inside track on all the shopkeepers. Two doors down from the boutique there was a shop that looked like a hoarder's paradise.

'Virgilio's shop,' Manu said. 'Nonna says it's full of ghosts because all the dead people's stuff ends up in there.'

Kathy shivered as she peered at the display in the window. It did look like the perfect shop for a ghost. Old rings and bracelets nestled in a layer of dust as thick as the velvet padding of an expensive jewellery box. None of it looked as if it would ever find another home. It was terribly sad to think of how treasured those tarnished old bits and bobs must have been once upon a time. Some of the rings must have embodied a promise. An engagement. A marriage. A lifetime of love.

While Kathy was looking at the window display, Virgilio himself suddenly loomed up behind the cabinet and flashed her a gappy smile.

'Quick! Run!' said Manu.

Manu set off at speed, with Faustino yapping along-side him. Kathy kept her nerve, of course, and politely nodded at the shopkeeper. Virgilio motioned that she should come into the shop and take a closer look at his wares. Kathy tapped the face of her watch, as if to say, 'In a hurry,' and, with a resigned nod, Virgilio melted back into the shadows.

'He knows witchcraft,' said Manu, when Kathy caught up with him.

'I'm sure he's just a perfectly nice old man,' said Kathy.

Still, she felt unsettled. Though perhaps not by Virgilio but from the stories his window held and thoughts of her own ring, which was Heaven only knew where.

Back at the Casa Innocenti, Roberta was waiting for them.

'Did you have ice cream?' Roberta asked, as she took the basket and dog's lead.

'I had *fragola* and *menthe*,' said Manu. It did not go unnoticed by Kathy that he'd neglected to mention the other three flavours. And the nuts. And the squirty cream.

'That sounds delicious,' said Roberta, adding, 'I bet it would have been even nicer with chocolate, vanilla and *stracciatella*.' Which were the other three flavours Manu had eaten. His grandmother knew him very well.

'Kathy,' Roberta said then. 'Your fiancé called.'

Fiancé. Kathy was still getting used to the word. She borrowed the house phone to call him back. This time, Neil picked up at once.

'What's happened now?' he asked. He sounded harassed.

'Nothing,' said Kathy. 'I mean, everything's fine. I'm just calling you back.'

'I'm in the middle of cooking lunch,' he said.

'The pasta sauce?'

'No.'

Kathy heard the microwave ping.

'The kids won't eat pasta. Sophie's gluten free, remember? Oscar and Amelie just don't like tomato. They're having Thai chicken curry.'

'I thought they were all vegetarians.'

'Not this week.'

'Neil,' Kathy asked, 'could you send over some money to the Innocenti? My account won't let me do international transfers.'

'What? I thought they were letting you stay for nothing.'

'They are, but I thought it might be a nice gesture.'

'And I'm sure they agree. I wondered when the requests for money would start.'

'They aren't asking. I am. They haven't even mentioned money.'

'That's a strange kind of hotel they're running.'

'They have this . . .' Kathy thought of telling him about the code but let the sentence tail away. 'They're just very decent people. Proud.' Neither did she tell Neil that he'd already met one of them.

'That's what they'd have you believe.'

He segued into a monologue about all the things he had to do that morning. When he finished, Kathy decided it was time to ask, 'Neil, have you had a conversation with the children about our getting engaged . . .

about the way they reacted?' It had been on her mind, along with so many other things.

'When was I supposed to do that? You have no idea what it's been like here today. The twins are in meltdown over their mocks. Sophie is pre-menopausal.'

'Pre-menstrual?' Kathy suggested.

'Whatever. She's being a nightmare. And to make things worse, Shelley and Dave made an announcement right after breakfast on Friday. After we'd already left for London.'

'Which was?'

'Shelley's only gone and got herself pregnant. At her age.'

Which was forty-two.

Kathy was suddenly glad she was alone in the attic room. She had been standing so she could look out of the window as they spoke. Now she sat down on the bed. 'She's pregnant?'

'I didn't think it was possible past forty,' Neil said.

His words went straight to Kathy's heart. He knew it was possible. Of course he did. Otherwise he wouldn't have . . .

He continued to talk. 'So, naturally everyone's gone completely doolally about it and there's no oxygen whatsoever left to discuss our good news. Typical.'

'Tell Shelley I'm really pleased for her,' said Kathy. 'And Dave, too. He must be thrilled.'

'No doubt they'll expect us to babysit,' Neil continued.

But your babysitting days are over, right? Kathy said to herself.

'And they'll probably time it that she drops the sprog just as we're having our wedding.'

'We can make sure that doesn't happen,' said Kathy. Though she supposed she should be pleased Neil was even thinking about a date. Perhaps it meant he didn't just think the ring was a holding gesture, as she had suspected.

'Look, did you want to tell me something?' Neil asked. 'Only I have got a lot to do here.'

'No,' said Kathy. 'It's fine. Like I said, I was just returning your call. Did you want to tell me something?'

'No, I didn't. Sophie wanted me to call you. She says can she borrow those weird red shoes of yours? The ones she borrowed at the wedding.'

While previously she would have been happy to know that Sophie liked anything in her wardrobe, Kathy found she was glad to be able to say that unfortunately those 'weird red shoes' were, of course, still with her in Florence.

When she got off the phone, Kathy sat on the bed in the attic room for a little while. Shelley's news had come as a surprise to her. Perhaps an even bigger surprise than Neil's proposal. Oh, she knew that Shelley and Dave had long wanted a baby, but three rounds of IVF had all been unsuccessful. She'd thought they'd given up after the last one. Yet here they were, announcing that they were going to be parents right after their beautiful wedding. How many weeks along were they? Kathy wondered. Had they waited until twelve weeks had passed to tell Neil's mum? Those weren't questions Neil would have bothered to ask. Neil failed to ask a lot of important questions.

Kathy was glad she hadn't heard the news direct from Shelley, face to face, and that she hadn't had to plaster on a smile and coo her congratulations. She would have had to hug her and tell her what wonderful, wonderful news it was. Had she not lost her phone, she would have had to text her congratulations. Kathy was glad she had an excuse not to do that too. She couldn't find the words. Not the words that would have been appropriate anyway. She wanted to be pleased for Shelley, she really did. She liked her fiancé's sister-in-law and could think of no one who deserved her happiness more. But why now? At least now she could react exactly as she wanted to, within reason. She couldn't scream – there were too many people downstairs – but she could lie face down and bite the white cotton pillow-case hard until the need to scream had passed.

Here in Florence she could prepare for the inevitable meeting at Neil's mother's house, for being invited to feel the bump and guess whether it was going to be a girl or a boy. She could prepare for having to grin and bear it. She could prepare for talking about her engagement afterwards. Her consolation prize. And right now she didn't even have the ring.

Kathy threw the phone at the pillows.

Chapter Twenty-eight

Ten minutes later, Kathy was back downstairs in the Casa Innocenti's kitchen, looking more serene than she felt (though the pillow she'd chosen to bite was probably a little sore). She was glad to see that everyone was busy again. It gave her another opportunity to offer help.

'Actually,' Roberta said gratefully, 'you could take some dishes out onto the terrace.'

Ernesto always had Saturday lunchtimes off. In his place, Roberta prepared the hotel guests' lunch. Most didn't want anything because they were out sightseeing. That day, however, a new pair of guests had just arrived and their room wasn't quite ready so Roberta had offered to fix them something to eat while she finished cleaning their suite.

'They're going in the honeymoon suite,' Roberta whispered, as she walked with Kathy to the terrace doors and told her what to do.

Outside on the terrace, a young couple – perhaps in their mid-twenties – were sitting at the table furthest from the doors. They were holding hands across the table and had eyes only for each other, despite the beautiful palazzo gardens and the crooked campanile that provided the day's backdrop to their love.

'Aren't they sweet?' Roberta said. 'As soon as I saw them, I knew I had to upgrade them to the best room in the place.'

The guests who had actually booked the best suite, arriving later that day, would have to be mollified with free Prosecco and a discount on the rate they had already paid. Henry was right that his mother ran her hotel in a very unconventional way.

'But I have a sense about them,' said Roberta. 'As well as being a refuge for the down-on-their-luck, the Casa Innocenti is famed for its romantic atmosphere. We've had a lot of proposals here,' she whispered. 'I'd put money on these two.' She seemed pleased with the thought.

Kathy took two plates and two sets of cutlery out to the table, forcing the two lovers to lift their hands so she could set their places, though they did not actually let go of each other for a second. They were in that stage of love where they couldn't believe how lucky they were to have found each other.

'This is our first time in Italy,' the young woman said.

Kathy was amused they might think it was otherwise for her. Less than a week ago, she'd never been to Italy either. The idea that she appeared to be a fixture at the Casa Innocenti was gratifying. She didn't seem out of place. Arriving at the house the previous evening, Kathy had worried that she would be in the way, but Carla had been right. She was already singing for her supper and she was grateful for the chance to do it. It was good to feel useful. It was good to have something to do other than dwell on her future sister-in-law's pregnancy.

'Italy is a very special country,' she said. 'And Florence, well, you'll love it.' What Kathy knew of it so far – with the exception of the bag snatch – was pretty good.

As Kathy brought out food and wine, she and the couple shared more snatches of conversation. They were from Bristol. They were called Jenny and Kyle. They'd been together for five years. They were celebrating Jenny's twenty-seventh birthday. They were planning to walk over the Ponte Vecchio that afternoon.

'Full of bloggers taking pictures,' Kathy warned them.

'We are bloggers,' Jenny said.

Once the new guests had eaten their lunch and were safely installed in the honeymoon suite, Kathy sat down for hers in the kitchen with Roberta and Manu. Faustino settled beneath the table, equidistant from all three of them, maximising the possibility of catching anything that might be dropped. He was lucky. Manu dropped a whole slice of mortadella. Actually, Kathy wasn't sure it was entirely an accident. Seeing that Kathy had spotted his sleight of hand, Manu gave her a shy smile.

'Manu taught me some Italian this morning,' said Kathy, to change the subject as Roberta was berating the waste of food.

'What did he teach you?' she asked.

Manu interrupted, waving his hands in Kathy's face. 'No. Don't say it, Kathy, please. She's not ready yet, Nonna! I still have to work on her accent.'

'Very good.' Roberta nodded at her grandson. 'The accent is important. I've never managed to get mine right. I've been here for more than forty years but I could never pass as a local. Unlike Henry and Carla.'

Just then Carla slammed her way into the house, throwing her bag down in the hallway like a teenager.

'Uh-oh,' said Manu, registering his mother's mood.

Carla sat down at the kitchen table. Roberta pushed the bread basket in front of her. Carla grabbed a piece of focaccia and stuffed it into her mouth. Her expression grew a little less 'hangry' as she ate but not by much.

'What happened?' Roberta asked. 'Is it Nico again?'

'He won't listen to me. The shop is failing and he says he's going to have to cut my hours but he refuses to stock anything anyone actually wants to wear. The window display is a mess. He's stuck in a time warp. People come in looking for something and go out laughing without buying so much as a hair clip. Still, he doesn't want to update his stock. He won't even look at my stuff.'

Carla explained to Kathy: 'I've designed some dresses that I think look good on every woman and I've been trying to persuade Nico to let me sell them through his shop since for ever. He keeps saying, "Next season, next season." All I want is a chance. I took in a suitcase of my new designs this morning and he hasn't even looked at them. Says he's too busy. Really I know it's that he doesn't want to have to change his vision. Which is to make every woman who comes into his boutique leave looking like she's just walked out of the nineteen nineties. A nineteen nineties' brothel at that.'

'What's a brothel?' Manu asked.

'I'll tell you when you're nine,' Roberta promised, obviously hoping that Manu would have forgotten he'd asked long before then.

Manu started calculating the wait on his fingers.

'My stuff is different,' Carla continued. 'It's modern. It's what women want. He just doesn't get it.'

'What Nico needs is to see the clothes on real people,' said Roberta.

'He sees them on me,' said Carla.

'But perhaps because he sees them on you, he thinks of them only as your personal style,' Kathy observed.

Roberta and Carla peered at Kathy with furrowed brows as the truth of what she'd said sank in.

'You're absolutely right,' said Carla. 'He needs to see them on other people. Not women he knows. But . . .'

'I'm not wearing them,' said Manu, looking worried.

'You won't have to,' Carla assured him.

It was Roberta who said it. 'Kathy, you should go to the shop and pretend to be a customer.'

'What?'

'When I worked in a boutique as a young girl we did it all the time. Whenever a customer seemed to be wavering about whether or not they liked something, one of the other sales girls would wander by – pretending to be a customer – and casually say, "That looks nice." It always worked. You could give Carla that extra validation by going into the shop and choosing something she designed.'

'But I don't speak Italian.'

'I could teach you some more words,' said Manu.

'You don't need to speak Italian,' said Carla. 'Nobody spending any money in the shops on that street is a local any more. They're all geared for the tourist market. It's just that Nico no longer knows the tourist market. Or any market this century. He doesn't even really know any women except his mother and me. And he won't listen to me.'

'Kathy will help you.' Roberta was decided. 'She'll come in and you can dress her up.'

'Kathy, will you?' Carla asked.

How could she refuse? More singing for her supper.

It was all agreed by the time Carla's lunch break was over. Kathy was to drop by the shop at around four o'clock, when Nico should be there. She would pretend she was looking for something for a party that evening. Carla would suggest one of her dresses, which she would bring out from behind the counter. Kathy would say she loved it and buy it – using petty cash borrowed from the hotel – *e voilà!* Nico would be convinced at least to display one in the window.

While the women were putting together a plan, Henry appeared. Having fixed the dripping tap in room six – 'which took far longer than I expected' – he was now dressed for the rest of his day. He wore a clean white shirt and black trousers, the outfit he'd been wearing when Kathy saw him on stage at the Palazzo Boldrini. This time, he also had a red tie draped around his neck.

When he saw Kathy, he gave her a small smile. A wary sort of smile. If that morning's chat in the corridor had been meant to clear the air between them and put her at ease, it hadn't worked. She felt immediately shy in his presence. She wondered if he felt the same.

'Let me sort out that tie,' said Roberta.

'I don't always dress like this,' Henry explained, for Kathy's benefit. 'I'm playing at a wedding this afternoon. The bride wants the band to match the floral displays. I hate playing at weddings.'

'My son, the romantic.' Roberta had adjusted his tie so that it sat more neatly against his collar. When she wasn't looking, Henry pulled it slightly loose again.

'You played very well at the wedding on Thursday,' Kathy said.

Henry shrugged. 'You know what I think? The bigger the wedding, the more likely the marriage is to fail. The more ostentatious the declaration of love, the more likely it is to be hollow. Don't you agree?'

Was he having a dig about Neil's proposal? When Roberta was out of the way for a moment, Kathy asked him, 'Are you sure you don't mind me staying in your room tonight? It's not too late for me to get a room elsewhere.'

'And if you do, my mother will go nuts. And I'll get another lecture on the Code of the Innocenti. *Deus ope, manus mea.*' Henry imbued the words with great drama. 'You stay here. I'll sleep on the couch. Apparently, it's good for my back. And it's definitely good for my soul.'

'I'm going to make sure Neil transfers some money, regardless,' Kathy insisted.

'There is no need,' Henry said.

'I know there's no need but I . . . I want to make things proper,' Kathy said, making it clear that she did not expect favours, or even friendship.

Henry winced.

Kathy decided to try to thaw the atmosphere between them by appealing to Henry's pride in his music. 'Whatever you think about weddings, I'm sure the bride and groom will love having you play,' she said.

'So long as nobody asks for "Yellow",' Henry said.

This time it was Kathy's turn to wince. 'I don't know how anyone could do such a terrible thing,' she said.

Henry nodded. 'See you later.'

On his way out of the house, Henry scooped up his

nephew and whirled him around, to Manu's squealing delight. Faustino jumped at Henry's knees, desperate to join in. Henry looked at Manu with the kindness she'd seen in him on the afternoon when they'd sat together at the Bösendorfer. He glanced back towards Kathy as he put Manu down and she thought she felt just a little of that warmth in the definite flicker of a smile he sent her.

Chapter Twenty-nine

At four o'clock, as agreed, Kathy retraced the route she and Manu had taken that morning to find the shop where Carla worked. This time, Carla wasn't alone. She was standing at the counter with a man who might have been any age from mid-forties to late sixties. He was heavily Botoxed and perma-tanned. His remarkably thick white hair was brushed into a high quiff and he wore his tight pink linen shirt open to show equally well-groomed chest hair. As Kathy walked into the shop, a bell ringing to announce her arrival, Carla and her boss both looked up. He gave Kathy a blinding grin. He had the sort of veneers so white that they look like old-fashioned dentures.

'How can we help you?' the man – who had to be Nico – asked.

'Oh, I'm just browsing,' said Kathy. She and Roberta had rehearsed that she shouldn't go straight into her speech about that evening's party. She had to make it look natural.

Kathy went to the rack closest to the door and started sorting through it. She knew at once what Carla meant about the stock. The dresses Nico favoured were for an altogether different type of woman from Kathy. They might have gone down well with the *Love Island* crowd – and Sophie and Amelie – but while they were bright and brief they were also very, very expensive.

Kathy flinched as she saw the price tag on something that resembled two net grocery bags stitched together with shoelaces. She got an electric shock of static from another garment that would probably burst into flames if someone stared at it for long enough. Hot in all the wrong ways.

There was nothing, absolutely nothing, on the rail that Kathy could imagine wearing. Not even if she lost three stone and her hair suddenly sprouted from her head like the luxuriant waves of the Girls' World toy she'd had as a child, rather than from her chin – as Sophie and Amelie liked to point out. (How was it that a chin hair could get as long as an eyelash without being noticed by the person sporting it?) Yet Kathy had to pretend she thought Nico – and Carla – might be able to help.

'Actually, I'm looking for something in particular,' she said. 'I have a party to go to this evening but the airline lost my suitcase and I've got absolutely nothing to wear. It's an emergency.'

'We can help you,' said Nico, stepping out from behind the desk, his hands clasped in a gesture of delight. 'Let me look at you properly. Your size . . . let me see. An Italian forty-four?'

Nico plucked the grocery-bag dress from the rack and held it against Kathy's back.

'Oh,' she said. 'I'm not sure.'

'It looks very different when you wear it.'

'The event I'm going to will be rather formal.'

'This is formal,' said Nico, clearly slightly affronted.

'Then a little longer?' Kathy suggested. 'I don't like my knees.'

Nico looked at Kathy's knees. His expression

suggested, disappointingly, that he wasn't about to persuade her that she'd overlooked their beauty. 'Then this?' He went back to the rail and pulled out a dress in shimmering black lamé. It would cover Kathy's knees but she couldn't see how the top half could possibly contain anything other than the flattest chest. It might have worked for Liz Hurley at a nineties' premiere. Kathy blanched but Nico would not take no for an answer.

'You have to try it on,' he insisted. 'You can't tell if you don't try it on.'

Which was Carla's point exactly. Behind Nico's back, Carla gave Kathy an extravagant eye-roll.

Nico ushered Kathy into a changing room, and while she struggled into the lamé tube, he handed accessories through the curtain. A pair of toeless suede stiletto boots that screamed, 'Twisted ankle!' A set of bangles that looked like standard police-issue handcuffs. They could be joined together by a glittering chain, Nico explained, as he passed that through the curtain too.

'You'll need a handbag as well,' Nico decided. The handbag he passed to Kathy was the size and shape of a large cooking apple studded with crystals.

'For the temptation. Like Eve,' he explained.

Kathy stared at her reflection. As she'd feared, the dress left very little to the imagination, and with the addition of each accessory, the whole ensemble somehow looked a little cheaper, though the price of the outfit had increased by several hundred euros. The end effect was less Project Runway than Project Run-the-hell-away.

'Come out and show me, *bellissima signorina,*' said Nico.

When Kathy emerged from the curtained cubicle, Nico was already leaning against the counter with a 'job done' look on his face.

He kissed the tips of his fingers. '*Perfetto.*'

Carla grimaced.

'It's not quite what I had in mind,' Kathy said at last. It was hard not to burst out laughing.

'No. No!' Nico wouldn't have it. He set about trying to make the dress look a better fit, pulling it in at the waist so that the front popped dangerously, revealing the best of M & S's lingerie.

Meanwhile, Carla was subtly preparing the next part of the charade. She had her case of samples on the counter now and was going through them as though simply folding them up to put them away. Kathy turned towards the counter and said, 'That looks interesting,' as Carla shook out a gunmetal grey dress with a fluttering hem.

'That?' Nico couldn't hide his disdain.

'Yes. May I try it?'

'It's not very formal,' Nico complained.

Carla seized the moment. 'The dress comes in only one size,' she said. 'But it is designed to be worn in several different ways according to the wearer's body. I think you should try it first with the deep V at the back.'

Kathy was only too pleased to hobble back into the fitting room and discard the excruciating shoes.

While she struggled out of the lamé dress, which was even more difficult to take off than it had been to put on, Kathy could hear Carla and Nico in discussion. She couldn't follow the conversation but she could tell from the tone that they were in disagreement. And she knew from the moment she held it in her hands that Carla's dress was a much better fit for her style, or the style she wanted, than the second-skin lamé extravaganza. The fabric was so beautiful. As Kathy slipped the dress over her head, she knew that it would fall in a flattering but not clinging fashion. This was a dress made by someone who understood other women.

She stepped out onto the shop floor. This time Nico grimaced. Carla ignored him. 'How do you feel?' she asked Kathy.

'It's very comfortable,' Kathy said.

'Comfortable!' Nico echoed the word as though it were a curse.

'Comfortable is good. You could define the waist with a belt,' said Carla, wrapping a red one around her. 'And, of course, you need some slightly higher shoes. Though only slightly higher.'

Nico affected a swoon of disgust.

Carla calmly handed Kathy a pair of sandals in a red to match the belt. 'And add a little fun with your bag.'

Carla passed Kathy the glittering apple again, with a sly glance at Nico to see his reaction. He was pretending not to be paying attention but this gesture definitely caught his eye. 'A special piece such as this one needs a plain background so that it can truly shine.'

'Yes,' said Kathy. 'I see what you mean. It is a lovely bag.'

Nico's ears pricked up.

Carla continued to lay on the patter. 'The great thing about this colour is that you can accessorise it with so many other accent colours. You can be subtle with black or a dark brown. You can be bright. You can go for a metallic.' Carla whipped the red belt away from Kathy's waist and replaced it with a stretchy elasticated belt in silver with a big shiny buckle. The apple bag was swapped for one shaped like a rocket. It was similarly impractical and flash. But somehow the gunmetal grey of the fabric made even the gaudiest gew-gaw Nico's shop had to offer look classy. It made any old piece of tat look like a deliberate touch of kitsch humour.

When Carla handed Kathy a pair of silver sandals, Nico stepped in. 'No,' he said. 'That's much too obvious. Too matchy-matchy. Try these.' He swapped the silver sandals for a pair of black sandals with a flat-form sole that gave them the look of a geisha's wooden shoes.

'They're . . . comfortable,' Kathy said.

This time Nico managed to laugh. 'Let's try it with white,' he said. 'Or blue.'

Kathy felt like Cinderella in the Disney cartoon as Carla and Nico whirled around her, draping her with scarves and necklaces, swapping bags and offering her different shoes to try.

While all this was going on, three more people had walked into the shop. Three women of what Nico would doubtless refer to as 'a certain age'. Like Kathy, they first pawed through the racks closest to the door, the disappointment easily readable on their faces as they realised that anything they picked up was too small, too bright, too skimpy and probably way too expensive. Clothes for a fantasy woman, unlike anyone they knew.

All the same, they came further into the store because they were fascinated by Kathy's transformation, which was unfolding like a piece of performance art. They pretended not to be watching but Kathy and Carla knew they were, and when the first of the three picked up a dress similar to the one Kathy was wearing from Carla's suitcase and stroked the fabric, Kathy knew they were interested too.

'Can I try this?' asked the woman. She was English.

'Of course,' said Carla. She opened a second changing cubicle. While Nico was distracted, tying a golden rope belt around Kathy's waist this time, Carla winked at Kathy over his head and mouthed, 'It's working!'

Moments later, the genuine customer was on the shop floor, twirling modestly, and Nico was in his element suggesting how she might liven up her 'Carla' dress.

'I never would have thought of buying a bag like this,' she said, as Nico handed her the silver rocket. 'But it works, doesn't it?'

'A piece so special needs a plain background to truly make it shine,' Nico said, echoing the sentiment of Carla's earlier pronouncement. Carla shook her head in delighted exasperation. 'Now, what would finish off this look is one of these.'

Nico flourished a necklace that looked as though it might have belonged to the pope. The English woman cooed, 'That is lovely.' When a second woman asked if she could try on the blue version of the dress Kathy was wearing, Kathy knew for sure the plan she and Carla had cooked up over lunchtime had worked.

'I sold four of my dresses straight after you left,' Carla confirmed, when she came back to the Casa Innocenti at the end of her working day. 'Four! At full price. And

Nico sold four of his hideous necklaces to go with them. They actually made quite a good combination. He was delighted. He's put one of my dresses in the window. You should have heard him talking to the other customers, telling them that true Italian style in the twenty-first century is all about understated chic. Understated chic! Nico! I nearly died from laughing.'

Carla grabbed Kathy by both hands and danced her round the kitchen. 'You were brilliant. I couldn't have done it without you.'

'I still feel a little weird about it,' Kathy admitted.

'Don't,' said Carla. 'This afternoon Nico made a thousand euros in genuine sales that wouldn't have happened without our little kick-start. He's happy. I'm happy. And you looked beautiful.'

Carla leaned back, still holding Kathy's hands, and observed her from arm's length. 'You should wear more colour,' she said. 'You have a beautiful complexion but all this black and white you wear drains you. I don't mean to be rude,' she added.

'I understand,' said Kathy. 'It's just that I don't know where to start when it comes to clothes.'

'Then it's lucky you have met me,' Carla said. 'You're a beautiful woman, Kathy.'

Inside, Cross-eyed Kathy blushed hard. And Chicken Licken blushed harder. It was difficult to feel beautiful when you shared your life with two teenage girls who had all the advantages of youth. There was no doubt that Kathy's style had changed since she'd been living with Neil. For the worse. It was easier to be invisible than be critiqued by a nineteen-year-old. But it had been fun dressing up. Really good fun. Kathy handed Carla the dress she'd pretended to buy. Nico had wrapped up a pair of red tassel earrings as a free gift with the purchase.

'I suppose you ought to have these back as well,' Kathy said.

'No way,' said Carla. 'Consider them your fee.'

They were the same red as the geranium on the windowsill across the street, Kathy noticed, when she was back upstairs in the attic room. She put them on and admired the way they moved in the old wardrobe mirror. Just a tiny splash of colour but they seemed to bring her face to life. Even the old black linen shift she was wearing looked better. The dash of red was like a pinch of salt for her appearance. She decided she would keep them on.

Chapter Thirty

Shortly afterwards, Kathy found herself alone in the kitchen with Ernesto, who had just arrived to prepare that evening's dinner. He nodded a greeting at her, which was an improvement on before, then busied himself with fetching out of the fridge the ingredients he would need for the guests. He was not one for small-talk, which was probably for the best, considering Kathy's lack of Italian.

He pulled out the vegetables Manu and Kathy had bought that morning. He sniffed them, squeezed them, put some back into the fridge and discarded others with a tut.

'What are you making this evening?' Kathy asked, embarrassed that she couldn't ask in Italian but sure that, spending so much time around Roberta and her family, Ernesto must have a smattering of English.

'Huh?' he asked.

'*Mangiare. Sta sera*?' she asked.

Ernesto gestured towards the tomatoes with a sharp knife.

'*Pomodori*. Good,' said Kathy. 'I mean, *bene*.' She knew that much.

Ernesto nodded.

So Kathy decided it would be a good moment to try out the phrase that Manu had taught her. She knew that Ernesto had made the pastries they'd eaten for breakfast from scratch. Kathy began haltingly, 'This morning . . . the *pasticcio* . . .' Was that the word? It sounded like it should be. 'The *pasticcio, molto bene*.'

Ernesto nodded. He was happy with that.

So then Kathy trotted out the phrase that Manu claimed was guaranteed to bring a smile to the face of any cook. '*Sei un grosso culo peloso.*'

Ernesto paused with the end of his knife on the chopping board. As he looked at Kathy, his expression recalled the one she'd seen on the face of the man in the *gelato* shop that morning: of confusion. Kathy remembered what Manu had said then about her accent. She was 99 per cent sure she had the words right and in the correct order but perhaps they needed different emphasis. She tried the phrase again. This time she added the hand gestures too.

'*Sei un grosso culo peloso.*'

And this time, Ernesto threw his knife down on the chopping board. Then he whipped off his chef's hat and tossed it into the corner of the room. By the time he took off his apron and stuffed it into the food waste bin, Kathy was beginning to get the idea that she had not said what she'd thought she'd said. Not at all.

Shouting something Kathy couldn't translate, Ernesto stormed out of the kitchen and away from the house. Even Faustino looked taken aback by his sudden and dramatic departure.

'What was that?' Roberta asked, when she appeared moments later. 'Who was shouting?'

Kathy stood in the doorway of the kitchen, blushing to the roots of her hair. 'I think I insulted Ernesto.'

'Don't be silly. Ernesto is impossible to insult. Unless he saw you adding salt to one of his dishes before you tasted it.'

'I just wanted him to know how much I like his cooking. I only said . . .'

For the third time in five minutes, Kathy repeated the phrase Manu had taught her. With the hand gestures and a perfect accent.

In response, Roberta clutched at the locket around her neck. 'You said that?'

Kathy nodded.

'To Ernesto?'

Kathy nodded again.

'But why, Kathy? Why would you say that? Hang on. Who taught you? Was it Manu?'

The penny dropped. Kathy remembered the look on the face of the ice-cream vendor again. Confused? Baffled? Insulted? 'It doesn't mean what I think it means, does it?'

'No,' said Roberta. 'I don't think it does. Emanuele!' she yelled up the stairs. 'Emanuele! Get down here at once.'

At the sound of his full name, Manu would know he was in for it. Even Faustino ran for cover beneath Roberta's favourite chair.

Of course Manu had taught Kathy a perfect insult. And in using it, she had upset the Casa Innocenti's cook of twenty-five years by telling him that he was a big fat hairy arse. Of course, as soon as Roberta had finished telling Manu he was in big trouble and would not have access to his tablet for the rest of the weekend, she called her chef on his mobile. Ernesto would not pick up. She left him a sweet, apologetic message but if he listened to it, he didn't call back.

'Manu,' said Roberta. 'You have taken advantage of our guest's good nature and caused a kitchen crisis!'

'I didn't think she would say it to Ernesto! I only wanted her to say it to Uncle Henry.'

Kathy had to smile at that.

The pan of water Ernesto had put on the stove for that evening's pasta course had boiled dry on the hob. He'd left at the worst possible moment, before he'd had time to get dinner even halfway prepared. Ordinarily, it wouldn't have mattered. The hotel was rarely full. But that night it *was* full and Roberta was expecting to serve dinner for fifteen at eight o'clock.

'It's all my fault,' said Kathy.

'It's not your fault,' said Roberta, firmly. 'It's not really Manu's fault either – though he needs to be discouraged from making a habit of leading people up the garden path. It wasn't that bad an insult. And, to be honest, it wasn't far from the truth.' Roberta allowed herself a twitch of a smile. 'I'm sorry to say that Ernesto is always looking for an excuse to take Saturday night off. He'll be in the bar telling everyone what a terrible boss I am and how he was so insulted he's going to call for a tribunal. He'll come back tomorrow with a hangover.'

'But that doesn't help you now.'

'No. It doesn't. But it's not the worst disaster the Casa Innocenti has ever had to deal with. Kathy, do you cook?'

'After a fashion,' she said.

In her mind's eye, Sophie, Oscar and Amelia all pulled their best 'yuck' faces. Prior to meeting Neil,

Kathy had enjoyed cooking for her friends. Cooking for a ready-made family turned out to be very different. It seemed no one was obliged to be polite. She wondered if her friends had just been kind for all those years when she'd plied them with her veggie lasagne.

'I can follow a recipe,' she concluded.

'Perfect. Ernesto's recipes are simple. It's all a matter of having the right ingredients and the patience to let them come together. For this evening, Kathy, you are my sous-chef. Manu will be on table service and washing-up.'

Manu slunk to the sink and started to fill it with hot water. 'What about Mamma?' he complained.

'Your mother has a date.'

'Not any more I don't.'

Carla tied an apron around her waist and joined them by the stove.

'Then I have a full brigade.' Roberta beamed.

Chapter Thirty-one

Roberta handed out instructions. Manu was to wash pots as needed and lay the tables on the terrace. Carla and Kathy were pressed into slicing onions, peeling tomatoes and chopping garlic for a first course of *pici* with tomato sauce. Sloshing olive oil into a huge pan, Roberta said, 'This is a cheat's sauce. A proper Italian mamma would never serve this. But I'm not a proper Italian mamma and since all the guests are English, except Signor Cagliari, no one will ever know anyway. The trick is to pretend that everything is going exactly to plan. After all, no one but us ever knew what the plan was.'

The onions were put on the stove to brown – 'for much longer than you think they need' – before the garlic and the tomatoes were added. Carla threw handfuls of basil into the mix. A generous amount of salt and pepper.

'And a magic ingredient.'

A big slug of grappa.

Meanwhile a big slug of Prosecco was to be poured directly into each of the guests. 'Because nothing makes waiting easier than a free drink,' said Roberta. She put on her best customer-service face and headed out with two bottles.

Manu circulated on the terrace with plates of Parmesan, prosciutto and stuffed olives, charming one and all. Except Signor Cagliari, who, according to Manu, had asked what the weird smell from the kitchen was.

'He's the one making all the weird smells around here,' Roberta complained.

'No, Mamma,' said Carla. 'That's Faustino.'

While Roberta and Manu were serving up the pasta, Carla and Kathy began cooking the *secondi*. There was a set menu for the evening, thank goodness, so everyone was having *tagliata di manzo*. Sliced steak, flash-cooked on a griddle – just like at Shelley and Dave's wedding. Kathy arranged rocket and slivers of Parmesan on fifteen plates, while Carla did the grilling, then held the cooked steak with asbestos fingers while she sliced it with one of Ernesto's best knives.

The kitchen that evening was like backstage at a fashion show, all creative chaos and last-minute adjustments. When Roberta and Manu went out to the guests bearing plates, they were the supermodels. Unflappable, serenely smiling, they accepted the coos and praise of the audience while the cooks sweated and swore out of sight, like the designer and the dresser. Wine was poured. Bread baskets replenished. Everyone was pleased. Even Signor Cagliari sent his compliments to the chefs.

'You're doing brilliantly,' Roberta assured her newest assistant, Kathy.

Kathy and Carla were getting used to working together, dancing around each other as though they had shared a kitchen their whole lives. Like good friends or flatmates. Like sisters. It was as though they were duetting, just as Kathy had duetted with Henry.

'What's for pudding?' Kathy asked, as the last of the steak went out.

'It's Saturday, so it's always bloody tiramisu!' Carla laughed.

Thankfully, Ernesto had prepared it that morning. Kathy scooped generous portions into colourful glass bowls.

'Save some for me,' Manu reminded her. He took a spoon and stole a bite in case Kathy forgot. While he was outside delivering the first few dishes, Kathy took a spoonful for herself.

'I saw that,' said Roberta. She had a spoonful too.

If any of the guests that night noticed that the food was not authentically Italian, no one said so. The plates that returned to the kitchen were already wiped clean. There were requests for seconds. Manu even got a tip. He showed off the two shiny euro coins proudly.

'Thank you, team,' said Roberta, when the last table was cleared. 'We all deserve a round of applause.'

'Do I deserve to be allowed my tech back?' Manu asked.

'I think that might be up to Kathy,' said Roberta.

Manu turned to Kathy with a pair of puppy eyes that could have put Faustino to shame. 'Do you forgive me?' he asked. 'I'm very, very sorry I told you to say those bad words.'

'I forgive you,' she said. 'At least now I know what you should never say when somebody gives you an ice cream. On the other hand, I also know exactly what I should say if I ever meet anyone who has a face like a big hairy bottom.'

'Like Uncle Henry!' Manu laughed.

Kathy could think of no one whose face was further from looking like a big hairy bottom.

Chapter Thirty-two

So, dinner was finished. The guests had been taken care of. The dishes were all clean and carefully put away. Manu had been sent to bed. Roberta had retired to her bedroom to read. Only Kathy, Carla and Faustino remained downstairs, though even Faustino was yawning. His pink tongue curled extravagantly in his mouth as he performed the classic 'down dog' stretch. But it was not bedtime just yet. Carla pulled a bottle of white wine – a Vernaccia di San Gimignano – from the fridge.

'We deserve this,' she said to Kathy. 'Let's sit on the terrace.'

Kathy followed her outside. It was still warm. The sun had gone down but there was just enough orange-purple light left in the sky to turn the umbrella pines and cypress trees in the palazzo's garden into a paper-cut silhouette illustration from a children's fairy-tale book. Bats flittered across the sky. Faustino made a half-hearted snap in the direction of one that dared to fly low over the terrace in pursuit of a moth.

Kathy and Carla pulled two chairs close to the terrace wall so that they could sit with their feet up. Carla had brought out a silver ice bucket – 1920s, from the palazzo, of course – to keep the wine cool. They settled down. Once he could see that Kathy was comfortable, Faustino leaped onto her lap, which seemed like a real seal of approval. Kathy was glad to have him there. The weight of his little body was comforting. She gently scratched at a spot behind Faustino's ears, sending him into a sort of happy trance.

'What happened to your date tonight?' Kathy asked, as Carla poured two glasses of the wine.

'Judging by the message, I guess his wife got into his Tinder account.'

Kathy's eyes widened.

'I didn't know he was married. He said he was divorced.'

Kathy nodded in sympathy. 'I've been there. Many times.'

'Internet dating makes you start to lose faith in humankind, doesn't it?'

'Just a small section of *man*kind,' said Kathy.

'Still, I'm sure I had much more fun at home tonight than I would have had on any date. I didn't even really like the look of the guy. His pictures were all of him posing in front of the bathroom mirror with his top off. Like pecs can make up for personality. The toilet in the background was a metaphor. I was just going on a date because I thought I should.'

'Because you thought you should?'

'Because my mother worries that Manu has no male role model. Apart from my brother, of course, and you've seen what an old misery guts he is. She also worries that there will be no one to take care of me when I'm old. I've told her that Manu will be like Henry. He'll take care of me. He'll never leave home. Not that I would wish that upon my boy.'

'I don't think I would ever leave home if I lived here.'

'Oh, I left as soon as I could,' said Carla. 'At eighteen

years old, I was out of this place and off to London. I was fed up with my parents' collection of waifs and strays. As a teenager, I really didn't appreciate having to spend every weekend with a bunch of nutty old people. I wanted the bright lights and the big city and people my own age. The minute I'd saved up enough cash, I was on a plane. I ran away . . . Where do people run away to when they already live in London?' Carla mused.

'Florence,' said Kathy. 'Like your mum did.'

They chinked their glasses to toast that idea.

'So, you ran away but your brother stayed here in Italy?' Kathy asked.

'No. He left too. The week after he finished school. But he went much further than I did. He went to the States to make his fortune as a musician. He was in a band. They had a deal, though nothing really came of it. But when they broke up, he was in big demand as a session player. He went on tour with loads of huge names.'

Hence the festival passes in his room.

'He flew round the world first class, stayed in some amazing places, played on loads of tracks you'd definitely have heard. He wrote some songs too, for other artists. And advertising jingles. Made quite a bit of money from that. When he wasn't on tour, he lived in New York. He had a great apartment there in the Meatpacking District. Really impressive. He was going to buy a bar with his best friends.'

'So why did he come back?'

Carla took a big slug of wine. 'I don't suppose he'd mind me telling you. He came back because our father died. This was three years ago. Henry was going to come back that summer for the first time in ages with his new girlfriend Amy. The way Henry told it, she was the most beautiful woman ever to walk the earth. The kindest. The cleverest. The sweetest. We were looking forward to meeting her. It sounded like she might be "the one".' Carla made little quotation marks with her fingers in the air. 'Though Mamma was starting to worry that if Henry married an American she would never see her grandchildren. Anyway, a meet-the-family trip was planned for the summer but Papa died at the end of April. It was quite sudden, though in retrospect, knowing what I know now, I think it was only sudden to Mamma, Henry and me because we didn't understand what had been going on behind the scenes. Papa seemed healthy for his age but he was under a lot of pressure.'

'From what?'

'From this . . .' Carla waved her hand to encompass the house behind them and the dark garden on the other side of the wall. 'The whole Innocenti myth. *Deus ope, manus mea.* My father loved the idea of being part of this noble ancient family. He truly felt himself to be a proper descendant of all those sour-faced old men and women who used to line the walls of the great hall. He wanted to be like them. He wanted to carry on the old traditions. The generosity, the charity, the largesse. But after the Second World War the family didn't have the money it used to have. Papa's father – my grandfather – sold off the country house. My father had to sell the palazzo. That was a great source of shame to him. But he continued to be more generous than he could afford to be, and by the time Papa died, he had racked up such huge debts that this place, the gatehouse, was in danger too.'

Carla looked up at the walls of her home, which seemed so solid and so eternal. Kathy commented as such.

'Believe me, it was falling down. Still is. Anyway, Henry came back from New York for Papa's funeral, but as soon as he got here, he knew he'd have to stay at least for a little while. Mamma was in pieces. She'd just lost the love of her life. She could barely dress herself. There was no way she could be expected to deal with the business side of Papa's death as well as the huge hole in her heart. And there was the hotel to run. So, Henry took over the practical side and little by little he uncovered a mess far greater than we had ever imagined. The only way to get out of it would be by selling this place. Or by Henry abandoning the idea of his club in New York and using the money he'd saved to patch it up instead.'

Carla's eyes went misty at the memory of that time.

'Henry knew as well as I did that asking Mamma to leave her home of forty years might be the end of her. Instead he sacrificed all he had dreamed of so that Mamma – and Manu and I, as it worked out – could stay here.'

'I had no idea,' said Kathy.

'Why would you? It's not something he would ever talk about to someone he's known just a few days. Especially since it turned out to be a bigger sacrifice than he'd originally thought.'

'In what way?'

'Well, Amy – the fabled girlfriend – came over with him for the funeral, of course. I think she was quite taken by the idea of moving to Italy and becoming the chatelaine of a palazzo. When she realised that the palazzo had been sold long ago, and all that was left was a one-star hotel full of down-and-outs in a crumbling gatehouse, she was suddenly a lot less excited. Especially when Henry told her he was going to have to sell the New York apartment as well as give up on the club.'

'Did she go back to the States without him?'

'Not immediately, no. While she was staying here, the palazzo was under renovation by its new owner, the Silicon Valley mogul. When Amy got wind of that, she would come out onto the terrace wearing floaty white linen, gathering huge armfuls of lavender, like she was starring in her own little film. Of course, she caught the dot-com billionaire's eye. She invited herself to "consult" on his interior design, using the Innocenti connection as her USP, can you believe? Within a month, she'd thrown Henry over for this new guy. She married him. They had a huge wedding. We could see it from here. I was surprised Henry didn't fire up the old Innocenti cannon and send a ball right into the middle of the party. Amy even had stationery printed with "from the desk of the Countess of Palazzo Innocenti". Whatever that means. Look at this.'

Carla tapped an address into the browser on her smartphone. It brought up a page from an online interiors magazine. 'This is her. Evil Amy.'

Kathy took the phone and had a look at the woman who had broken Henry's heart. The petite brunette, who wore her hair in the sort of severe bob only someone with really delicate features can get away with, was pictured wearing a flowing white dress against a backdrop of flowing white curtains dressing a window that opened onto a soft green lawn.

'That's the ballroom inside the palazzo. She took out most of the distinguishing features and made the whole thing like a warehouse. "Sensitive restoration". Huh! It used to be painted with a *trompe l'oeil* scene of the hills around Fiesole. She just slapped white paint over everything. She's wrecked the place. I'm just glad Papa never saw it.'

'She's very beautiful,' Kathy grudgingly admitted.

'On the outside.' Carla took her phone back. 'Believe me, there's a pit of greed behind those eyes. Look at her Instagram account.'

Kathy scrolled through more pictures of Amy in white, gazing out over various views, interspersed with motivational quotes. Including 'If you want to feel rich, just count the things you have that money cannot buy' and 'All you need is love.'

'It wasn't enough for her.' Carla snorted. 'I can't believe Henry was ever taken in. As soon as she saw a chance to live the rest of her life in luxury, she took it. She literally jumped over the fence. Fortunately, she and her husband live in San Francisco most of the time. I don't think they visited the palazzo once last year.'

'I'm not surprised Henry's sworn off women now.'

'He picked the wrong one, that's for sure. And he's convinced himself that all women are only interested in money and he won't try again. He's got prickly since it happened.'

Kathy wondered if Carla had noticed how odd Henry had been with her.

'You'll have to forgive him,' Carla said. 'He's a true softie at heart.'

So that was the story of how Henry had come to be living with his mother and his sister as he neared forty.

Kathy felt ashamed for having thought less of him for his circumstances, given she hadn't had any idea of the truth behind them. No wonder he was so angry that, three years after he'd made his sacrifice, his mother was still filling the hotel with people who couldn't afford to be there, or people who could afford to be there but were squatting in his bedroom. And to have to wonder whether Evil Amy might pop up in the palazzo gardens gathering armfuls of lavender at any moment.

'My brother drives me absolutely crazy but he's the best brother a girl could ever have. Without him, I don't know what we'd do. Any of us. Me, Mamma, Manu. He really stepped up when I left Manu's father and had to come back from London. He practically saved my life . . . No, he really saved my life. I was in a relationship with a seriously controlling man.'

But Carla didn't get to tell the story.

Chapter Thirty-three

Faustino, who had been napping quite contentedly in Kathy's lap, suddenly sat up very straight with his ears pricked, like two pointy, furry satellite dishes. Having confirmed that he'd heard what he wanted to hear, Faustino leaped from Kathy's lap and skittered into the house and down the stairs to the entrance hall.

'Henry must be back,' said Carla.

She was right. As the two women listened in silence, they heard Henry greeting the dog in the hallway below.

'Whoa! It's the flying fluff ball of fury. How are you, Faustino? How's my favourite member of the family? You know I love you the best, don't you? Don't tell the others . . .'

Carla rolled her eyes. 'He says that to all of us.'

Downstairs, Henry continued to chat to the dog. 'You want to know how the wedding was, Faustino? The wedding was the usual load of bullshit. The food was good, though. I brought you some ham. No, Faustino! Would I give you any old prosciutto? This is the good stuff.'

'No wonder the dog's diet isn't working,' Carla observed.

Moments later Henry walked onto the terrace, holding Faustino as if he was cradling a human baby, cooing as he tickled him under the chin.

'Oh. You're still here,' Henry said. 'I mean, you're still up.'

But Kathy knew he had meant to say the first thing. She was still there. Though he'd said otherwise, he *had* been expecting her to find somewhere else. Hoping she would find somewhere else, more like.

'Busy night in the kitchen,' said Carla. 'Ernesto went AWOL.'

'Again?'

'Again.'

Kathy was comforted to hear that Roberta hadn't been overstating Ernesto's regular disappearing acts to make her feel less guilty about having been the cause of today's episode.

'What happened this time?' Henry asked.

'I'm afraid I told him, "*Sei un grosso culo peloso*,"' Kathy admitted.

'Good accent,' said Henry, with a nod of appreciation. 'And you're not wrong.'

'I'm sorry it caused so much trouble.'

'You can guess who taught her how to say it,' Carla said. 'Still, Kathy saved the day by helping in the kitchen. It went well. She knows her stuff. We made *pici all'pomodoro*, *tagliata*—'

'Tiramisu?'

'Always bloody tiramisu!' the siblings said in unison.

'The guests didn't notice the difference,' Carla continued.

'Well, anything is better than Ernesto's tomato sauce,' said Henry.

'How was the wedding?' Kathy asked.

'Expensive. Showy. Pointless.'

'Your favourite kind,' said Carla.

'Never seen a more badly suited couple. I could see what the groom saw in her – everyone could, the dress was barely there. But what she saw in him . . . Hidden assets, no doubt. So, I give them twelve months. Or as long as it takes to file for divorce in America, these days. They were American, of course, living the Tuscan dream, Four Seasons-style.'

Henry's eyes drifted to the trees in the palazzo garden.

'Join us for a drink, big bro?' Carla asked.

'No.' Henry didn't hesitate. 'You ladies probably want to gossip. I don't want to break up your party. I'll just hang out with Faustino for a while, then get some sleep. Thank you, Kathy, for helping Mamma and Carla with dinner. I appreciate it.'

Kathy was pleased to be thanked but couldn't help feeling that, had she not been there, Henry would have sat down with his sister. Perhaps she ought to go so that the siblings could talk. Carla didn't seem too worried, though. 'Suit yourself,' she told her brother. 'There's pasta left in the fridge if you're hungry.'

Still carrying Faustino, Henry went into the house. 'Let's get comfy on that old sofa eh?' he said, to the dog. 'You've got me as your bedmate again tonight.' Kathy felt another wave of guilt. She guessed she was supposed to.

'I hope he's not going to turn into a mad old dog lover,' said Carla. 'All I want is for him to be happy. But tell me about your man, Kathy. How did you meet him? Are you excited about getting married? It is your first time, isn't it?'

Kathy was suddenly very aware that if she and Carla

had been able to hear Henry talking to the dog, then Henry could probably hear them talking to each other.

'Neil's a good man,' Kathy said. 'I wish he were here with me in Florence. I think he would like it. I've always wanted to visit this city.' Rather than talking about Neil, Kathy chose to tell Carla about her parents, their honeymoon and her middle name.

'Then you were destined to come here,' Carla agreed.

By the time Kathy went to bed, Henry was already asleep on the sofa. Faustino was asleep alongside him, flat out on his back with his four paws in the air. The dog looked extremely comfortable, Henry slightly less so, perhaps, as he did his best not to squash the dog.

Kathy remembered what her father had once told her about dogs. Dogs know who the good guys are. They can tell whom to trust. The Courage family dog – Benji – was utterly devoted to Kathy's father. Faustino always sought Henry out when Henry was in the house. Maybe it was just the prosciutto but Kathy doubted that. Faustino was devoted too.

Neither Henry nor the dog stirred as Kathy crept by, which gave her a moment to observe them. Henry's hair stuck up from his head and she could see in his sleeping face the young boy he must once have been, when he still dreamed of being a star musician, before the responsibilities had started to pile up.

Carla's revelations about why Henry was back in Italy had painted her brother in a different light. He wasn't mooching off his family. He was holding it together.

Just then, Faustino let out a fart so violent that he shook himself awake – doubtless a result of the illicit prosciutto – and his sudden movement caused Henry to begin to wake up too. Kathy tiptoed at speed to the staircase.

Upstairs in the attic room again, she looked at those festival passes with a fresh perspective, as remnants of a life Henry had left behind for the most admirable of reasons. What a sacrifice he had made for love. She understood it, though. Absolutely. Henry was in Italy for the same reasons Kathy had never made it this far before.

Chapter Thirty-four

Despite her late night talking to Carla on the terrace, Kathy was up early again. If this was to be her last full day in Florence, she didn't want to miss a moment. Besides, there was already an awful lot of noise coming from downstairs. Specifically, an awful lot of yelling and clattering and crashing.

When Kathy walked into the kitchen, it was a whirl of activity. For activity, read coordinated chaos.

'Ernesto didn't show up,' said Carla, as she pressed an apron into Kathy's hands. 'You don't mind helping Mamma and Manu, do you? Henry's doing the tables outside. Everyone in the hotel has decided to have breakfast at once and so early. I don't know what's the matter with them all. It's a nightmare.'

Kathy tied on the apron and joined Roberta and Manu on the cooked-breakfast production line as they scooped and slopped the contents of various pans and dishes onto plates and into dishes. Meanwhile Henry and Carla took orders from the guests and kept the flow of plates to the terrace constant.

'I'm sorry about Ernesto,' said Kathy. 'He must be very upset.'

'He must be very hung-over, more like,' said Roberta. 'He's not upset. This happens all the time. Any excuse to have Sunday morning off. Well, I'll give him a real excuse. Next time he turns up he can hand in his chef's hat and look for somewhere else to work.'

'You don't mean that, Mamma,' said Carla, who was momentarily in the kitchen to fetch more eggs.

'You're right. Ernesto was taken on by my husband's father,' Roberta explained. 'He's been here since he was Manu's age. However irritating the old man is, he comes with the house and that is that. Ernesto is practically fixtures and fittings.'

'And about as useful as half of them,' said Carla, giving the temperamental oven a kick as she passed it. 'Kathy, would you come out and give me a hand clearing some of the tables?'

Out on the terrace, the guests were having a wonderful time. Jenny and Kyle, the young couple who had arrived the previous afternoon, were busy taking selfies. They were so delighted in each other and in their surroundings that Kathy offered to take a photograph of them so they could both be properly in the frame. Though they were on opposite sides of the breakfast table, the two were constantly touching, their hands intertwined over the crumb-dusted cloth. As soon as they'd finished looking at Kathy for the photograph, they went back to gazing at each other. Every glance they had for each other said, 'I can't believe how lucky I am to have found you.'

'There you are,' said Kathy, handing back the phone. 'I hope you have a lovely day.'

'Oh, we will,' said Jenny.

'Every day is lovely with you,' Kyle agreed. Jenny feigned embarrassment but Kathy knew she was thrilled.

'Cute, huh?' Carla observed, as they met by the buffet table. 'Young love.'

It seemed that young love was infectious. An elderly couple at the hotel to celebrate the wife's eightieth birthday also held hands as they left the terrace to begin their day. And not because they needed to hold each other up, as Henry suggested, while Carla was cooing over them too.

The sight of the older couple holding hands moved Kathy even more than the young lovers had. Young love is easy. Devotion after such a long time was of a different class.

'How do you know they've been together for years?' Henry asked, when Carla suggested that Kathy was right. 'They probably got together on Tinder last Wednesday. I hear it's full of old people after a final fling.'

Carla frowned at her brother. 'You and your cynicism.'

After what Kathy had heard the previous evening, she thought perhaps he deserved to be cynical.

'I like to see people in love,' Carla said.

The young lovers got up and walked, as if in a dream, back to their room, with their arms wrapped so tightly around one another it was a miracle they didn't fall over.

'Ugh! Kissing!' said Manu, when he saw them. He covered his eyes and mimed puking into a flowerpot.

'That's my boy,' said Henry.

Back in the kitchen once breakfast was over, Roberta glanced at her watch. 'We have half an hour to get changed and get to church.'

Manu flopped over a chair in a dramatic fashion. 'Church! But we've already been working for hours.'

'And that makes a difference because? Manu Innocenti, we've been working for hours already because you taught Kathy a bunch of insults when she thought you were being a good Italian host teaching her some polite and useful phrases. Get upstairs. Put your tie on.'

Manu mimed being choked by his collar.

'Do you need to speak to your fiancé?' Roberta asked Kathy then. 'You must use the phone whenever you want to.'

'He'll be doing his run,' said Kathy. When they'd first met, he'd told her, 'I run ten kilometres every Sunday morning, rain or shine, unless I've got a beautiful reason to stay in bed.' The implication being, of course, that she was a beautiful reason. He started running again two weeks after she'd spent her first Sunday morning at his place.

Now there was no interfering with his routine, which was to leap out of bed at six thirty, pulling the sheets off Kathy as he did so. She'd once suggested that he might be a little less energetic on a weekend morning, but he'd told her that she was welcome to go back to sleep while he was 'making the most of the day'. The thing was, she could never really go back to sleep, but would just lie there waiting to hear him come through the front door, at which point she would jump out of bed and pretend she'd got up moments after he'd left for his jog. If Neil caught her still in bed, he wouldn't ever say he was disappointed in her, but she could definitely feel it in his regard.

'I'll call him later,' Kathy said. 'Can I come to church with you too?'

'I hoped you'd ask.' Roberta beamed. 'We'd be delighted to have you with us.'

Chapter Thirty-five

Before they left for the church, Roberta gathered a small bouquet of the pretty roses from the terrace and wrapped them in a curl of brown baking paper. The church was not far away as the crow flew – it had once been part of the Innocenti estate – but since Roberta and her family could no longer wander freely across the palazzo's gardens, they had instead to walk right around the perimeter walls to get to their ancestors' place of worship. With five minutes to go before the service started, a small crowd had gathered on the steps in the sunshine. Greetings and kisses were exchanged. Manu expertly dodged a crowd of *nonna*s eager to press their powdery faces to his pretty young cheeks. He then dodged a crowd of girls of his own age, keen to do the same.

'Come inside.' He dragged Kathy into the nave, using her as a sort of human shield. It was so dark in there compared to the day outside that it took a little while for Kathy's eyes to adjust so that she could see. Manu took her to the family pew, which was very near the front. He went in first, wriggling so that he was right at the end of the bench and behind a pillar. 'So that the priest won't see me if I fall asleep,' he explained.

'What about me?' Kathy whispered. 'What if I need to fall asleep too?'

Manu was delighted at the idea.

Having greeted her friends at the door, Roberta joined them in the pew. 'Manu is taking care of you. Good. These are the family pews,' said Roberta. 'Scratched with the names of generations of Innocenti children. Those are my husband's initials.'

'And Uncle Henry did that,' said Manu, pointing out a very good picture of Bart Simpson carved into the back of the pew in front. 'It must have taken him ages,' he added, with admiration.

'It took him as long as I had my eye off him, which wasn't ever very long when he was your age. He was a terror. Still, he's made up for it since.' She smiled with fond pride.

Henry had gone on ahead because on Sundays he played the organ. He was already playing the congregation in with some perfectly holy-sounding stuff that he was in fact making up on the spot. Carla was not with them. She'd had to go into work.

'On a Sunday.' Roberta sighed. 'But . . .'

Nico was keen to give the store an entire overhaul in light of the previous day's sales successes. He was finally ready to let Carla try things her way and, understandably, she wasn't going to let the opportunity pass her by.

As the congregation filed in, Kathy admired her surroundings. Though the church itself was fairly simple, the artwork on the walls was anything but.

'That's Francesca Innocenti again,' said Roberta, noticing that Kathy was looking at one painting in particular, 'as St Catherine being martyred on the wheel.'

It was gloomy subject, but this time Francesca's slightly disappointed resting face fitted the painting well, Kathy thought. For once she was suitably pained.

'That's her over there as well. As St Fina, patron saint of spinners. St Fina was from San Gimignano – as was Francesca before her marriage.' In this picture, Francesca was depicted lying prone on a board as rats danced around her feet.

'Fina had a terrible life,' said Roberta. 'One story is that she had some sort of osteomyelitis that robbed her of the use of her limbs but she refused a sick bed and instead lived out her days on that table. Though why she would refuse a proper bed, I don't know. Another story is that she strapped herself to the table to prove a point after being unlucky in love.'

'Her body got stuck to the board with gunk and she was eaten by rats and worms,' Manu added gleefully.

'After she died,' Roberta picked up the story, 'violets sprang from where her body had lain. People who touched her remains were cured of all sorts of things.'

'Have you ever touched a dead body?' Manu asked Kathy, as if it were an entirely normal conversational gambit.

Roberta silenced him with a glare.

Next Roberta nodded to a man Kathy recognised as Virgilio, the owner of the antiques store. He sat down a couple of pews away. 'Terrible old crook,' Roberta muttered. 'Your hair would go white if I told you what goes on in the back of that dingy old shop of his. But this is God's house and it's not my place to judge anyone here.'

'Since Grandpapa died, Virgilio keeps asking Nonna if he can marry her,' said Manu. 'He says he'll save the house. He's got lots of money.'

'We don't need that kind of money,' said Roberta. 'It's not just dead people's things that end up being sold through Virgilio's shop.' She turned to Kathy. 'Where I come from, he's what we used to call a fence. Do you know what I mean?'

'Of course.' Kathy was amused to hear such a thoroughly British term in a very Italian setting.

They both glanced round at Virgilio, who smiled and winked this time.

Then Henry upped the tempo to a processional and the priest and his attendants filed in. Roberta prompted Manu to stand up and stashed his tablet in her handbag. His silently mimed protest got no response. As they sat back down, Manu fished a safety pin out of his pocket. The devil makes work . . .

The service was in Italian and Latin and Kathy couldn't follow much of it. So while Roberta mumbled along with the bits you were supposed to join in with and Manu scratched with the safety pin at the seat of the pew on the side of him Roberta couldn't see, Kathy admired the Innocenti church. The painter with a penchant for cat-faced elephants had been at work in here too, she noted. He'd painted two of the unlikely pachyderms guarding the entrance to Heaven. Or was it Hell? Kathy wasn't sure she ever wanted to meet a cat-faced elephant.

She took a longer look at Francesca Innocenti too. She thought perhaps she was beginning to know her a little better. Behind the pious exterior, there was something Kathy recognised. A need for approval. Those paintings of Francesca as various saints were surely the Renaissance equivalent of selfies.

How lovely it must be for Carla, Henry and Manu

to have so much family history. At the same time, how sad, Kathy thought, to know what had once been. She didn't know much about her own family beyond her grandfather's generation. She sometimes thought she should write down what she did know but there was no one to pass it on to. No one who would care. Her ancestors were not Sophie, Oscar and Amelie's ancestors. And now the chances of there ever being someone who would truly care about Kathy and her parents' stories were . . . well, they were gone.

Kathy mind drifted to what Neil was doing that morning. Were the children still with him or had they already headed back to their mother's house in search of something decent to eat? Often on a Saturday night they would stay with friends, coming home only to eat Sunday lunch before they were gone again. Neil complained that they treated the house like a hotel but he rarely pulled them up on it.

'They went through a lot,' he'd once explained, 'with the divorce, so I want them to feel they can come here whenever they like and relax. If I tick them off too often, they won't want to be here with me.'

Kathy understood Neil's instinct to treat his children delicately in the wake of his split from their mother – and when they'd first got together she'd admired it – but she was beginning to wonder if they were taking advantage of him. It seemed there was no amount of thoughtless behaviour that couldn't be excused by the effects of growing up in a broken home. She thought of Sophie pretending to faint when her father had proposed. They held Neil to ransom. Were they going to hold Kathy to ransom too?

Kathy gazed up at Francesca as St Fina, strapped to the board for love, while the rats chewed through her shoes. What good had her sacrifice done anyone? Was she saintly or plain daft?

Chapter Thirty-six

As soon as the service was over and people stood to leave, Virgilio made a beeline for Roberta. He snatched her hand and kissed it gallantly. 'My dear Roberta,' he said. 'I haven't seen you for a few days. I was beginning to worry. Are you well?'

'Quite well,' said Roberta.

Even though Roberta claimed to have no time for Virgilio, there was the Innocenti magic again. Kathy could understand why Virgilio had set his cap at the English widow. Roberta asked solicitously after the old man's health. He responded with a gesture that made Roberta blanch and Manu giggle.

'I'll translate for you later,' Manu said.

'Please don't,' Kathy whispered to her young friend. 'But tell me, is this an appropriate moment for me to use my best phrase? Is he *un grosso culo peloso*?'

'Definitely!' Manu was delighted.

Kathy did not tell Virgilio he was an arse. Instead, she nodded along politely to the conversation she didn't understand and could only hope Manu was translating semi-accurately.

'I hope I will see you soon,' Virgilio told Roberta. 'Perhaps you would like to take a walk along by the river one evening.'

Roberta shook her head. 'If only I had the time,' she said. 'You know what it's like, running your own business.'

'Oh, I do,' said Virgilio. 'But one must always make time for pleasure.'

'Indeed.'

With that, Virgilio turned his attention to Kathy.

'This is our new friend, Kathy Courage,' said Roberta. 'From England.'

'An English rose.'

'Who is very keen to see more of the church. If you'll excuse us, I'd like her to have a closer look at Francesca Innocenti as St Catherine.'

Roberta pulled Kathy out of harm's way.

'You put him off very elegantly,' Kathy said, as they looked up at Francesca on the wheel.

'And it's not working. I should probably try putting him off with the toe of a Ferragamo instead.' Roberta linked her arm through Kathy's. 'Come along. It's about time you met my darling husband.'

With Manu leading the way, they stepped outside. The sunlight seemed especially bright after the best part of an hour spent in the cool gloom. Roberta greeted more friends on the steps. Manu also found his pals and soon a gang of children of all ages and sizes was tearing around the church, filling the air with laughter and squeals of indignation or delight. The game mostly seemed to involve the girls chasing the boys with the threat of kisses if they were caught.

'He'll be happy playing for a while,' said Roberta.

With Manu taken care of, Kathy followed Roberta to the churchyard. The back of the church was slightly less well cared for than the front. The churchyard was overgrown in places but for all that it was still quite beautiful. The pink, blue and white wild flowers that had colonised the cracked paths and abandoned graves buzzed with butterflies and bees.

'The Innocenti family tomb is actually in the grounds of the palazzo,' Roberta said. 'But Henry rightly suggested it would be better to have his father here, so that we can visit whenever we want to. I'm glad that's what we decided.'

The idea that the Innocenti family could no longer visit their forebears seemed sad but understandable, Kathy thought, given that the palazzo's chatelaine was Henry's ex-girlfriend.

Roberta and Kathy walked towards a part of the churchyard that seemed better tended, where the graves were newer and fresh flowers suggested that the dead who lived there were still fondly remembered. Roberta stopped to admire the abundance of flowers on the grave of someone only recently lost.

'Chiara was a lovely woman,' she commented. 'She used to run the salumeria. Faustino absolutely adored her. We all did. She always had time for everyone.'

Roberta pulled a single flower from the bouquet she'd picked from the casa's terrace and added it to Chiara's tribute. Then she stood back and sighed at the thought of her old friend. 'Oh, never get old, Kathy,' she said. 'Never get old.'

Roberta pulled Kathy a little closer for the rest of the walk to Ugo Innocenti's grave.

Chapter Thirty-seven

'Here he is.'

His memorial was a relatively modest stone. The white marble was decorated with black lettering, giving his name and his dates, and also, to Kathy's surprise, a black-and-white photograph in a gilt-edged frame that was set into the stone. Kathy was not used to seeing photographs on headstones but they were everywhere in the Italian graveyard. Some showed the dead as they were in old age. Others showed them as they had been in their prime. Kathy found it odd, but when she thought about it, she supposed it was really no stranger than keeping a photograph of a long-dead loved one on a mantelpiece.

Roberta touched her fingers to her lips, then pressed a kiss to the picture of her husband's face. 'That's one of my favourite photographs of him,' said Roberta. 'Of course it was taken a long time before he died. I think he must have been nearly forty then. About the age Henry is now. It's how I like to remember him. He was a very handsome man.'

'He was,' Kathy agreed.

'It wasn't just the way he looked,' Roberta continued, as she tidied up the old flowers and replaced them with new. 'It was the way he could make people feel. He was everybody's friend. Everybody mattered to him. He even had time for Virgilio. They were at school together. Ugo said that Virgilio was horribly bullied on account of being so small and that was what had made him mean as an adult. So he did his best to bring Virgilio out of himself by offering him the friendship he didn't have as a child. Ugo saw the best in everyone.'

Roberta's eyes gazed softly into the distance, into the past. 'I miss him so much,' she said.

'That's understandable,' said Kathy. Right then, Roberta reminded her of her own mother whenever she spoke about Kathy's dad, Eddie. Grief came over her face, like a small cloud crossing the sun. The shadow was brief but you couldn't miss it.

'He was the centre of my life for so long. Of all our lives. He was the centre of the family. I remember the very first time I saw him. I was nineteen years old. I was caring for the children of a family who lived just up the hill from the Palazzo Innocenti. Ugo came to a party there in the middle of the summer. I can still picture him standing in the garden. He was wearing a pale blue suit. Flared trousers, which were very fashionable then. And a pink kipper tie with fishes on it. I still have that tie somewhere. I saved it for Henry. Or it might be fashionable again by the time Manu is old enough to wear it.

'Anyway, I was too shy to speak to him and he was too shy to speak to me, but I knew he had noticed me. We spent the afternoon of the party moving around the garden as though we were at opposite ends of an invisible bar, never getting any closer but never any further apart. Each keeping an eye on the other. I knew exactly where he was all the time.

'Later, the father of my host family insisted that Ugo

play the piano to entertain us all. He was a wonderful musician. Henry takes after him of course. When he sat down at the piano, all his shyness was gone. He could let the music express how he felt. When he played a love song, he finally had the courage to look straight at me. I looked straight back at him – and boom! I knew at once that I'd found the love of my life. He plucked up the courage to ask me on a date three days later. We went to the cinema. We never looked back. We saw each other whenever we could after that.'

The memory of her courtship had blown the cloud away from the sun and Roberta's face was transformed again. Now Kathy could see the young girl from Brentwood, dazzled by the handsome Italian.

'One afternoon, towards the end of the summer, he took me to the Uffizi. Even though I was supposed to be going back to London to study art when I'd finished my time as an au pair, I couldn't understand why he wanted to take me on such a stuffy date. And he was so nervous about it too. It was so strange. He took me to see the *Doni Tondo*. Do you know it?'

'I learned about it just last week,' said Kathy, remembering the beautiful picture in the guide book.

'Isn't it lovely? I'd seen it before, of course, but I'd never really looked at it. Not the way he had. When we were standing in front of it, Ugo took my hand and told me that when he looked at that painting – of Mary and Joseph with the infant Jesus – he saw the life he wanted to have. He saw a man and a woman working together for their family. He saw a strong woman, who could hold the whole world in her arms and build empires with her love. He said he saw me in the Madonna. Can you imagine?'

Roberta touched her fingers to the centre of her chest as if in surprise.

'And then he asked me to marry him. He got down on one knee right in the middle of the gallery and asked me to be his wife. I said, yes, of course. I knew I loved him the first time I saw him. I realised then that he truly loved me back. I'd never felt like I could be anything special before that moment. I was just a girl from Essex. I grew up with a family who didn't really expect anything of me. I was silly and stupid and vain, as nineteen-year-old girls are. Ugo made me see myself differently. He made me want to be a better person, for him. I knew then that he would always be there for me, and with him beside me, I could do anything.'

Roberta fished a handkerchief out of her handbag.

'That's a lovely story,' said Kathy.

'I was such a lucky girl. I still talk to him, you know. The thing about having known someone for as long as I knew Ugo, and having known them so well, is that they can never really be lost to you. When you need to talk to them, you still can, and you will hear them answer because, having loved them so hard, you know what they would have said in any given situation.'

'Mostly Papa would have said, "Yes, dear,"' said Henry, who had managed to sneak up behind them without either of them noticing.

Roberta turned to him with a mock-stern look. Then she nodded. 'That is exactly what he would have said.'

Henry put his arm around his mother's shoulders and pressed a kiss to her hair. 'Where's Manu?' he asked.

'Playing with his friends. Let's pick him up and get back to the house,' said Roberta. 'I have no idea whether or not Ernesto will be in the kitchen today.'

'If he isn't, we will be,' said Henry. 'Isn't that right, Kathy?'

'Yes. Yes, of course,' Kathy agreed. The fact that Henry had included her in his assertion surprised her. It also made her very happy. She felt they were at least becoming friends.

Henry offered his mother his arm as they turned to walk back down the path. 'Shall we?' he asked.

Kathy lingered behind them for a moment or two, taking in the tranquillity of the churchyard. She took a last proper look at the photograph on Ugo Innocenti's headstone. She could see Henry's face reflected there, she realised. In the shape of his cheeks and his chin. In his curling brown hair. In his eyes. His kind dark eyes.

'Nice to meet you, Signor Innocenti,' she said. She wished she might have met him in person.

Kathy made to catch up with the others. Ahead of her on the path, Henry was making his mother laugh about something. Kathy noticed the care with which he helped Roberta navigate the steps, which were more difficult for her to walk down than up. There was so much love between them it was almost palpable. And then Manu joined them, running around them in circles all the way back to the street, like a little human bumble bee, dancing with all the happiness of an early summer's day.

Chapter Thirty-eight

Kathy was all ready to do her bit in the kitchen again, but when the family got back to the Casa Innocenti, it was to find Ernesto already at the stove preparing lunch.

'Well, well, well,' said Roberta, when she saw him. 'That's the fastest result I've ever had from a Sunday-morning prayer.'

Kathy asked Manu for a genuine translation of her apology, which she delivered to Ernesto as soon as she was able. He paused in chopping vegetables to nod his acceptance. He even attempted a smile.

Kathy was pleased that Ernesto was back for Roberta's sake but there was a tiny part of her that was disappointed not to have a chance to be in the kitchen with Henry, proving to him that she wasn't just a freeloader. She'd have to wait until it was time to serve the food. She could help again then.

Manu was also disappointed: since Henry wasn't needed in the kitchen he was able to give his nephew a quick piano lesson.

'You haven't practised all week,' Henry said.

Manu groaned. He hunched over so far that his knuckles nearly dragged on the floor as he reluctantly followed Henry to the upright piano in the sitting room.

'Fifteen minutes,' Henry said to him. 'That's all. You'd happily play Piano Tiles for twice that time,' he observed, referring to the game Manu had installed on his mother's phone.

At Roberta's insistence, Kathy sat down to watch from the other end of the room.

Once Manu had stopped playacting his disgust at having to practise, he sat down next to his uncle quite happily. Faustino followed, standing with his front paws on the edge of the piano stool as though he, too, was ready to read the music Henry put on the stand. Manu played a few tentative scales. Faustino made a few tentative *rrrrowl*-type noises in response. Henry had Manu play some arpeggios as a warm-up. Again, Faustino squeaked and grumbled in response.

'You must watch this,' Roberta said to Kathy.

'OK, Manu,' said Henry. 'Let's try the Mozart.'

Manu's brow was furrowed in concentration as he began to play 'Eine Kleine Nachtmusik'. As he plonked at the keys in laboured concentration, Faustino sang along in full howling canine voice. The dog had quite good tone.

'He's putting me off!' Manu complained.

'You're doing brilliantly,' Henry told his nephew. 'Faustino wouldn't be singing along if he didn't appreciate your playing.'

'I can't hear myself playing!'

Every time Manu stopped to tell Faustino off, the dog stopped singing. Every time Manu started playing again, the dog would start howling. Little dog and little boy turned Mozart's most famous tune into a terrific cacophony, leaving Kathy and Roberta doing their best not to cry with laughter, while Henry tried to keep Manu on task.

'It's like this every week,' Roberta whispered. 'Every single time.'

Eventually, Henry scooped Faustino up, with the intention of putting him in another room so he couldn't sing along but, despite his complaints, Manu didn't want that. Instead boy and dog continued their painful duet until fifteen minutes had passed – Manu had set an alarm on his tablet – and Manu jumped up from the piano stool like a jack-in-a-box.

'Hooray!' Manu pumped the air and bolted for his bedroom, followed by his grandmother, who wanted to be sure he hung up his Sunday best once he'd changed out of it.

With Manu gone, Faustino remained by the stool as though hoping for an encore. He put a paw on one of Henry's knees and cocked his head to one side as though to ask, 'Is that all?'

Henry ruffled Faustino's fluffy head.

'As you can see,' said Henry to Kathy, 'we're a very musical household.'

Watching Henry at the piano with Manu and Faustino had brought back some bittersweet memories for Kathy. She was reminded of her own younger self, sitting alongside her father, with Benji, their dog, looking on. As was the case with Manu, there had been times when Kathy didn't want to practise. There were times when she'd been rude to her dad, telling him that music was boring and she didn't want to learn any more.

'Just fifteen minutes.' He'd said that to her too. Kathy had played grudgingly, eager to get back to a more interesting game. She hadn't realised as a child what a gift her father had been offering her. She wished she'd been more enthusiastic. More grateful. She hoped he'd understood before he died how much she had enjoyed playing alongside him as she'd got older. She knew he would have enjoyed seeing Henry, Manu and the singing dog.

That morning in the Casa Innocenti, Faustino continued to paw at Henry's leg. 'You want another tune?' Henry asked the pup. 'Perhaps Kathy can play for you.'

Kathy sat up a little straighter. Was Henry inviting her to play with him?

'A duet?' she suggested.

Henry shuffled to the edge of the piano stool to make room for her but then the phone rang. And it was Neil.

Henry handed the phone across and left the room so that Kathy had some privacy.

'Chicken?' Neil asked.

'I'm here,' said Kathy.

'I've been trying the phone all morning. Where have you been?'

'We went to church.'

'What?'

'I said we went to church.'

'Really?' Neil seemed surprised. 'Are you staying in some kind of cult? Are you going to have to hand over all your money before they let you leave?'

Kathy ignored him. Neil attributed the worst of motives to just about everyone.

'How are you?' Kathy asked. 'How are the children?'

'Nightmare,' said Neil.

He launched into another litany of complaints. It was as though he'd only just noticed that his three children could be difficult. Possibly that was the case. It was the first time in a long time that Kathy hadn't been there to divert the flak. Or act as a taxi service.

'And then Mum called,' Neil continued. 'Wouldn't stop going on about Shelley and Dave's baby. You'd think they were the first people on earth to be having one.'

'It's an exciting time for them,' said Kathy.

'It's an exciting time for *us*,' Neil countered. 'Dave wasn't the only one to make a big announcement last week.'

The timing of the engagement began to sound more and more like a move calculated to divert the spotlight. Now Neil was upset that it hadn't worked.

Kathy waited for Neil to say something that would make her smile, laugh, feel a little happier. He didn't. In the background, Amelie asked, 'When's she coming back?'

Back. Not home.

'I need some stuff washed.'

'Tomorrow,' said Kathy, answering the question. 'Tomorrow night.'

And she wasn't looking forward to it at all.

Chapter Thirty-nine

After talking to Neil, Kathy helped Henry serve lunch to the hotel's guests on the beautiful terrace.

Fortunately, that evening there would be no dinner service in the hotel to worry about, should Ernesto not feel like turning up for work. The guests already knew they would have to go further afield if they wanted anything more than olives and crisps to go with their drinks from the honesty bar.

'So you can have the night off,' Roberta joked to Kathy.

'Not me, though,' said Henry. 'Your humble minstrel has another gig. Surprise sixtieth birthday party at the Michelangelo Plaza Hotel. Two hundred guests. It's going to be quite the bash.'

'What's it like,' Kathy asked, 'going to party after party but not as a guest? You must see some things.'

'Yes,' said Henry. '*In vino veritas*. The best punch-ups I've ever seen have been at wedding receptions and not between the men. I once saw a bride tuck her wedding dress into her knickers so she could take a flying kick at her new husband's female best friend. That was impressive. And I've found that the richer the guests, the more likely they are to be badly behaved. They think money makes up for a lack of manners.'

Kathy thought again of Neil, tucking the cash into Henry's top pocket and telling him, 'Buy yourself a decent shirt.'

'What tonight will be like, I don't know. The playlist they've sent me is pretty good. No Coldplay.'

Kathy ignored the dig.

'What will you do this evening?' Henry asked.

Kathy shrugged.

'You can come to church again with me,' said Roberta.

'I don't suppose Kathy's soul needs that much attention,' said Henry.

'Who's singing with you tonight, Henry?' Roberta asked.

'Giuliana,' said Henry.

'She's back from the South of France, then?'

Roberta explained that having met a music producer in a bar in Florence, Giuliana had travelled to St-Tropez in the hope of a second meeting. She'd hatched a plan that she would turn up there with a couple of girlfriends and wangle a lift on his yacht.

'Didn't work out,' Henry explained. 'The producer already had a fearsome Russian supermodel in tow. Giuliana had no hope of getting on deck with Miss Moscow already in position.'

Roberta sighed and shook her head. 'I wish she'd find herself a nice local fellow instead of chasing after all these rich men who see her as nothing more than entertainment. Still, at least it means she's back to play with you tonight.'

Unfortunately, that wasn't the case. It turned out that Giuliana had other plans for the evening.

Two minutes after Henry went up to the attic room to fetch a clean shirt from his wardrobe, he was back downstairs with a face like thunder.

'She claimed she didn't know we were working

tonight!' Henry was outraged. 'When I asked if she could cancel her new plans, she told me she was taking my phone call in Prague.'

'Prague? Oh dear,' said Roberta. 'How will she get back from there in time?'

'Well, of course she's not going to, is she?'

Henry got another message on his phone. He jabbed at the screen to open it. 'Trixie's out of town as well.'

'Then who's going to sing for you?' Roberta asked.

Kathy was sitting with Manu, while he showed her his favourite clips from *The Simpsons* on the tablet. She was pretending not to listen in to Henry and Roberta's conversation, but she gradually became aware that Henry was looking straight at her.

'You can do it,' he said.

Kathy turned. Was he talking to her?

'You can sing with me tonight. What do you say? It'll be fun. We'll split the fee.'

Roberta, Manu and even Faustino looked at her expectantly.

'Oh,' said Kathy. 'I don't really think so.'

'You can do it.'

'I can't.'

'I've heard you sing.'

'You didn't say so,' said Kathy. When she'd realised Henry was watching her at the piano in the Palazzo Boldrini she hadn't known how long he had been watching her. Now he told her he'd been there when she warbled her way through three verses of 'The Man I Love'.

'I didn't know.'

'You sang it beautifully,' Henry insisted. He appealed to Roberta and Manu to back him up. 'She sang it *wonderfully*. She has a lovely voice. Easily as good as Giuliana's.'

'Oh, Kathy. Wouldn't it be fantastic if you could step in tonight?' said Roberta. Her face was bright with the prospect. 'It would save Henry so much trouble, and I'm sure it would be quite the experience for you. The Michelangelo Plaza is a lovely hotel. You really ought to see the gardens there. I'm sure they'll treat you very well.'

But Kathy was thinking of the number of guests Henry had quoted back when he first mentioned the gig. There were to be two hundred at that party. Two hundred! Kathy was still cringing at the thought that she'd been heard singing by one solitary person she hadn't even known was listening.

Now four pairs of eyes, including Faustino's bright brown ones, gazed in her direction, willing her just to say yes and make everything better for everyone with a single word. Her cheeks were burning as she told them, 'I can't. I'm really, really sorry. I just can't.'

'Oh.' Roberta did her best to hide her disappointment.

Henry did the same. He nodded. 'I understand. That's OK. It's perfectly fine.'

Taking his mobile, Henry headed for the terrace. 'Right, I suppose I'd better start phoning around.'

Chapter Forty

Feeling embarrassed, small and more than a little pathetic, Kathy excused herself to go upstairs to the attic room. She took the house phone with her. Standing next to Henry's music-covered desk, looking out of the window, Kathy called her mother. She hadn't spoken to her since Friday morning in the airport.

'I was beginning to worry,' Clare said.

'There was no need for that,' Kathy told her. She didn't mention the bag snatch. She pretended instead that her mobile was on the fritz. She confirmed that she would be back in London the following day.

'And then we can talk about the wedding properly,' Clare said.

'Yes,' said Kathy. 'Yes, we can.'

'Are you enjoying Florence?' Clare asked.

'It's beautiful,' Kathy said. 'Even better than I imagined.' Kathy told her mother about her day in the centre of the city, giving her all the details except for the mugging.

After talking to Clare for five minutes, she phoned Neil again to finish the half-conversation they'd had earlier. Landline first. The phone rang out. She could imagine it echoing in the empty hallway of the house in Fulham until the answer-machine picked up. Then she tried Neil's mobile number. Having read the number so many times over the past couple of days, she had almost come to learn it off by heart by now. Again, Neil didn't pick up. What time was it in London? Two o'clock? He was probably at his mother's house. She served Sunday lunch at one thirty prompt. Chicken, lamb or beef in rotation, but always with Yorkshire pudding. She wondered if Shelley was there too, officially celebrating the good news about the baby with her nephew and nieces. How would they react to the prospect of a new cousin? Probably entirely differently from the way they would have reacted to a new half-brother or sister. Still, Kathy would never have to test that.

When Neil's voicemail kicked in, Kathy left the usual sort of message, saying she hoped Neil was having a good day and that everything was OK back there in the UK, that he had everything he needed and that he was happy. The sort of message she didn't think he had ever left for her, now that she came to think about it. With that little flash of annoyance, she also realised that she was glad she didn't have to speak to him for once. Their phone calls over the past few days had not left her feeling uplifted. She always put the phone down feeling that Neil was disappointed about something and that something was probably her.

Kathy ended the call by stabbing the off button. She sat down at Henry's desk, looking out at the sky. The swallows were putting on their usual acrobatic display, swooping between the tall houses like mini fighter jets. The geranium on the windowsill opposite had put out more bright red flowers over the past few days, drawing the gaze with their vibrancy. But Kathy's eyes were pulled back into the room, to the pile of sheet music Carla had tidied so hastily on Friday evening. She picked the top sheet off the pile and opened it.

Tucked inside the commercially printed sheet music was a scrap of hotel notepaper, from the Palazzo Boldrini. Kathy had a pad of the same paper stashed away in her suitcase, with a couple of lavender stems she'd taken from the garden pressed inside it. On the piece of paper there was a wobbly stave, hand-drawn in biro. Kathy realised it must be one of Henry's own compositions. She tried to hum the notes he'd scribbled. They went up and down a scale, tripping lightly, like raindrops or water in a brook. Like laughter. One of the notes was in the shape of a heart. Whether accidentally or on purpose, Kathy couldn't tell.

Kathy carefully replaced the notepaper in its hiding place and put it back on the pile. She had no right to look.

Still feeling she couldn't go back downstairs yet, while Henry was likely to be calling round for a new singer, Kathy lay down on the bed. Above her head, the cherubs fired arrows of love at one another. Kathy reached up and took one of the dangling festival passes between her fingers. It was for Coachella in California, one of the world's biggest, she knew. The height of Sophie's ambition was to go to it for her twenty-first birthday. What must it have been like to play there, to be on stage in front of thousands of people? It must make playing to two hundred seem a bit of a comedown.

'But two hundred is still an awful lot if you've never really sung in front of an audience before,' Kathy muttered to herself, justifying her decision.

'You've sung in front of nearly that many people before,' came her father's voice from nowhere.

'Dad?'

'You know you have. And you gave an excellent performance.'

'Are you talking about the school concert?' Kathy asked.

'You were wonderful,' her father's voice said.

Was what Roberta had said by her husband's grave-side true? That when you've known and loved someone well, you can still talk to them even if they aren't in front of you or at the end of a phone? Doesn't mean they stop talking to you either . . .

'OK, what would you do, Dad?' Kathy asked the empty air. 'About tonight.'

And in her head, her father answered, 'I'd go to the party, make a terrible job of singing, then drink all the free booze.'

Kathy laughed at the imaginary answer.

'Seriously,' her father continued, 'what have you got to lose? Courage is your surname. Time to show some. Unless you're really Kathy Coward and you're not my little girl after all. Be Kathy Brave.'

Kathy sat up in bed. That was what her father used to call her. Kathy Brave. He'd first called her that when she was going into the hospital operating theatre for the procedure that would fix her eye. 'You could not be more beautiful to me,' he said, when she asked him if it would make her pretty. 'In any case brave is better than beautiful and brave is what you are.'

He reminded her to be brave all the time. Not just when she was facing physical pain, as with all the medical tests, the injections and the months with an eye patch. He reminded her when she was facing exams, when she was facing the humiliation of another sports day, when she was facing the knee-shaking terror of having to stand up in front of the whole school to sing a solo with the choir, aged fifteen.

'They'll all be looking at me,' she had complained.

'Let them look,' Eddie told her. 'Let them remember the girl with the fabulous voice. If you don't get up there on stage, you'll be letting the choir down, of course, but, ultimately, you're the only person who will really miss out. If you do get up there, you won't regret it.'

On the day of the school concert, her father had had to tell her a thousand times that he believed in her. And he'd been right: singing that solo had been the highlight of her school career. Afterwards, people seemed to treat her differently. They talked to her in the classroom in the morning before the day started. They talked to her in the canteen queue at lunchtime. She was invited to some parties. That solo was the beginning of a new era.

By the time she got to university, Kathy was no longer Cross-eyed Kathy. She had plans, she had ambitions, she had friends. So, when had Kathy got so cowardly again? She knew exactly when. Her self-confidence had started to shrink after Eddie died. It turned out that even though she was away at university she still needed him as a cheerleader.

Why had she never been able to hear his voice like this before? Was it just that she'd never really listened for it? Was it that other voices had come to seem louder in her head? There were always people talking for her. Her mother projecting her fears, which had only got worse after Eddie's death. 'Be careful. Take care. Are you safe?' Neil projecting his need always to be the strong one, which meant Kathy always had to be weak.

His children casually expressing their disbelief that a woman her age could possibly still have dreams and ambitions of her own. A dream like standing on a stage again? That was nuts.

Where had Kathy's voice gone?

'It's still there,' her father's voice said in her head. 'Use it.'

'All right, all right,' she said. 'I'll do it.'

She imagined her father opening his arms to give her a hug as he had on the morning of the school concert. 'You will never regret being brave.'

Chapter Forty-one

Even so, as Kathy went back downstairs, part of her was still secretly hoping that Henry would have found an emergency singer and her gesture would have to be nothing more than that, a gesture that would leave her feeling absolved.

Henry was still on the terrace, sitting on a chair by the wall, scrolling through the contacts on his phone. Kathy crept out there and joined him. 'Henry, are you still looking for someone to sing with you this evening?' she asked.

He was. 'Got two hopefuls more to call. Otherwise I'm going to have to do the singing myself, which is not ideal. Not for the requests the client wants.'

'If they can't do it,' said Kathy, 'maybe. . . maybe I can sing with you if you're desperate.'

Henry put his phone back in his pocket. 'I'm desperate,' he said.

'I'm a bit rusty so it would be good if we could have a quick practice before we go, but if you really think I'll be good enough . . . I mean, obviously you should phone those other singers first in case one of them is available but . . .'

Henry jumped up and planted a kiss right in the middle of Kathy's forehead. 'You're a lifesaver,' he said. 'Kathy, you've saved my bacon. Thank you. Thank you.

Thank you. You'll be great. This is brilliant. I cannot tell you what a bloody relief it is.'

He seemed so pleased. Meanwhile, Kathy was beginning to get scared. 'Are you sure you shouldn't phone the others?'

'I'm not phoning anyone else. You're coming with me to the Michelangelo Plaza. You're going to sing like an angel. You're going to have a wonderful time. And I might just forgive you for having nicked my bed for three nights.'

When Carla came back shortly afterwards and heard the news, she, too, was delighted. 'I'll dress you,' she said.

'And I can lend you some of my jewellery,' said Roberta. 'A singer should always have sparkle.'

'I can teach you some useful phrases to say between the songs,' said Manu.

'Don't teach Kathy any more useful phrases,' Carla and Roberta said in unison.

Even Faustino seemed to understand that something exciting was about to happen. He danced around Kathy's feet as Carla shuffled her into her room and flung open her colourful wardrobe to find the perfect outfit. Roberta joined them with a huge jewellery box that was like a pirate's treasure chest, over-spilling with diamanté and *faux* pearls.

There was much to be said about the principle of 'Fake it until you make it.' Standing in an apron in the kitchen, Kathy had dismissed out of hand the idea that she could sing in front of an audience. But now that she was putting on the outfit, she started to feel differently. In Carla's beautiful gunmetal dress – the one

she'd 'bought' from Nico's boutique the day before –
Kathy instantly felt the need to stand a little straighter
and hold her head a little higher. Meanwhile Roberta
persuaded her to wear a pair of chandelier earrings
that dangled almost down to her shoulders. Every time
she moved her head, they sent fireworks of glittering
light across her face and décolletage. It was like having
personal lighting.

She needed make-up too, the women decided.

'You have such beautiful eyes. You need to wear lots
of mascara.'

Carla applied so much that Kathy felt she could
hardly open her eyes, let alone bat her lashes.

'And lipstick,' said Roberta, unscrewing a tube of
bright carmine.

'I never wear lipstick,' said Kathy. It was truer to say
that she hadn't worn lipstick since meeting Neil's children. Sophie didn't think anyone over thirty should
bother adorning themselves. 'It's like putting glitter on
a turd,' was what she'd once said. Roberta and Carla
believed the exact opposite. They treated Kathy's transformation like an art project.

Roberta and Carla stepped back to admire their
handiwork. 'You certainly look the part,' Roberta
declared.

'You look very nice,' said Manu, shyly.

'Not like *un grosso culo peloso*?' Kathy joked.

'Like *una bellissima principessa*,' said Manu, before
running away to hide his furious blushes.

'What do you think, Dad?' Kathy silently asked her
father.

She thought she could hear him say he loved it.
Especially the lipstick.

Chapter Forty-two

By five o'clock, Kathy and Henry were as ready as they would ever be, having spent half an hour practising, with Faustino providing accompaniment. The party was being held on the other side of the river, in the gardens of the exclusive Michelangelo Plaza Hotel. As they walked there, Henry brought Kathy up to speed with the evening's plan.

'We have to play from seven. The birthday girl arrives at eight. It's a surprise party. I hate surprise parties,' Henry added. 'If anyone ever threw me a surprise, I would turn round and walk out. I don't think it's fair to dump someone in a room full of all the important people in their life without giving them a chance to get prepared first. I once played at a party for a man turning fifty. That was a surprise. The even bigger surprise was that the wife had booked the mistress to do a belly-dance that evening.'

Kathy winced in sympathy.

'Kathy,' Henry said then, 'I can't tell you how grateful I am. I've been really unfair to you. When I first realised I was sleeping on the sofa because Mamma and Carla had given you my bed – you, the Queen of Sheba – I was angry. I made all sorts of assumptions about you based on what little I knew of you from two brief encounters at the Palazzo Boldrini. But you've mucked in and got your hands dirty. You helped Carla sort things out with Nico. Manu adores you – he wouldn't have played that hairy-arse joke on you otherwise. You let Mamma talk to you about Papa. That's worth more than any amount of money. Thank you. It's been a pleasure having you as the Casa Innocenti's latest official waif and stray.'

'I've really enjoyed myself,' Kathy said honestly.

'Let's hope you enjoy this evening too.'

Soon they were at the hotel. It was as grand as the Palazzo Boldrini. It must once have been the home of someone very important indeed. Now it was the latest addition to a luxury hotel chain, catering to a glamorous international crowd that could feel at home anywhere in the world so long as the chain's familiar crossed-keys logo was found above the door. The traditional Tuscan interior was offset with glitzy furniture that would have looked right anywhere from Los Angeles to Lagos.

One of the management team showed them to a staffroom where they could change. Henry merely ran his hands through his hair, leaving it sticking up and looking, if anything, slightly less tidy than before. He also opted to discard the red bow tie he'd been wearing.

'I don't think it's going to be that sort of crowd tonight. Thank goodness.'

Kathy had to change her shoes and put on an extra layer of lipstick. She was properly nervous now. She imagined the acid in her stomach churning and bubbling like one of Ernesto's pasta sauces. But she was also excited. In the dress Carla had lent her, with Roberta's enormous sparkling earrings, she felt at least she looked as though she might be able to pull off this adventure.

She patted her hair, tucking a stray strand behind her ears. Henry's face appeared in the mirror beside hers. He untucked the strand she'd just tidied away.

'That's better,' he said, while Kathy was still startled by the sudden intimacy of the gesture. 'Now let's go and set up.'

The hotel garden – which was every bit as beautiful as Roberta had said – was already dotted with early party guests, catching up with old friends and new gossip as they sipped Prosecco and ate canapés. It was a boho sort of crowd, artistically dressed in floppy linens and tie-dyed silks that evoked the hippie trail yet were obviously expensive. They had the carelessly glossy look of the very rich. Which is what they were, Henry assured her.

'The husband is an industrialist. The wife is the daughter of a politician. The guests are some of the city's most wanted – as far as guest lists are concerned, anyway. This party is costing a fortune.'

Henry procured a couple of glasses of Prosecco from a passing waiter.

'Now, I wouldn't normally countenance drinking on the job,' he said, as he handed Kathy one of the glasses, 'especially as you're going to be singing. But in exceptional circumstances such as this . . . Here's to your Florentine debut, Ms Courage.'

The bubbles felt like glitter on her tongue. She hoped they might gild her singing.

Henry checked his watch. One minute to seven.

'Let's get started,' he said. He sat down on the piano stool and played a little tune of his own composition to get an understanding of the piano. Meanwhile Kathy stood at the music stand, with the sheaf of lyrics Manu had printed off from the Internet and the set list in her shaking hands. There was lots of Abba and Adele – both had an easy range – and Henry had put some thought into the order in which they would play, beginning with a song Kathy knew well, a number she would be able to sing easily though her voice – and, indeed, her whole body – was trembling with nerves.

'Just think of it like posh karaoke,' Henry had suggested on the walk over.

Kathy had never done karaoke sober, let alone in front of such a crowd.

Henry played the first few bars of the Carpenters' classic 'We've Only Just Begun'. Kathy looked across to him. Their eyes met. He gave a nod of encouragement and Kathy began to sing.

Chapter Forty-three

And from the moment she started singing, Kathy knew for sure that it was going to be OK. As her voice floated over the garden, no one looked up and winced, wondering what that awful noise was. No one covered their ears. For the most part, the party guests continued to chat to their friends but a couple actually moved closer to the stage and seemed to be listening appreciatively.

Kathy and Henry moved smoothly from one song to the next. As promised, Henry matched the key of every new tune to Kathy's capabilities. Somehow, she thought, he knew how to make her sound better than she really was.

'No,' said her father's voice in her head. 'The truth is you really are better than you think you are.'

How could Kathy have forgotten how much she loved this?

The birthday girl – all sixty years of her – arrived exactly on time to the tune of 'Happy Birthday'. Kathy led the whole party for that. Unlike Henry, the birthday girl seemed to love the idea of a surprise party. Her delight was obvious as she went from guest to guest bestowing kisses and hugs, her smile growing wider and wider as she saw more and more of the people she loved. Kathy felt uplifted by her happiness. The birthday girl raised her hands in a gesture of thanks as she got to the stage. She didn't seem disappointed in the least by the last-minute change of singer.

Henry and Kathy took a break while dinner was served.

'How are you feeling?' Henry asked.

'Exhilarated,' Kathy admitted. 'I can't wait to get back up on stage.'

'You've been singing really well. Better than when we were practising.'

Henry unfolded a little pile of paper slips onto which people had written requests.

'Not that one,' he said, putting one song aside. 'Or that one.'

'But people want to hear them.'

'The nature of a request is that it's a request and not an order,' said Henry. 'Oh, look. Someone wants your favourite song.'

He passed the slip over.

'"Yellow" is not my favourite song. But it was a song that was played a lot when we first got together,' she said, defending Neil's choice. 'I told you what my favourite song was.'

'And I played it. You didn't dance.'

'I couldn't. You know that. But I heard it and I appreciated it. Thank you.'

'I'm glad.'

Then it was time to be back on stage. This time Kathy was looking forward to it.

They sang for another hour, as Henry had agreed when the gig was booked. As their time on stage drew to a close, Henry thanked the crowd for being a good audience. He told them it was time to say goodnight, but someone shouted, 'Encore!'

'I didn't think they were paying attention,' Henry said.

'Encore!' another shout went up.

'Encore!' said the birthday girl, striding to the front of the stage. 'Encore, encore!'

They could hardly refuse her.

'Are you up for it?' Henry asked.

Kathy nodded. 'OK. But what shall we sing?'

'I know exactly what we should sing,' he said. 'I'll give you three bars to guess it.'

It was 'The Way You Look Tonight'. Of course it was. Those drip-drop notes at the beginning were unmistakable. But though Kathy had loved the song for more than twenty-five years and sung it to herself a thousand times, she'd never before performed her favourite song for an audience. Not even an audience of one. As Henry began to play, she looked to him pleadingly. She wasn't sure she could do it. She hesitated. Henry began the introduction again.

'You can do it,' she heard her father's voice.

'You can do it,' Henry mouthed from behind the piano.

'I can do it,' Kathy told herself.

'"Some day . . ."' she began, in a whisper. Her voice seemed too small for the challenge but then she heard Henry's voice join with hers, backing her up, encouraging her, just as he'd encouraged her on that afternoon at the piano at the Palazzo Boldrini and the song became a perfect duet. It was as though they were singing only to each other.

Their audience was captivated and hushed. Down on the dance-floor, couples sought each other's arms and swayed together in the dark.

As the last note faded away, Kathy and Henry held each other's eyes. Each of them was telling themselves they were just doing what professional performers do. They were acting out the feelings for the benefit of the audience . . . That was all.

Whatever, the crowd was delighted. There was more applause and more calls for an encore. This time, however, Henry was firm. They were leaving the building, like Elvis. There was, in any case, a DJ waiting to go on after them, ready to spin the tunes from the seventies that would take the guests back to their heyday. Kathy and Henry walked off stage to Earth, Wind and Fire's 'September'. The disco beat danced the tension of that last moment at the microphone out of Kathy's head.

The birthday girl's husband stopped them as they were leaving. He praised them both in mellifluous Italian, then handed Kathy a thick envelope, kissed her on both cheeks and pronounced her '*bellissima*'.

'He was pleased,' Henry confirmed.

As soon as the man was out of sight, Kathy opened the envelope at Henry's request to find that it was stuffed with cash. Some five hundred euros in smart new notes. 'This is yours,' she said to Henry.

'No,' he said. 'We've already been paid. This is a tip. We split it.'

'No,' said Kathy. She stopped short of saying, 'You need it.' The whole Innocenti family needed it to fund their nutty life. 'I can't possibly. You take it.'

Henry did take the envelope, but he pulled out just ten euros – for a couple of drinks – and passed it back to Kathy.

'I insist,' he said. 'For your running-away fund.'

Kathy opened her mouth to protest that she didn't need a running-away fund.

'Don't argue, please. Just take it. Everyone should have a running-away fund,' said Henry. 'Even if they don't know they need it.'

Kathy put the envelope in one of the big pockets of Carla's dress. One part of her was already planning to get the money back to Henry and his family somehow, in a way that wouldn't leave Henry offended. The other part of her was processing the truth of what he had said. Everyone should have a running-away fund.

'Plus, you deserve it. The whole evening was a triumph,' said Henry, as they got back to the changing room and he poured her another glass of Prosecco. 'A triumph!'

Kathy had never seen him so enthusiastic.

'You were fantastic,' he said. 'Far better than any of the regulars I play with. You have a wonderful voice. You're a natural.'

Kathy blushed. 'I couldn't have done it without you,' she said.

Henry looked pleased with that.

It was late but Kathy still felt wide awake, thanks to the adrenalin of the performance, and when Henry suggested that perhaps they shouldn't go straight back to the house but have a nightcap instead, she was only too happy to agree.

But where could they go? As they walked back towards the river, most of the restaurants and bars they passed were already closed for the evening. Those that weren't closed were in the process of winding down. In one, a waiter stacked chairs on tables all around a couple who were holding hands over a half-eaten bowl of tiramisu, oblivious to the heavy, clattering hints that it was time to go home.

'These are all tourist places anyway,' said Henry, dismissing them with a wave of his hand. 'Let me take you to my Florence.'

Chapter Forty-four

As soon as they were away from the main tourist drag, the streets were quiet and empty. If it weren't for the occasional streetlight, they might have been transported back centuries to the time when Florence really was the centre of the cultural world.

They came across a piazza that wasn't as busy as most. One side was taken up by an austere grey building, with green-shuttered windows that were closed against the night.

'Look up,' said Henry. 'Do you see that window? The one that isn't shut. That's the old Palazzo Grifoni. They have to leave the window open because of the ghost.'

'The ghost?'

'One of the Grifoni sons went off to war, leaving his young bride behind. He promised he'd be back soon but he never returned, though she waited by the window for years. Until she died, in fact. When they closed the window that day, it was as though an earthquake hit the house. Books came flying off the shelves, paintings fell off the walls. It didn't stop until someone opened the window again and they've left it open ever since.'

'She must have loved him very much.'

'I imagine after three years of waiting that feeling started to wear off . . .'

It was as she was looking up at the window, with

its shutters slightly ajar, that Kathy felt her ankle begin to go over. She instinctively grabbed the closest thing to hang onto. Which was Henry. Carefully, he helped her to right herself, but once he'd done so, he didn't let go. Instead, he took her arm and wove it through his own. 'Don't want you falling over again,' he said. 'That's all,' he added, as though she might be thinking otherwise. As though he was thinking otherwise.

Through the tiniest alleyways Henry could find, they wound their way closer to the river.

'Just for you,' Henry said, 'we'll walk over the Ponte Vecchio.'

'I'd hate to force you.'

'Everyone should do it at least once and at this time of night there is a faint chance that we'll actually be able to walk without having to stop for a teenage blogger intent on getting their pout right.'

With Kathy holding tightly to his arm, Henry picked his way through the last of the day's crowds. The jewellery shops that flanked each side of the bridge were shuttered for the night, which helped Kathy to imagine how it might have been in the days before Instagram.

Henry told her, 'There is a secret passageway across the top of the bridge that goes all the way from the Uffizi to the Palazzo Pitti, so that the grandees of the town never had to face their angry public. My father took me across it when I was a child. He loved this city. There wasn't anything he didn't know about its history. I wish I'd listened when he talked about it but, of course, when I was a kid, I wasn't interested in history. I was interested in football and music and how I could get out of going to school on Monday morning.'

'He sounds like a wonderful man, your father.'

'Yes. He's a hard act to follow.'

A group of rowdy students were crossing the bridge in the opposite direction. When it looked as though they might collide with Kathy and Henry, he pulled her against him for a moment, so the students could pass.

That left Kathy flustered. Henry, too, she thought.

Once they were on the other side of the river, he seemed to relax again. They meandered down the road where Kathy had walked with Manu. They passed Carla's boutique and Virgilio's junk shop with its sad, dusty window display.

'You met Virgilio this morning,' Henry commented. 'One of the local characters. The secrets his shop could tell.'

The secrets the whole city could tell. Every street was overlaid with years upon years of memory. At every turning, there was another story to be told and Henry knew it.

At one point he said, 'This is the corner where Galileo might have had a flash of inspiration, where Michelangelo might have spotted the boy who would be *David*, where Dante dreamed of his Beatrice. But when I pass by here, I remember Giuliana Tordoni, who offered to show me her bra in exchange for the equivalent of two euros.'

Kathy burst into laughter. 'What did you say?'

'Of course I paid it.'

'I find that hard to believe.'

'Back then,' said Henry, 'I was not the handsome beast you see before you now. I had one of those braces with the wire that goes around the back of your head to pull your teeth forward. My schoolfriends would come up behind me and play me like a harp. Nobody ever kissed me except for a dare. Needless to say, two euros seemed like a bargain for a glimpse of a real live woman.'

Kathy shook her head.

'It got a little better when I joined a band. Though keyboard player doesn't quite have the same cachet as guitarist. But for most of my youth, I couldn't get a woman to look twice at me. You'd have walked on by.'

'Only because I would have been too shy to talk to you,' said Kathy. 'I had my own challenges at school.'

'Batting away the attentions of all the boys?'

'I don't think so. They called me Cross-eyed Kathy,' Kathy said. 'Something was wrong with my eye when I was born. I had to have an operation.'

'Then we would have made the perfect pair,' Henry said. 'My friends called me Metal Mickey. Like the robot in the old TV show.'

'I hate nicknames,' said Kathy.

'Even Queen of Sheba?'

'That one's not so bad.'

'Good. I think it suits you.'

Chapter Forty-five

They walked past the turning for the Casa Innocenti and kept going. The bar Henry had in mind was up a hill behind. He offered to give Kathy a push up the worst of it. She declined with a giggle. He took both her hands and pulled her up instead, walking backwards.

Kathy was almost sad when they reached the top and she had to let go of him. The bar was right there.

'This place looks rough,' said Henry, conceding that the façade of La Fenice – the Phoenix, like the opera house in Venice – was peeling and dirty, 'but they make the best cocktails in the city and that is all that matters tonight. I want you to have the very best.' He pushed open the door and waved her in.

The cellar bar was certainly busy – and with locals rather than tourists, Kathy quickly discerned. There was a brief moment of affronted hush when she stepped through the door – a stranger – but as soon as the proprietor saw she was with Henry, the atmosphere changed. Just as when she'd accompanied Manu and Faustino to the market and Roberta to church, Kathy found herself swept into the community and heartily welcomed. Henry's favourite drink was on the polished bar within seconds.

When the barman asked what Kathy would have, Henry warned her, 'Don't ask for an Aperol Spritz.'

So Kathy answered, 'I'll have the same as he's having.'

'Good choice,' said Henry. 'Have this one.' He passed her his drink.

She took a sip. 'It's pure alcohol.' She coughed.

'Pretty much. Kills all germs, though. There's a squeeze of lemon juice in it too. For the vitamin C.'

When Henry's drink was ready too, they clinked glasses.

'*Cincin*,' said Henry.

'*Cincin.*'

'That's all the Italian you need.'

'I won't be trying out any of Manu's phrases here,' Kathy said.

She looked around her. The bar was dim and dank and smelt, Kathy had thought when she first walked in, overwhelmingly of damp. The floor was sticky. The bar itself, when she made the mistake of leaning against it, was sticky too. But as she sipped her drink, and Henry filled her in on the gossip about the regulars, Kathy relaxed into the scene. The bar might be scruffy but the crowd was remarkably chic. Not dissimilar to the guests at the party on the other side of the river. They were artists, jewellers, sculptors, songwriters and television stars, Henry explained. This was a Florence she would not have been able to get to know were she not with a local.

Henry introduced her to a few people. A man who looked like Italian star Toni Servillo kissed her hand and declared himself enchanted. His elegant female companion, whose carefully made-up eyes had sparked with obvious affection when she saw Henry walk in, regarded Kathy with interest and perhaps, thought Kathy, even a little envy.

'Henry Innocenti,' she said. 'We haven't seen you here in ages. Has this Kathy been keeping you away from us?'

Kathy was secretly flattered that she looked like the kind of woman Henry might be interested in.

The Servillo lookalike offered to get Kathy another drink. Still warm inside from the rocket-fuel cocktail that was Henry's favourite, Kathy asked for something a little lighter. A tall cocktail that was mostly soda water duly appeared.

'Your first time in our city?' said Servillo's double. 'Then you are very lucky to have this man as your guide. He can show you the real city.'

Henry looked up from his conversation with Servillo's girlfriend. Seeing that Kathy looked a little lost, he took her hand and pulled her closer. She felt inordinately pleased.

There was a piano in the furthest corner from the door. It was not a beautiful grand, like the one at the Michelangelo Plaza, or the Bösendorfer back at the Palazzo Boldrini, but a battered old upright that had seen a great many nights like this. A crowd of glasses covered the top.

Henry did not take much persuading to sit down at the keys again. He took requests from the other guests in the bar. He was like a one-man karaoke machine. He could play anything anyone asked for. Even, Kathy noted with some amusement, if what they asked for was Coldplay.

While the whole bar sang along to 'Yellow', Henry didn't seem to be hating every note.

He played some of his own compositions too. The crowd was delighted as Henry made up lyrics off the cuff about the place's most notorious regulars and 'the grumpy old sod behind the bar'. Then, as Kathy had feared might happen, he insisted that she join him at the piano.

'Introducing *l'uccellino di Londra*. That's the London sparrow,' he translated, for Kathy's benefit, as he took her hand and pulled her close. 'Known to me as the Queen of Sheba.'

Kathy gave a little bow.

'You ready for this?' he asked.

'I suppose I'll have to be.'

They sang the classics, old and new, reprising their performance at the party. And, just as had happened at the party, Kathy felt the applause filling her with energy and a lightness she hadn't experienced for a long time. Not since before her father had died. Not since long before she'd met Neil. She wished the night would never end.

At nearly one in the morning, having played for another hour, Henry stood up and gave a deep, deep bow as he bade their audience goodnight.

'I need to make sure the queen gets her beauty sleep,' he said.

'Are you suggesting I need it?' Kathy joked.

'Far from it,' said Henry, meeting her eye to eye.

It took a while to get out of the café, as Henry's fans insisted on offering them a drink or at least sharing a couple of words before they left for the night. But once they were on the street outside, Henry offered Kathy his arm again. Without hesitation this time, she tucked hers through it. Maybe it was tiredness, maybe it was the drinks, but Kathy leaned a little more heavily

against Henry as they began the homeward stretch.
And he leaned a little more heavily in her direction.
She could feel the warmth of his body against her bare
arm and she liked it.

Chapter Forty-six

Back at the house, Henry opened the door that led into the loggia with his own version of the big iron key, but instead of turning into the house, he took Kathy's hand and pulled her through into the garden.

'Come with me,' he said.

'Where are we going?'

'Just follow me.'

He led her to the wall that marked where the grounds of the Casa Innocenti ended and the sumptuous gardens of the palazzo began. He dropped her hand to vault over the wall, disappearing into the darkness beneath.

'Henry!' Kathy exclaimed, as loudly as she could without waking anyone up. 'Henry. Where are you?'

She peered down into the gloom.

'I'm here.' His face loomed out of the shadows. 'Come on. You do the same.'

'I can't get over that wall. I'll break something.'

'No, you won't. There are piles of compost sacks down here to break your fall. Plus I'll catch you. You've got to come and see this. Trust me.'

'Aren't we trespassing?'

'No one will know. Actually, that's not true. The guy who owns this place is a tech nerd. He's probably got CCTV cameras all over the place. They're probably so good he can count my nose hairs.' Henry waved to an invisible camera. 'Hey there, Mr Nerd!'

He looked back at Kathy, who was leaning over the wall, still staring down into the darkness, trying to work out just how big the drop actually was, compost sacks or no.

'It's nothing. Manu does it all the time. And Carla, when she's had enough of Mamma and wants to run off into the woods for a quick smoke and scream.'

'Right.'

'Come on, Kathy Courage. Kathy Brave.'

The sound of her old nickname made Kathy look up in surprise. 'Did you just call me Kathy Brave?'

'Courage. Bravery. Same thing, right? Though you're not showing much of either right now. Come on, Queen of Sheba. After tonight, I thought you were all about new experiences, taking chances and living life to the full.'

'Where did you hear that? Not when it involves potentially breaking my neck. Plus I'll rip the dress.'

'Tuck it into your knickers,' Henry suggested.

The suggestion made her laugh.

'I want to show you something really special. If you don't get down by yourself, I'm coming up to get you.'

'You may have to.'

Henry shone his phone against the wall. 'Look, you don't have to jump. There are foot and hand-holds everywhere. Sit on the wall and swing your legs over.'

'This is crazy.'

'You're having a crazy day.'

Kathy took off her shoes. Swinging her legs over the wall as Henry had instructed, she took a deep breath. Henry kept the light on the wall until she found her first foothold. From there, she felt confident enough to drop straight onto the soft compost. Thankfully, the bags didn't split.

'We need to stay low,' said Henry, 'since technically we're not meant to be here.' They set off across the lawn. The grass was springy beneath Kathy's feet. As it was crushed beneath her toes, it released the unmistakable green scent of summer holidays that mingled with the perfume of the jasmine that always seemed stronger at night.

Henry held tightly to her hand as they dashed across the grass like children. He knew exactly where he was going. Through the trees behind the crooked campanile. Stepping carefully through the grove behind him, Kathy caught her first glimpse of the Palazzo Innocenti, silent as a tomb in the night. The vast pink- and yellow-plastered house – perfect in its symmetry – was dark but for a single light on the topmost floor.

'The security guard,' said Henry. 'Probably watching a blue movie on his laptop. He won't bother us.'

Henry kept hold of Kathy's hand to take her right past the palazzo in the direction of another wall. Thankfully, there was a door in this wall and it was unlocked and open. He guided Kathy through.

'Where are we going?' Kathy asked.

'Sybilla Innocenti's private garden. She was the daughter of Francesca.'

Hidden behind the wall was a formal garden of exquisite beauty, laid out in an intricate knot design of low bushes. In the centre was a fountain, with a statue of a woman, standing on a half shell. Kathy recognised her at once as Aphrodite, born from sea-foam and carried into shore on an empty clam shell blown by friendly winds. Yet she was different from Botticelli's *Venus*. Her look was less far away and more engaging. Around her feet, dolphins ridden by cherubs played in the waves.

'This fountain is by Bandinelli,' Henry said. 'Rival of Michelangelo. The Venus is Sybilla herself.'

'It's beautiful. She's beautiful.' Kathy stepped closer. Her eyes had grown used to the darkness now and the white marble seemed to glow.

Henry hovered behind her. 'Not a lot of people know this exists. I wanted you to see her because I think she looks exactly like you.'

In the quiet peace of the garden, Kathy did a double-take. 'I don't—'

'She does. She looks like you. You look like a goddess. I thought it the very first time I saw you, playing the piano at the Palazzo Boldrini. The curve of your cheek is exactly the same as hers. The way your hair falls when it's loose.'

'I . . . I don't know what to say.'

'You don't have to say anything. But I wanted you to see this. It's almost as though you've been here before.'

'Like reincarnation, you mean?'

'Something like that. When we first met, I felt as if it wasn't actually the first time, didn't you?'

'It was like we'd met before,' Kathy agreed.

'To see you sitting at that piano, looking so happy and so right at the keys, was really strange. That piano, the piano in the Palazzo Boldrini, is the one on which I learned to play. It used to stand in the music room of the Palazzo Innocenti, until it had to be sold along with just about everything else of any value. Of all the things the family had to give away, that piano hurt the most for me. It felt like giving away a living thing. A dog or a horse. Seeing you playing it felt oddly right. Like you were supposed to be there.'

Kathy felt a shiver of recognition.

'Then we duetted and it was so natural. After I left you in that room and went back to Florence, I couldn't stop thinking about you. And this little tune started to come together in my head. A tune that was all about you. It tumbled through my head, like a musical notation of the way you laughed when we finally got the "Queen of Sheba" right. I scribbled it down. I was sure it was going to be a song and one day I would play it to you and you would provide the words. All that on the basis of having sat next to you at the piano for an hour or so and thinking you looked like my favourite statue. I didn't know you at all and yet I felt I knew you very well indeed.

'I was so looking forward to seeing you at that wedding. When your fiancé proposed to you at the end of the dinner, I felt like such a fool. I was jealous. Of course you were there with someone else. A woman as beautiful as you simply had to be in someone's heart. I knew that. But when we were playing, I put that out of my mind and enjoyed the fact that you were a kindred spirit. Then when you turned up at the house . . . I was rude. I'm sorry. I was just so surprised to see you there, and embarrassed when I thought about Wednesday afternoon and Thursday night and how I'd practically written you half an opera without knowing anything more than your name.'

Henry paused and snuck a glance at her. 'You think I'm nuts,' he said.

'No,' said Kathy. 'No. Not at all.'

She knew how brave he must be to have said any of it and how true it all sounded to her.

'In that case, come here,' said Henry.

They sat down on a marble bench facing the statue – a bench not much wider than the piano stool – with their hands on the cool seat between them. Silently, their fingers crept towards each other until they touched, jumped apart, then touched again. Kathy turned her face towards Henry's. There was just enough silver light coming from the moon above and the ambient glow of the city around them for Kathy to see Henry's soft, enquiring eyes and the slight, uncertain smile on his lips.

Their fingers touched and intertwined, finally coming together as though magnetised.

No more words passed between them but a whole conversation took place in those few moments as they leaned their heads closer and closer together. They rested forehead against forehead. Henry lifted his free hand and laid it on Kathy's cheek. She could hear nothing but the pounding of her own heart. She leaned into his caress.

In that touch was a thousand questions. Henry's heart was asking, 'Do you love Neil? Do you really love him? Or do you feel as I do? Did you feel it when we shared that piano stool, just as I did? Could you throw it all away to be with me?'

And Kathy's heart was asking in return, 'Is this real? Or am I crazy? Is it possible to fall in love like this? This fast? If I jump now, will you catch me?'

Henry's hand cupped Kathy's chin and gently he brought her face forward so that their mouths were millimetres apart. It was going to happen. They were going to kiss. But then . . .

Chapter Forty-seven

An alarm rang, tearing through the peace of the soft, warm night, and the dark walled garden was suddenly flooded with light, as a security system they'd somehow managed not to trigger on the way across the lawn, sprang into life.

Swearing, Henry grabbed Kathy's hand again and they ran back in the direction they'd come. There was no time to savour the beauty of the palazzo's vast lawn now. Its openness was only a problem. They ran and tumbled over the grass. At the wall to the casa, Henry gave her a leg up, lifting her as high as he could. Kathy feared for her knees, for her hands, for Carla's dress, but close behind them, they could hear barking and not the friendly kind, as the palazzo's security guards unleashed their dogs.

'Come on!'

Henry climbed the wall alongside her and, getting to the top first, he hauled Kathy the last couple of feet.

From inside the Casa Innocenti, Faustino was barking too. As Henry and Kathy fell onto the terrace, rolling onto the flagstones, like two commandos fleeing enemy fire, Faustino came barrelling out through the glass doors. Barking, barking, then squeaking his delight at seeing Henry, Faustino ran to be with his favourite person on earth.

When Kathy looked back in the direction from which

Faustino had come, she saw Carla silhouetted in the doorway by the light from inside the house.

'What's going on? What's with the sirens? Is that the palazzo's security system going off?'

'I have no idea,' said Henry, unconvincingly.

Carla didn't even pretend to believe him. 'What were you doing over there, you idiot? Are you crazy?'

'Do I look crazy?'

'Don't make me answer that,' said Carla. 'Amy's husband will have you put in jail.'

'He'll have to catch me first.'

Carla held out her hand to Kathy and helped her to her feet.

'I wanted to show Kathy the statue,' Henry said.

'In the walled garden? Henry, you're mad.'

'How was I to know they'd installed some mega security system since I last went over there? They must need a licence for an alarm that loud. It will have woken all our guests up.'

Carla's mouth straightened into a *moue* as she looked at her brother and shook her head. 'I don't think they can take responsibility for that. Oh, Henry, you might have got Kathy bitten on the bum by one of the dogs.'

Henry grinned at the thought.

'It's not funny.'

Kathy grinned too.

'If you've woken Manu up, you can deal with him being grumpy in the morning,' Carla told them. 'How was the gig?' she asked Kathy then.

'It was amazing.'

'I knew you'd be good.'

'She was magnificent.' Henry's eyes twinkled in the dark.

Kathy knew they shouldn't be looking at each other like that in front of Carla but she found she didn't care.

'It's a shame you've got to go home tomorrow,' Carla said.

Kathy and Henry were still gazing at one another, as though sharing a private joke.

'Actually, Kathy, while you were out you had a phone call. From your fiancé, Neil. I took it. He seemed quite upset that you weren't in to talk to him. He says he's flying out tomorrow.'

'What?'

'He's flying out to meet you here in Florence. Tomorrow. He said he'll come and pick you up so if you could be packed and ready by midday . . .'

As she processed what Carla was telling her, it was as though Kathy had stepped off a kerb into a deep, cold puddle. The chill of shame crept through her body. Neil had phoned. The romance of the evening, as fantastical as it had been, disappeared in an instant. She had a fiancé. He was real and he was coming to fetch her.

Henry at once stood up and dusted down his trousers. He cleared his throat. 'Well, I suppose I should be going to bed. Come on, Faustino.'

The little dog followed him inside, leaving Carla and Kathy alone on the terrace. Kathy watched Henry go. Carla watched Kathy watching Henry.

'I'll never get back to sleep now,' Carla complained once her brother was gone. 'Sit out here with me for a bit?'

Kathy followed Carla to the chairs they'd sat in the night before. They settled down side by side and Carla lit up a cigarette and began, 'I didn't finish telling you about Manu's dad.'

Kathy felt herself start to sober up as Carla told her about Manu's father Nathan, an English man, with whom she'd fallen madly in love. Who had made her feel so cared for and so loved. At least at first. As long as Carla was doing exactly what Nathan wanted. Over five years, Nathan went from being caring to controlling and when Manu came along, Carla realized that it was never going to get any better.

'I wanted Manu to have a father in his life but every evening before Nathan got home, I had to make sure Manu's toys were out of sight,' she explained. 'Even when Manu was a tiny baby, I would whisk him out of the way before his crying disturbed his father. I spent so much time making sure Manu didn't disturb Nathan's tranquillity in any way. Everything was about keeping Nathan happy.

'Now I know I made the right decision in leaving. Manu loves being here. He can be a child. He was already starting to be affected by the way his father was. He was creeping around like a mouse. No five year old should be afraid to laugh and shout.'

Kathy agreed.

'But it was hard. I felt embarrassed when I first left Nathan. I felt like everyone was judging me and thinking I was crazy for leaving such a "good" man, when surely I should have been grateful he wanted me. And he had been great at first and I'd invested so much time in him. It was hard to walk away from that. But when I think of how it really was behind closed doors. How I had let him chip away at my dreams . . .'

Carla stubbed out her cigarette and plastered on a smile.

'It's good news, isn't it, that Neil's flying out to meet you?' she suddenly asked. Her eyes searched Kathy's for the real answer.

'Of course,' said Kathy. 'I'm just amazed that he's going to. Tomorrow is a bank holiday in the UK but he's probably got an early start on Tuesday and . . .'

'He did say he wants to make sure everything is sorted out properly for the insurance, with the police. Regarding your bag. And the ring, I expect.'

'I haven't told him about the ring,' Kathy admitted. 'I didn't know where to begin.'

'Well, I don't think I mentioned it,' said Carla. Concern wrinkled her brow. 'But he won't mind, will he? When he finds out. The ring is just a thing. All that matters is that you're safe and happy. You don't need to worry about how he'll react.'

Do you? was the unspoken question.

When Kathy passed through the sitting room, Henry was on the sofa. He had his face buried in a pillow though he couldn't really have been asleep. Faustino was busy trying to get into a comfortable position, kneading Henry into the right position with his four paws. Nobody could have slept through that.

'Goodnight,' Kathy said quietly. 'Thank you. I had the best time.'

'Me too,' she thought she heard Henry say.

Up in the attic room, Kathy got into bed but couldn't sleep. She felt giddy when she considered what had almost happened in the walled garden. It was just a 'nearly kiss', fuelled by a night filled with adrenalin and alcohol. It was nothing significant. Nothing to feel guilty about. And tomorrow she would be going back to London. Back to her ordinary life in the house in Fulham. Back to Neil and his children. Back to her job search. Back to planning a wedding. Back to the life she was meant for.

Chapter Forty-eight

Waking up in the morning, Kathy felt the effect of every single sip of alcohol she'd had the night before. It was as though someone was holding a dance-off in her head. It hurt to open her eyes to the light that insisted on pouring through the window. Kathy was far from ready to start the day.

Dragging herself from her bed, Kathy looked at her reflection in the foxed mirror inside Henry's wardrobe, sticking out her tongue to further diagnose that she'd had too much. As if she didn't know. She couldn't remember when she'd last had so much to drink in a single evening. And while elements of the previous evening were hazy, other moments shone out in her memory, like loose sequins on a dusty floor.

Henry's eyes meeting hers as they finished singing 'The Way You Look Tonight' at the party.

The after-party in the bar. What on earth was in that awful cocktail?

The face of Venus on the fountain in the walled garden.

Henry's eyes so soft and questioning, as he leaned in to kiss her.

The questions that had arisen in her own mind.

The answers she'd given herself.

Then finding out that Neil was on his way.

Kathy pinched the bridge of her nose and took a deep breath in and out. The thought of going downstairs and facing Henry and Carla filled her with something like dread. But she had to do it.

Kathy did not know exactly what time Neil would arrive. He'd told Carla that he would be there 'in the morning' and that Kathy should be ready to go by lunchtime but she had not made a note of which flight. He hadn't offered the information.

'Seemed in a hurry to get off the phone,' Carla said.

Of course Kathy couldn't text Neil for more clarity since she still didn't have a phone. All she could do was wait at the house until he turned up.

Kathy still couldn't quite believe that Neil was coming out to Florence to fetch her, to be sure she caught her flight. She wasn't quite sure what to make of it. Was he coming because he thought she was too stupid or incapable to get to the airport herself? Or was he coming because he wanted her to feel safe and loved? Had being engaged made him feel suddenly romantic? When they'd spoken on the phone over the past few days he'd seemed distant, disgruntled, almost angry with her that she was still in Italy while he was back in the UK, as though she'd planned the whole thing from the start.

Playing for time, alone in Henry's room, Kathy folded her clothes back into her case. The dress she had borrowed from Carla hung from the back of the door, like a costume for a play about a woman who'd run away to Italy and found true love. It was a dress for another woman. A woman running away from reality. Not one engaged to be married to a man she had loved for five years. Kathy gave the fabric a fond stroke. She wondered if she would ever find something so beautiful to wear again.

* * *

Downstairs, the kitchen was busy. Ernesto was absent, though Roberta didn't seem unduly worried.

'He'll be back again tomorrow. His football team had a big match yesterday evening. I have no doubt he was out celebrating until late.'

Without Ernesto, all hands were on deck and Kathy quickly slotted into the team again. The first she saw of Henry was when she took a dish full of freshly scrambled egg out onto the guests' terrace, overlooking the garden where – Kathy calculated – only around five hours ago, he had taken her hand and . . .

Don't think about it.

Now they performed an elaborate dance to avoid bumping into one another as they juggled plates.

'You go first,' said Henry, conceding the gap between tables and stepping out of Kathy's way. He didn't meet her eyes as he did so. He had closed down to her again. Even when they were together in the kitchen and Roberta asked them both about how the previous day's gig had gone, he was almost monosyllabic. 'It went well.'

Perhaps it was just that he had a hangover. Kathy's head was still banging, and Henry had drunk more than she had. He didn't hate her for what had happened in the garden. He probably couldn't remember what had happened.

Though, of course, he was right to distance himself a little if he did, as should she. Her fiancé would be arriving at any moment. Her fiancé . . . Kathy glanced at her ringless left hand.

Kathy went out onto the terrace to collect the last of the plates and glasses. As she did so, she bumped into the young blogging couple, who still couldn't keep their hands off each other, so deeply in love were they.

'Excuse me,' Jenny said to Kathy. 'Can we borrow you for a moment? We're leaving this morning, but before we go, we want a photograph with the garden behind us to send to our parents.'

Kathy took Jenny's phone, which was already set up to take a shot. All she had to do was point and press.

'You see,' Jenny continued, 'we got engaged last night.'

She stretched out her hand in Kathy's direction, so that it dominated the phone screen. On the third finger of her left hand, a chip of diamond glittered proudly in the morning sun. Jenny stepped closer so that Kathy could take a proper look. Kathy held Jenny's hand gently, just as the other women at Shelley and Dave's wedding had done when she was given her own engagement ring. She bent nearer to see the ring properly. The diamond, which was the size of a lentil and cut into the shape of a heart, was set in a yellow gold band.

'I picked it out myself,' said the proud fiancé.

'It's exactly what I wanted,' Jenny assured him, with a beaming smile that said she was telling the truth.

'She's got really delicate fingers,' said Kyle, 'which is lucky because I couldn't afford anything bigger. I'll get her something better when I'm promoted.'

'You could have put an elastic band around my finger and I would have been happy. What matters is that we're getting married, right?'

Jenny looked to Kathy for back-up.

'Absolutely right,' Kathy agreed. She forced a bright smile. 'Shall I take those pictures?' She let Jenny's hand go and moved back so that she could get both the happy couple in the frame. Once she'd taken a few decent shots she handed the phone back and grabbed a couple of plates to show that she was busy and couldn't hang around talking about love all day.

'Congratulations.' She threw the word over her shoulder as she hurried back to the kitchen.

The young lovers were too busy gazing at each other to notice that Kathy had rushed to get away.

'So, they got engaged,' said Carla. 'Love's young dream.'

'I hope he's got a good lawyer,' Henry grumped.

'They won't need one.' Carla was sure.

'What time's your fiancé coming, Kathy?' Henry asked.

'I don't know,' Kathy said. 'Soon, I hope.' It seemed like the right thing to say. How had they gone from sharing secrets to this staccato exchange?

Faustino sounded the alarm as they were in the kitchen washing up. Before any of the human beings heard the sonorous tone of the doorbell that had announced centuries' worth of visitors to the Casa Innocenti, Faustino was skidding across the parquet floor in his haste to see off this latest intruder. Henry went to answer the door.

Chapter Forty-nine

Just three days had passed since Kathy had last seen Neil as he disappeared through airport security with his children, yet somehow it seemed much, much longer. It was almost as though he belonged to a different lifetime. To see him step through the blue gate into the loggia at the Casa Innocenti was surreal. He didn't belong there. He looked oddly unfamiliar, in his khaki trousers and the plain blue cotton shirt that was a total bugger to iron.

He was shaking hands with Henry.

'Neil Sherwin,' he said. 'You must be . . .'

'Henry Innocenti. We've met before,' Henry reminded him.

'Have we?'

'I played in the band at your brother's wedding.'

'Ah! So you did! You were on the keyboard. Great playing. I do remember you now. Pretty good rendition of "Yellow" you did back there. Anyway, thanks for looking after the little lady,' he said. Then, when he saw Kathy: 'Chicken Licken, there you are!'

She wished he hadn't used her nickname. At least, not at once.

'So this is where you've been hiding. Not bad,' he added, taking in the height of the loggia's ceiling and the huge brass carriage lamp above his head. He turned his eyes to the view beyond the arches. 'Is that your garden?'

'No,' said Henry. 'Alas, our property stops at the wall.'

'I see,' said Neil, walking to the wall to get a better look. Faustino was still barking. Henry scooped the little dog up and gently muzzled him with his hand. Faustino's wide eyes declared his disgust at the betrayal. How could he guard the family when no one let him bark? Henry tried putting him down again, only to have to grab him once more when he made a yapping, snarling beeline for the bottom of Neil's trousers. Henry caught him just in time, lifting him up again so that his snapping jaws clamped around thin air.

'Dogs,' said Neil, teasing Faustino with a poke to the nose. 'Can't live with them . . .'

Once he'd had a good look at the garden, Neil came back to where Henry and Kathy were standing. He offered Kathy his cheek. She duly planted a kiss on it.

'You must come inside and have some coffee,' said Henry.

'That sounds like an excellent idea. I had one hell of a journey to get here. The airport was a nightmare as usual. How half those idiots have passports, I don't know. There should be a test. Then I got into a taxi driven by someone who was clearly out to rip me off.'

'That's unlikely,' said Henry. 'It's a flat fee from the airport to the centre. There's a sign in all the cars.'

'Well, he made a real dog's breakfast of getting me here, is all I can say. He went all round the houses. I swear we passed the end of this street three times.'

'The one-way system can add time to a journey,' Henry conceded.

'So.' Neil paused to admire the staircase. 'This is all original, is it? The carving and the paintings and stuff?'

'Yes. They're original,' said Henry.

'Anyone important? The artist?'

Kathy was glad that Neil was showing some interest in the house but she was braced for what might come next.

'Must cost a bit to keep all this up.'

Roberta was waiting at the top of the stairs, just as she had been when Kathy first arrived, dishevelled and shocked by the robbery, on Friday evening. She had taken off her apron, put on her best pearls and was her usual elegant self. She held out her hands to Neil. He stuck out his right hand to shake hers.

'It's lovely to meet you,' she said, undeterred by the formality of the greeting. 'We've heard so much about you.'

'Have you?' Neil looked at Kathy with a raised eyebrow. 'All good, I hope.'

'Of course. Come in. Sit down.'

Henry was dispatched to the kitchen to bring out the coffee. Manu helped carry in biscuits. Carla shut Faustino in her bedroom, whence he could be heard complaining throughout Neil's visit. Yap, yap, yap. And the occasional threatening growl.

'It's because you're a man,' Carla said. 'Faustino is normally in charge here. He only really tolerates Henry and Manu.'

'The little ones are the worst,' said Neil. 'Smaller the dog, snappier the temper. It's probably because they think they need to keep barking to make sure nobody steps on them. You could hoover him up without noticing.'

Manu looked horrified at the very idea.

'Tell me about the house, Roberta,' said Neil. 'I'm assuming this used to be part of the main place. The Palazzo Innocenti?'

'Yes,' said Roberta. 'It was the gatehouse.'

'A very grand gatehouse.'

'The Innocenti were a very grand family.'

'That's a lot to live up to,' said Neil. 'And, as I was saying, the upkeep must be pretty steep. Enough to keep you awake at night.'

'Oh, no,' said Roberta. 'The house looks after us.'

'We're sorry you're here on such a fleeting visit,' said Carla, changing the subject. 'Time for lunch and that's about all before you fly home, I imagine.'

'Oh, no,' said Neil. 'We're not going back today.'

'We aren't?' Kathy was surprised.

'That's right, Chicken. I had Melanie book us onto a flight tomorrow. You didn't think I was just flying out here to pick you up and fly straight back on the same day. That would be crazy.'

'Well, yes, but . . .'

'I know I've got a lot going on at the office right now but sometimes you just have to say, "What the hell?", right? Work can wait.'

'Then you must have lunch with us,' said Roberta.

'No, no. I think we've prevailed upon your hospitality quite enough,' said Neil. 'I'm going to take Kathy out for lunch in the centre. Somewhere nice. But before I go, I wanted to give you this.'

He opened his overnight bag and pulled out an envelope that was almost as thick as the one Kathy and Henry had been awarded at the party the previous night. 'Who should I give it to?'

Roberta visibly recoiled. 'Really, Neil. It's been our

pleasure to have Kathy stay with us. Our family motto is *Deus ope, manus mea.*'

Neil shook his head.

'It means "God's work through my hands". Which translates as meaning we should help whenever we can. Which is all Carla did when she saw that Kathy had been robbed. If anything, we probably owe your fiancée a weekend's wages after her time here. She's been such a help to all of us.'

'Come on,' said Neil. 'She can't have done that much.'

'Actually,' said Carla. 'She has. She won me a lot of business, by encouraging my boss at the boutique to stock my designs. I'm a dress designer,' she added, by way of explanation.

'And she saved the day by stepping into the kitchen on Saturday evening after the chef decided to go AWOL,' said Roberta.

'She helped me at the market,' said Manu.

'And she helped me too,' said Henry.

'She stood in for Henry's usual singer,' Carla explained.

'You sang?' Neil looked at Kathy in astonishment.

'At a sixtieth birthday party.'

'Now that I really didn't expect to hear. I don't suppose the guests expected to hear it either. Can you sing, Chicken? I didn't know.'

He did know. He must know. Kathy knew she'd told him about those long-ago school-choir days back when they were first together. When she'd still thought he was listening.

'It wasn't something I ever expected to do,' Kathy admitted.

'But she did it brilliantly,' said Roberta.

'You weren't there.' Kathy tried to be modest.

'But she's right,' said Henry. 'You did brilliantly. Your fiancée is a very talented woman, Neil.'

Neil raised his eyebrows and tucked in his chin as if to say, 'Really?'

'Well, she still eats like a horse,' he said. 'So, please, take this money to cover her bodyweight in pasta. I'm sure she ate at least that much.'

In an echo of the previous Thursday evening, after the proposal, Neil took the initiative and tucked the envelope into Henry's top pocket. 'Have a couple of days off busking,' he said.

Kathy felt her entire body and spirit cringe as Henry took the envelope from his pocket and put it on the table, flattening it out as he did so. His expression said it all. He was going to say something he couldn't take back. Ever the diplomat, Carla jumped to the rescue, 'Thank you, Neil. Manu has been saying that he'd like to learn to play the trumpet so we'll put it towards getting him some lessons.'

'Or some new games for my tablet,' Manu suggested. His mother and grandmother's faces told him 'Little or no hope.'

'Right. That sounds nice,' said Neil. 'Come on, Chicken. Let's leave these good people to get on with their day.'

While Neil and Kathy made their goodbyes, Manu disappeared. Where he'd gone to became clear moments later as Faustino came barrelling along the hallway, puffed up to his maximum circumference, teeth bared and snapping.

'Faustino!'

Four adults lunged for the dog as the dog lunged for the bottom of Neil's trousers. Henry lifted the dog into the air just in time again so that his sharp white teeth snapped and closed on nothing.

'I'm so sorry,' Henry said. 'Faustino never does this.'

'How did he get out?' Carla asked rhetorically. They all knew how he'd got out.

From the darkness of the corridor, Manu smirked.

'You should get him muzzled,' Neil suggested. 'One day he's going to go for a paying guest. Then you'll have a real problem on your hands.'

Henry carried Kathy's suitcase to the bottom of the stairs and opened the door onto the street. After another perfunctory goodbye, Neil set off towards the river, leaving Kathy to drag her own case. When she tried to tell him he'd set off in the wrong direction, he disagreed. They stood in the sun on the street corner for five minutes, while Neil waited for his iPhone map app to catch up with them.

Chapter Fifty

Neil had booked them into a hotel near the city's central station. Kathy tried not to be disappointed as she followed him into the lobby of the huge grey building, which was decorated in the style of so many corporate hotels from London to Laos – an uninspiring mixture of cream and coffee tones. She knew that the most uninspiring façade could hide hidden beauty in this city – a secret garden or a courtyard with a tinkling fountain. Alas, it didn't seem to be the case here.

Their room was ready early. They went upstairs and padded along a corridor where the walls were actually lined with the same carpet as the floor. The windows of their bedroom looked out onto an inner courtyard, which was full of air-conditioning equipment.

'Room with a view,' Neil joked. The only view in the room was a faded reproduction of, incongruously, one of Turner's paintings of the River Thames. 'Still, it's only for one night and we won't be spending much time in here,' Neil said.

Over lunch in a nearby restaurant – a tourist trap that had a menu with photographs – the true story behind Neil's sudden appearance in Florence came out.

'You didn't need to come to get me,' said Kathy. 'I would have been back by tonight.'

'I know,' said Neil. 'But, as it happened, it's turned out to be a very good thing, you getting yourself into such a mess.'

Kathy was puzzled. Not least by the idea that she'd got herself into the mess.

'I'm out here to meet a client from the Majestic Hotel Group.'

It was based in New York, Kathy knew. Neil had acted for them on several finance deals. She'd heard all about them.

'Since Florence is closer than New York, it made sense to have a face-to-face here. He's in town looking at a number of properties. Old hotels that need fixing up. I should suggest he looks at the Casa Innocenti.'

'It's not for sale,' said Kathy.

'They clearly can't afford to keep the place together. It looks like it's ready to fall down.'

Kathy felt the sting of Neil's words as though they were aimed at her personally. 'They won't sell,' she insisted.

'The son busks to make a living.'

'He doesn't busk. He's a professional musician.'

'Whatever you want to call it. And you saw the way the daughter leaped on that cash. They're desperate. They'll sell if MHG make an offer. If they do, you can thank me later.' He kissed her on the forehead. Kathy recoiled.

'Oh, don't be such a softie. They'll be much happier when they let go of their delusions of grandeur. They'll get a decent price. They can send the kid to private school. Grandma can get a nice flat all on one level to save her knees. The lord of the manor can afford to get a proper haircut. And you, well, with the fee my firm could get from acting for Majestic this year, you might just get some nice earrings to match your . . .'

Kathy followed Neil's eyes down to her left hand. Her bare hand.

'Your ring. Where's your engagement ring?'

Now at last it was all going to hit the fan.

'Neil,' Kathy began. 'I've been meaning to tell you.'

'Where is your engagement ring?'

'You know on Friday afternoon, when I was sitting in the café and you called and we talked on the phone and while we were talking—'

'Where is the ring?'

It was 'the' ring now. Not hers any more.

'It was so loose. It kept slipping over my knuckle. I was afraid I was going to lose it while I was walking round the city.'

'After I told you to stay in the airport . . .'

'I was so afraid . . .' Kathy shrank into herself as she watched Neil's face harden '. . . I thought the best place for it was inside the zipped pocket in my handbag, which I had been wearing across my body for safety, until I sat down and I put it on the table and—'

'You're telling me the ring was in the bag that was stolen?'

'Yes,' said Kathy. 'It was. Neil, I'm so, so sorry.'

'Do you have any idea how much that ring cost me?' Neil asked. 'Do you have any clue? And you put it in the pocket of your tatty old handbag?'

'I know it was a stupid thing to do. I should have put it on the chain around my neck or something.'

'You put a five-thousand-pound engagement ring in your handbag, which you left on a table in full sight of everyone in a town with the highest number of pickpockets in the world.'

Kathy decided not to dispute Neil on that statistic.

Neil bashed his own knuckles against his forehead. 'I am surrounded by idiots everywhere. Everywhere! Is there a single person in my life who isn't an absolute moron?'

'Neil.'

She had expected him to be upset about the ring but not this upset.

'I'm beginning to wonder why I asked you to marry me in the first place. Perhaps I should take it back.'

Exhilaration flashed through Kathy's mind so fast she almost didn't notice it.

'For crying out loud.' Neil threw another wodge of cash on the table and stormed out of the restaurant. Kathy followed him, apologising as she went to the people he'd shoved out of the way.

'Neil! Neil!' She tried to keep up with him but he was striding ahead, not stopping for anything. He almost sent a moped rider flying as the young man had to brake hard to avoid knocking him over as he strode across a street without looking.

'Neil!'

He didn't turn to look back at her once on the walk to the hotel.

Kathy was scared and worried yet there it was again: that flash of exhilaration. Of clarification? Of relief? She had never seen Neil so angry. Surely they couldn't survive this.

Neil did not speak to her all afternoon. They certainly did not go out for dinner at a fancy restaurant that evening, as he had promised when he picked her up at the Casa Innocenti. Instead he ordered room service. Kathy said she didn't feel hungry and it was true. Her stomach churned.

Though they couldn't move around the small hotel room without bumping into one another, Neil was doing a pretty good job of pretending that Kathy wasn't there. He didn't say a word to her. He turned on the television and flipped through the channels, jabbing at the buttons on the remote, which was sluggish. The batteries must have been running out. Deciding there was nothing to watch, he turned the television off and picked up his phone, scrolling through videos of goals from Fulham's triumphs past, which Kathy had come to understand was his way of self-soothing. Ordinarily, knowing this, she would have snuggled into his side and asked him if he was OK. But since she was the reason he wasn't OK, there was no point trying to help him unpack his unhappiness tonight.

Eventually, at around ten o'clock, he got up and went to the bathroom. At home, Kathy always went through the bathroom first, since Neil's bedtime routine was more extensive than hers, but he was continuing to act as though she wasn't there so this time he got bathroom priority. Afterwards, he got into bed, climbing under the single sheet and turning away from her. While she was in the bathroom, he turned the air-conditioning down as low as it would go. As though the atmosphere needed any help to make it icy.

Even wearing a T-shirt and socks, Kathy was too cold beneath that single sheet on the bed. She lay awake. She might have been anywhere on earth. She could hear none of the comforting sounds of the city she had come to love. It was too late for swallows but neither could she hear the bells, nor the chatter of happy people on their way home from restaurants, nor the odd snatch of opera as a chef grabbed a break from the kitchen. Just the air-conditioning, which for some reason right then made her think of being inside one of those big stainless-steel drawers in a morgue.

'You don't have to do this,' her father's voice said.

Chapter Fifty-one

A good night's sleep did not improve Neil's mood. He got up without kissing her good morning. He showered and dressed before he even glanced in her direction, and when he did there was no trace of affection in his regard.

'I've got my first meeting in an hour,' he said eventually.

Though she had nothing planned, Kathy got out of bed and began pulling on her clothes so that she might at least look as though she was ready to do something too.

They went to breakfast together. It was served in a dining room on the top of the building, the eighth floor, a 1970s addition with floor-to-ceiling windows. At seven thirty, the room was already packed and there was a long queue for the self-service coffee machine. Kathy said she would stand in the queue for both of them, knowing Neil would not mellow with the wait.

'What are you going to do today?' Neil asked, as they ate.

'I don't know,' said Kathy. 'I didn't know how much time I'd have.'

'We need to leave here at five this afternoon. I'll have the hotel get us a car. If you could just manage to stay out of trouble until then. Try not to lose any more of the things I've bought you.'

Neil looked Kathy over from head to toe so that she, too, glanced down at what she was wearing. Not one of the items she had on, from her shoes to her earrings, was something Neil had bought her. She'd bought everything for herself, with money she had earned before she'd lost her job. She didn't argue, though. The absence of the ring meant everything right then.

When Neil left for his meeting with the client from New York, Kathy lingered over another coffee, trying her hardest not to cry. Ahead of her, through the large windows of the restaurant, was the roof of the Duomo. She had come to Florence and she had seen it. That was worth being happy about. And Neil would get over the loss of the engagement ring. And if he didn't?

'Does it matter?' she heard her father's voice again.

After breakfast, Kathy went back to their room. She turned off the air-conditioning and opened the window. Mosquitoes be damned. She needed real air. Then she flipped through the hotel's service guide to find the page on using the phone and the code for dialling internationally. She had to make a call.

Her mother picked up after two rings.

'Hello?' Clare sounded tentative.

'Mum, it's me.'

'Oh, darling! I was wondering when I'd hear from you. You haven't called or texted since Sunday! I was beginning to worry. Are you at home?'

'Not yet.'

Kathy explained the situation. Neil's unexpected business trip. 'So he thought he'd come and fetch me.'

'I'm so glad,' said Clare. 'I hate to think of you flying alone.'

Which was ironic, thought Kathy, since the prospect of going to the airport with Neil was far from relaxing.

'I found your father's letter,' Clare carried on. 'Not that I'd ever have lost it. I always knew exactly where it was. I went up into the loft to get it out of the safe on Sunday. So now it's ready for your wedding day. Have you had any more thoughts as to when that might be?'

Kathy dodged the question. 'Mum, I know the letter was meant for the wedding reception, but will you read it to me now?'

'But why, dear? Are you worried what it might say? You know your father won't have written anything embarrassing.'

'Of course not. I just want to hear it. I want to hear something in Dad's voice.'

'I can't do your dad's voice!' Clare said.

'I know. That's not what I meant. I meant I just want to hear what he wanted to say to me. I need . . . I need . . . Oh, I don't know. I guess going through such a big thing as getting engaged without him has made me miss him more than usual.'

'I know what you mean, love. There's nothing I'd like more than for us to be sharing all this with him.'

'Hearing the letter will be like having him there now reacting to the news about me and Neil.'

'Well, if you're sure it won't spoil the real big day, having already heard it . . .'

'It won't spoil the real big day, Mum. Please.'

'OK,' said Clare. 'If that's what you want. Just let me get my glasses.'

The wait while Clare found her glasses seemed endless. Kathy spent the moment staring at Turner's view of the Thames. Soon she would be swapping the Arno for that more familiar river.

'Right,' said Clare. 'I'm back. Are you ready?'

'Have you read this letter before, Mum?'

'No, I haven't. It was for you from your dad. I'd never have read it before you had a chance to see it. I hope it's not going to make us both cry.'

'You know it's going to make us both cry, Mum.'

Kathy heard her mother tearing open an envelope.

'Oh,' Clare exclaimed.

'What is it, Mum?'

'It's just seeing his handwriting . . .'

For a moment, Kathy felt bad, putting her mum through this when she was too far away to give her a hug, but she had a feeling that after she'd heard her father's words everything would make sense.

'Are you ready, sweetheart?' Clare asked.

'I think I am.'

Clare began to read.

Chapter Fifty-two

'My darling girl,
So here it is at last. Your big day! How I wish I
could be there with you in person. You'll have to
settle for having me there in spirit. Or at least in
print.

'I'm writing this letter on a Sunday afternoon
in May. You're away at university, studying hard
for your degree. You always were a clever clogs.
Did I tell you how proud your mum and I are that
you're at university, Kathy? We're so proud. I tell
everybody I meet. People at the bus stop, people
in the supermarket, people in the hospital. I've
told the doctors they'd better keep me going until
you graduate. I'm not going to miss that too.'

He had missed that too.

'But, without a miracle, I know I'm going to miss
your wedding, and unless you marry that nice boy
who does the MOTs at the garage on the
Chelmsford Road, like I'd strongly advise you to,
then today you're going to be marrying a stranger
– at least a stranger to me. So I have this to say
to him and to you.

'Kathy, you are my only child. That alone makes
me certain that you're the best woman in the

world. But even people who don't have my bias can see that you're a one-off. You're clever, you're funny, and you're kind. You can light a room with your smile. You can also block out the sun with your moods but I'm sure your future husband already knows that.

'There's not a single day goes by when I'm not chuffed to be your father. If I listed all the ways you've made me proud over the years, there wouldn't be enough paper in the world to get them all down. But here are a few of my favourites. Your first word. "Dada", of course. Your first steps. Your first day at school. Your first nativity play. You were the best second sheep that school ever saw. You getting your grade-one musical-theory exam when you were only eight. The day you had your eye fixed and showed us how you could be "Kathy Brave". You singing a solo in the school choir when I know how hard it was for you to get up in front of such a big audience. All those exams you aced. Your university place. First one in our family to go!

'So many proud-dad moments you gave me, but my very best memories of you are of the times you and I spent together at the piano, side by side, playing our favourite duets. I can still see the concentration on your face as you tried your hardest to keep up with me until one day it was me struggling to keep up with you. Whenever you asked me to join you at the keys after that, I felt like the luckiest man alive to have a daughter so talented and so patient, who still had time to play the odd tune with her old man. Such a gift you gave me.

'To the future Mr Courage – I'm sure that men will be taking women's surnames soon – I say this: Look after my daughter as I know she will look after you. Help her to be her best self. Support her, listen to her, always try to understand her point of view. My girl knows what she is doing. Help her to achieve her dreams and I know she will help you achieve yours. Treat her kindly at all times, or I promise I will haunt you from the grave. Make your life together a real duet.

'That's all from me for now. Have a wonderful day, future son-in-law and my beautiful Kathy Brave. I love you, sweetheart.

'With big hairy kisses,

'Your Dad.'

'Oh, Kathy!' When she'd finished reading the letter, Clare burst into noisy tears. Alone in the hotel room in Italy, Kathy did the same. They cried down the line for what felt like ages, until Clare laughed. 'Of course he had to mention that you said "Dada" first.'

'Typical Dad,' Kathy agreed.

'Oh, he loved you. And I love you too,' said Clare. 'Everything he wanted for you, I want as well. Everything.'

Especially a duet partner for life.

Chapter Fifty-three

With her head aching from having cried so hard, Kathy knew she needed to get outside. She had at least four hours to kill before Neil came back from his day of meetings. In that time there was only one thing she really wanted to see and that was the Uffizi.

There was a long wait to get into the galleries, of course, but Kathy was prepared. As the queue shuffled forward inch by inch, she thought about her father's letter and she thought about Neil.

For the first four years they were together, Neil hadn't talked much about the future and Kathy hadn't known how to broach it. The dozens of books she had read on the subject of dating a divorcee had warned against pushing for too much too soon. She had to let Neil come to the conclusion that it might be good to formalise their relationship. At the same time, Kathy was acutely aware that they didn't have all the time in the world. Not if they were going to have a baby together. She'd said in her dating profile that she wanted children. She was thirty-five when they met. Now she was thirty-nine.

As they came up to the fifth anniversary of their first date, she decided to broach the subject in a very roundabout way. By mentioning that she was thinking of coming off the pill. 'I've been on it for quite a while.

It's probably not doing me much good.' Neil had nodded vaguely. She put that down to the fact he wasn't keen on talking about anything to do with menstrual cycles. They were a feminine mystery he preferred to stay that way.

'The only thing is, what do we do for contraception if I'm not going to be on the pill any more?'

Kathy's musing was supposed to open a conversation as to whether they really needed to be using contraception at all. They were both grown-ups. They had money. They had space. Why shouldn't they just try for a baby?

'That's a tough one,' said Neil. 'Condoms, I suppose.' Then he went back to watching the news.

The conversation didn't come up again, but Kathy was beginning to understand that that didn't mean Neil wasn't thinking about it. Sometimes it would take him weeks to come back to her on something she'd suggested.

'I've got you a very special present,' Neil told her a month later. It was the week before Dave and Shelley's wedding.

Kathy felt her heart make a bid for escape via her mouth as she wondered what that present might be. It had to be a ring. It could only be a ring.

'I had a vasectomy,' Neil said.

'You what?' Kathy snorted. It was a terrible joke.

'I said I had a vasectomy.'

The smile melted from Kathy's lips. If it was a joke . . . 'Stop mucking about,' she said.

'I'm not mucking about. I thought you'd be pleased, Chicken. It means you can come off the pill, like you said you wanted to.'

'Tell me you've just made an appointment but it hasn't actually happened yet.'

'No. I had it done while you were at your mum's three weeks ago. Still a bit sore, to be honest. And it takes a couple of weeks for the last of the sperm to get flushed through the system. I've got to go back for a test tomorrow to make sure my semen is free of the little wrigglers but after that . . .' Neil grinned and moved his pelvis in a fashion that made Kathy turn her head away.

'You had a vasectomy without telling me?'

'Yes. Because I knew what you'd say. You'd tell me I didn't have to. You'd tell me it was too drastic and you'd never expect me to go that far for your sake. But you don't want to keep taking the pill and I certainly don't want to have to use condoms.'

It had never crossed Neil's mind that Kathy might want him not to have a vasectomy for reasons other than her hormones and his contraceptive comfort.

'You had it for *my* sake?'

'Yes.' Neil looked pleased with himself. 'And mine, of course. If you're coming off the pill, then the last thing we want to risk is you getting pregnant. We're just coming out of the woods with Sophie and the twins. I can't face going through all that again. My babysitting days are over.'

'But we've never talked about having kids,' said Kathy. 'You never asked me what I wanted.'

'Didn't seem much point. Been there, done that. I don't know why you're looking so slab-faced about it. I'm the one making the sacrifice.'

That night, Kathy cried herself to sleep. She kept it together all day, but as soon as Neil was snoring Kathy let loose.

What had she been hoping for? She should have guessed that, because Neil had never raised the subject of children, he had no intention of having any more. Had he assumed her silence meant she was in agreement? He could hardly be blamed for coming to the wrong conclusion since she hadn't given him anything more than hints in the time they'd been together that she wouldn't be against the idea of a baby.

Yet to take such a drastic final decision without even mentioning it? He was being disingenuous, wasn't he, when he said he'd done it for her sake? He knew she'd be against the idea. He knew she would have begged him not to. But maybe he was that stupid. Maybe he thought that when she'd talked about coming off the pill, she still wanted to be protected. Neil didn't seem to understand what his unilateral decision represented. He seemed even more proud of himself when he came home from the doctor and announced that he was officially technically infertile. His seminal fluid contained 'no more swimmers'.

'So in ten years' time, I'll be free of school fees and university fees and free to spend some of my money on myself at last.' He didn't even seem to include her in that ten-year plan.

Every day since then the situation had been like a stone in the bottom of a shoe. There was barely a single hour when Kathy didn't give it some thought. She tried to be rational about it. Neil's vasectomy might not have made a difference anyway. As the magazine and newspaper features she read were always pointing out, after thirty-five a woman's fertility falls off a cliff. Kathy was knocking on forty. She might never have got pregnant even if Neil wanted her to.

And perhaps if Kathy had really wanted to be a mother she'd have come off the pill without telling him. Was it only the slamming of that door that had made her sensitive to what she was saying goodbye to? Was that the truth?

No, it wasn't. Kathy had always wanted to be a mother. It was just that she'd been disappointed in love so many times that she hadn't allowed herself to become too attached to the idea. Hadn't allowed herself to say it out loud.

Since the moment Neil revealed what he'd done, Kathy had wrestled with what she should do, talking herself in and out of the relationship a dozen times a day. She would lie awake in the middle of the night, feeling scared and alone, even though Neil was sleeping alongside her. She would convince herself that she had to leave. Then she would convince herself that if she did leave, there was nothing for her outside her relationship. It had taken her a long time to find someone as solid and reliable as Neil. Was it really the right idea to walk away from everything they still had – even if she would never be a mother – only to find herself single for ever? She still wouldn't be a mother but she wouldn't have a partner either. Surely it was better to resign herself to having half the life she wanted. At least she wouldn't be alone.

Neil was oblivious to the arguments that raged in Kathy's head. With Shelley and Dave's wedding approaching, like a runaway train, she couldn't find the right moment to bring it up with him. Perhaps it was because she knew what he would say. He would tell her she could either like it or lump it, wouldn't he? And then she really would have to make a decision.

Easier to pretend that she would do that when they got back to London or at least come to a place in her mind where she was content with what a future with Neil had to offer her. But then he asked her to marry him. Was it because he felt safe at last in the knowledge that Kathy would only ever have him to worry about and care for? Now she really had to fish or cut bait, as her father might have said. Was she going to take the consolation prize?

In the Uffizi Gallery, finally standing in front of the *Doni Tondo* – the beautiful picture of the perfect family – Kathy at last allowed herself to feel the truth of her situation with every cell in her body. She was engaged to a man who saw their future life unfolding exactly as *he* wanted it. There was no 'we' in her relationship with Neil. There never really had been. Sure, at first he'd made her feel that what she wanted was important, too, but the truth was, he was the captain of his life and she was to be his helpmeet. Her wants, needs and dreams were always secondary to his, if he even thought about them at all. He certainly hadn't thought of her when he'd had that bloody vasectomy.

She was on the verge of giving up everything for Neil. He'd only asked her to marry him because he didn't want to grow old alone and he'd decided that – now he would never have to worry about more children – Kathy was his best bet. And over the five years they'd been together, he'd chipped away at her so steadily that she'd come to believe that he was hers.

His life was going to be easier. Hers was not.

What on earth was she doing? How had she come to accept that this boorish man was her destiny?

Her life with Neil was no duet. She was second violin to his sodding trumpet solo.

Kathy tried to press the ache of an impending crying jag away but it was no good. She burst into ugly tears.

'Are you OK?' one of the museum attendants asked her gently. 'Would you like to sit down for a moment or two?'

The kindness pushed fresh tears to Kathy's eyes, but she shook off the offer of a place to rest. 'I'm fine,' she said. 'It's just the paintings. They're all so beautiful and so moving.'

'They get to some people more than others,' the attendant agreed. 'They call it Stendhal Syndrome.'

Kathy called it realising you've travelled an awfully long way down the wrong path and not having a clue what, if anything, you can really do about it now.

Chapter Fifty-four

After that Kathy left the Uffizi straight away. She didn't stop to see the Botticelli *Birth of Venus* or the Caravaggios. She just knew she had to get outside again before she made a complete fool of herself. The piazza della Signoria was crowded and noisy. The happiness of the people visiting Florence on a proper holiday seemed to mock her. She took the straightest route back to the hotel and went directly upstairs, without looking left or right, desperate to make sure she didn't catch anybody's eye.

In the room, she examined her face in the bathroom mirror. The lighting was unflattering at the best of times but now she looked frighteningly awful. She splashed cold water onto her face to wash away the tear tracks. She just wanted to get back to London now.

When she walked back into the bedroom, she saw that the light on the telephone was flashing to announce a message. She expected it to be from her mother, checking she was feeling better after their earlier emotional phone call. But the message wasn't from her mum: it was from Carla.

'Hey! Kathy, I hope this is you and I hope you haven't set off for the airport already. The craziest thing ever has happened. We think we've found your engagement ring. If you're still in Florence, come over to the house as soon as you can.'

Of course she called Carla back at once.

'You'll laugh when you hear what happened. It's the most ridiculous coincidence you've ever heard. We're sure it's yours. It's Tiffany. A square-cut diamond with two smaller square diamonds on the shoulders. A platinum band. A large size.'

'It sounds right. Where did you find it?'

'You'll never guess.'

'Don't keep me in suspense.'

'Virgilio from the junk shop brought it to the house this morning. He used it to propose to my mother!'

'What?'

'She said no, of course.'

'But how did Virgilio have it?'

As she asked, Kathy remembered Sunday morning in church and Roberta explaining in a whisper that Virgilio was a well-known fence – someone who received and passed on stolen goods. 'When Mamma asked him, he tried to say he'd bought it in Rome a few weeks ago, but when she pressed him, he admitted he'd bought it off a local junkie last night. I don't suppose he paid anything near what it's worth. After Mamma refused his proposal, he tried to take the ring away with him again, of course, saying, "Finders keepers," but Mamma pointed out that the very last thing Virgilio wants is for the police to get a warrant to examine the contents of his safe. So he left the ring with us. I gave him the money Neil paid us in that envelope to make up for his out-of-pocket expenses. Given how little he seemed happy to take, I almost feel sorry for the junkie who sold the ring to him. He obviously got a terrible deal. Not that I should feel sorry for someone who robbed my dear friend, of course!'

'Thank you,' said Kathy. Those words, 'my dear friend', were among the kindest she'd heard since she'd left the Casa Innocenti the previous day. 'If it is my ring, it will get me out of a lot of trouble.'

'Neil was upset, huh?'

'That's an understatement.'

Carla exhaled loudly. 'Well, now he'll be happy again, won't he? And so will you?'

Kathy mumbled her agreement.

'Come by later? We'll have tea, English-style. Half past four?'

Neil returned at three o'clock. He'd undone his tie. He looked hot and bothered. He definitely didn't have the average Italian businessman's knack of looking pristine, no matter how stifling the weather.

'How was your day?' Kathy asked him out of habit.

'Hot. I don't know how anyone gets anything done in this heat. But it was a good meeting. The client was very pleased with the information I gave him about the Casa Innocenti too. He thinks it could be worth a look.'

'I've got some good news,' Kathy said, cutting him short.

'Oh? You don't look like you've had good news.' He referenced her puffy face. 'Did you get an allergic reaction from something you ate?'

'Perhaps.' Kathy was going to fake it for a little longer. She didn't know what else to do. 'The engagement ring has turned up,' she said.

'What? Where? Did the Italian police actually do something?'

'It turned up at the Casa Innocenti. I said we'd swing by and fetch it on our way to the airport.'

'How did it get there?'

Kathy told Neil the story. His face was sceptical throughout. 'Why didn't they just bring it to the hotel?'

'Because they're all working,' said Kathy. 'They have a full hotel. Besides, it's on our way, isn't it?'

'Not really,' said Neil. 'We'll have to get the car early.'

Kathy couldn't wait to leave.

'If you ask me, it all seems slightly dodgy. The woman who chased the thief who took your bag ends up finding the ring?'

'I don't think it's dodgy,' said Kathy. 'The man who brought it to Roberta is a well-known fence. I expect half the stolen goods in Florence end up under his nose.'

'Well, he needs to go to prison.'

'Let's look on it as Fate,' said Kathy. 'And be happy that we're getting the ring back.'

'If it is the same ring.'

Kathy was praying hard that it was.

When they got to the Casa Innocenti, Neil declined to come in. Instead, he insisted on staying in the car, with the air-conditioning running at full blast, while he checked the emails that had been coming in since his earlier meetings. He said they were urgent. Kathy suspected that Faustino was another part of the equation. Indeed, Neil added quietly, 'And the last thing I need is to get bitten and have to have a tetanus jab as soon as I get home. I'm assuming you'll know whether the ring is yours or not. I mean, you did have it for the best part of twenty-four hours before you managed to lose it. Be quick. You don't want to miss tonight's flight too.'

Chapter Fifty-five

Faustino greeted her at the door. In contrast to the way he had welcomed her when they'd first met, this time he reacted as though she was a long-lost love he hadn't dared to imagine might ever come home. He danced around her, squeaking the happy squeaks she'd thought he reserved for Henry. Kathy picked him up and he licked her face. She ignored the fact that his breath smelt of anchovies and concentrated on the wild expression of love he was offering her and the sensation of his soft foxy fur as it tickled her face.

Manu was next down the stairs.

'She's here!' he called up to his mother and grandmother. 'Kathy's back!'

Roberta appeared. 'Isn't this wonderful?' she said, clasping Kathy's hands when she got to the top of the stairs. 'We've found your ring. And it's better than that,' she added. 'It turned out that Virgilio bought your rather lovely handbag as well.'

It was definitely Kathy's handbag. The Radley number that she'd stalked in the winter sales. Her purse was gone, alas, as was her phone. The thief had even removed the fluffy gonk key-ring Kathy had attached to the zipper on the inside pocket. That hurt. But at least she had the bag back. And the ring.

'It is your ring?' Carla asked.

'I think so,' said Kathy. 'I hardly had a chance to get

to know it but it certainly looks like the one Neil proposed with.'

'Put it on,' said Roberta.

Kathy slipped it onto the ring finger of her left hand. 'It's going to have to be adjusted,' she said, moving it onto the fatter second finger, which it fitted perfectly.

'Will you have a cup of tea?'

'I can't. I ought to go. We're late for the airport.' Kathy took Carla's hands. 'Thank you again for everything. Thank you. I don't know what I would have done, Carla, if you hadn't found me and brought me here. Thank you, Roberta, for taking me in.'

'Come back soon,' said Roberta. 'There is always space for you here with us. Henry will be sorry he missed you.'

Would he?

Kathy's eyes prickled. 'Where is he?' she couldn't resist asking.

'He had to go to Rome last night,' said Carla. 'A big meeting. Someone is interested in his music.'

'It could be the lucky break he needs,' said Roberta, crossing fingers on both hands.

'I have to go,' Kathy said, hearing the sound of a car horn outside. 'Thank you, Manu, for teaching me some very useful Italian.'

Manu let Kathy kiss him on the forehead, then hid behind his mother's legs so Kathy wouldn't see how sad he was. Even Faustino seemed sorry to see her go.

'Thank you, all of you.'

Knowing that she would cry if she stayed a moment longer, Kathy made haste for the door. 'Tell Henry . . . tell Henry I said goodbye.'

* * *

Outside, Neil made a point of looking at his watch as Kathy climbed into the car. She was trying her very hardest not to cry but couldn't hold back a sniff. She surreptitiously wiped at her eyes. Neil took her hand. Kathy turned to smile at him, grateful that he seemed to understand. But then he raised her hand to his face and lifted his sunglasses from his nose so that he could see better.

'Yes. That looks like the ring I bought,' he said. 'Of course we'll only know for sure when we have it checked over back in London and matched to the details Tiffany have for it.'

Satisfied, he let Kathy's hand go again, so that it fell to the empty strip of seat between them. He hadn't even noticed that she was wearing the ring on the wrong finger.

Chapter Fifty-six

The traffic was bad. It took longer to get to the airport than they'd expected. By the time they were on the road around it, where cars jostled for lane position, like ancient Roman chariots in a race to the death, Kathy could tell that Neil was ready to kick off.

A few minutes later, she followed him into the terminal, anxious to get ahead or at least alongside him and smooth the way. But Neil knew where he was going this time and he was on a mission. They joined the queue at the check-in desks. It was long.

'We could have avoided this is if we hadn't stopped to pick up your ring.'

Though they would have left slightly later, had that been the case, Neil preferred his narrative. Neil always preferred his narrative.

Kathy could feel the engagement ring on her finger. Because it was too big and kept slipping so that the stones got stuck in the tender dip between her fingers, she couldn't get used to the sensation of wearing it so that she hardly felt it at all. It reminded her at every moment that she was wearing an engagement ring. A ring she hadn't expected. A ring she was beginning to realise she would not have asked for. Not now.

The check-in queue lurched forward. Neil sighed impatiently and she could tell he was winding himself up for a complaint.

This is going to be your life. You're signing up to spend your life in this man's wake, forever smoothing the feathers he ruffles. Forever trying to make him happy. He will always be centre stage. His needs will always come first.

'Make your life together a real duet,' her father had written.

Kathy would only ever be Neil's chorus.

They got to the front of the queue. Sabina was on duty again. She gave Kathy a subtle nod of recognition as Neil handed over the passports. Tap, tap, tap: she typed their names in. The tip of her tongue poked out of the side of her mouth as she studied the screen. Kathy sensed that something was awry.

'I can't find Miss Courage on the passenger list,' said Sabina at last.

'That's ridiculous,' said Neil. 'Look again.'

Sabina typed in Kathy's name one more time.

'I'm sorry. She's not on the passenger list for this flight. Do you have the booking confirmation with you?'

'Of course.'

Neil pushed the printout under her nose.

Sabina nodded. 'Yes. Ah. I see. You are on this flight but she is not. The date for your flight is today. The date for *la signora*'s flight is a whole month away. Someone put in the wrong month when they were doing the booking.'

'That can't be right.'

Sabina helpfully put her finger beneath the date so that Kathy and Neil could see it easily.

It was right. Good old Melanie, the world's best PA.

'For Heaven's sake!'

Kathy closed her eyes and waited for the explosion.

By the time Neil had been persuaded that nothing could be done again, there was no chance of getting Kathy onto the same flight. They compromised by accepting a seat on a flight that would leave in two days' time. Once again, Kathy and Neil stood together by the security gates, knowing that only one of them would be going through that day.

Neil was surprisingly calm this time. 'Well, this is sub-optimal,' he said. 'Have you got any euros?'

'About five hundred,' said Kathy.

'Where did you get that from?'

'A tip for my singing on Sunday night.'

'OK,' Neil said. 'So you can get a hotel. If you need more, ring me and I'll give my card details. I'll see you on Thursday.'

Kathy nodded.

'I don't know why nobody can seem to get anything right,' Neil complained.

Kathy hesitated. It would have been so easy to kiss Neil on the cheek and let him go to catch his flight without saying anything, but that would not be the brave thing to do.

'Neil,' Kathy piped up, 'what if today's flight mix-up wasn't a mistake? What if it was a sign?'

'What are you talking about?'

'Before we went to the wedding, I'd been wondering whether we were really right for one another.'

Neil squinted at her.

'I know you're probably surprised to hear it,' she continued, 'but I'd been thinking about our life together and whether it was what I wanted. I love you and I always will, but over the years there have been days when I wondered if you really loved me back. The real me. The me who is sometimes clumsy. The me who is sometimes lazy. The me who doesn't always know what to say at a fancy event. The me who had dreams of her own before she met you.'

'What dreams?' Neil asked, as though the very notion was preposterous.

'A dream of a family of my own,' Kathy told him.

'Is this about the vasectomy? For Heaven's sake.'

'Of course it's about the vasectomy. And what it represents.'

'I did it for you.'

'You did it for *you*,' Kathy countered. 'You definitely didn't do it for me.'

'I don't know what you're talking about. I had an operation to make you happy.'

'You had an operation to make sure I could never have a child of my own.'

Neil shook his head. He wasn't going to be told he was wrong. He would never be told he was wrong.

A call went out over the tannoy. Final boarding for the London flight.

Kathy slid the engagement ring from her finger. 'You should take this back with you.'

'What now? What's this about? Are you telling me you don't want to get married?'

'Yes, I am. And, honestly, I don't think you really want to get married either.'

'But I wouldn't have asked you if I didn't! Women! We can never get it right where you're concerned.'

The tannoy announced Neil's flight again.

'Neil, you need to go through security,' Kathy said. 'We can talk about this when I get back to London, but when you think about it properly, you'll see that I'm right. We can't get married. Not now. Your children will be relieved at least.'

'They certainly will,' said Neil, dropping the ring into the breast pocket of his jacket, and the way he said it told Kathy that he would soon adjust his thinking to accommodate this new state of affairs and make it a good thing.

'Exactly. So now there's no need for them to be upset.'

'There is that. Mum will be pleased as well.'

'Quite.'

Neil seemed about to say something else and, for just a moment, Kathy thought he might try to change her mind. Perhaps he might find the words that could make everything all right. Looking into the blue eyes she had fallen in love with five years earlier, Kathy half wanted that to happen. But the moment passed. He gave her a curt nod and left.

This time when Neil went through security, Kathy was glad he didn't look back. She was certain that when he really thought about it, he would see that she'd made the right decision. In all probability, by the time he got back to London, Neil would have decided that the end of the engagement had been his idea. As she articulated her feelings in words, it was all becoming clearer to Kathy, too, that she'd been pondering the future of her relationship with Neil for a long time. Since long before the vasectomy.

She loved Neil and she thought that, in his own way, he loved her, but if he was willing to close the door on one of her fondest dreams without consulting her first, how could they be right for one another? She was sure now that after the vasectomy Neil had felt the change in her feeling and, sensing her slipping away, he'd tried to lock her in with the engagement. It was always more about being seen to do the right thing than about being in love with her.

The more she thought about it, the more confident Kathy felt that she'd done the only thing she could. Taking a deep breath, she turned towards the escalator and headed out of the terminal towards . . . towards a new life?

'Stay brave, Kathy Courage,' she heard her father's voice.

Chapter Fifty-seven

Kathy couldn't go straight back to the Casa Innocenti, much as she wanted to. That would be unfair. Roberta, Carla, Manu and Henry had been so kind to her already and this was an adventure she needed to begin alone. She decided she would find an inexpensive hotel for the next two nights and spend the time she had left in Florence writing down all the things she would need to do to make sure that officially splitting up with Neil was as painless as possible.

This forty-eight-hour period was crucial. She had to start to visualise a happy life on her own so that she didn't change her mind as soon as she got back to the UK and saw Neil in his house – the house that had never really been her home. At least her leaving wouldn't make a big mark. She'd never even hung one of her own pictures on Neil's walls.

She found a small family-run hotel near Santa Croce, a part of the city she had yet to get to know but which Carla had spoken about with enthusiasm. They had a single room left.

'Can I pay in cash?' she asked the hotelier. He seemed happy enough with that.

As she counted out the notes from the small wedge Henry had given her on the night they'd sung together at the sixtieth birthday party, she felt proud. Henry was right. Everyone should have their own running-away fund. Had she known that she would need hers so quickly . . .

The hotelier handed Kathy the key to her room on the top floor.

A room with a view.

In the room, she made a cup of tea and called her mother, fudging the reason why she was still in Italy, saying it was just another flight mix-up. A proper explanation would have to come later, face to face.

'It's like Florence has decided to keep you!' Clare said. 'You know, the funny thing is, I always thought you might end up in Italy one day. I was surprised when you never left England.'

'Oh, Mum.' Kathy sighed. One day she would tell her why that was so frustrating to hear.

The hotel had a small garden. When she'd finished her phone call, Kathy went downstairs to ask if she could have an early supper outside in the shade of a tree. The hotelier grimaced. 'We have a party here this evening,' he said. 'We need to set the garden up. But perhaps if you are quick . . .'

'I'll be quick,' said Kathy.

The staff were already laying out tables for the evening's event, spreading them with pristine white linen. One of them broke off to ask Kathy how he could help her. She ordered a plate of antipasti and an Aperol Spritz. Sod it if it was unfashionable. Right then it was exactly what she wanted.

When the bright orange cocktail was placed in front of her, Kathy raised a toast to herself. 'Kathy Courage.

Kathy Brave. From this moment on, I follow my own rules.'

The Aperol Spritz was delicious.

Scribbling on a hotel notepad, Kathy made a list of things she would need to do when she got back to London. It started practically. She'd need to chase her replacement credit cards. Start looking for a new flat. And a new job . . .

But, gradually, the list became more interesting. She'd look into joining a choir. Or a band. Definitely get some singing lessons. When she had her own place, she'd get a keyboard. Or a real piano, depending on how much space she had. As for a new job, she was going to make sure that this time it was a job that fulfilled her. Maybe she should go back to university instead.

Kathy's dreams filled the whole notepad, like a list of old friends' names. As she sipped her Spritz, the future unfolded on paper in the most wonderful way.

Then . . .

'*Cazzo!*' From behind the jasmine-covered trellis, came a burst of angry Italian, in a voice that wasn't entirely Italian but which Kathy recognised at once. '*Cazzo. Cazzo. Cazzo.* Arse.'

Kathy leaned back in her chair so that she could see around the trellis to the kitchen door. And there he was, swearing at the screen of his phone.

'Henry?'

'Kathy?'

They both asked at the same time, 'What are you doing here?'

Stepping round the trellis to get a better look at her,

Henry said, 'Sheba, tell me you're not drinking a bloody Aperol Spritz?'

It turned out that Henry was to be the hotel's musical entertainment for the evening except that, just as happened on Sunday, he was a singer down.

'She's got flu,' he said, miming the speech marks with his fingers. 'By which she means she has a wealthy new boyfriend, and an evening with him seems like a far better investment than doing a gig she agreed to three months ago. I came back from Rome for this.'

'How was Rome?' Kathy asked.

'Bloody amazing.' Henry grinned. 'I've been asked to write the score for a movie.'

'Congratulations.'

'Means I can give up the weddings and birthday parties.'

'Which will be a great loss to the Tuscan party scene.'

Henry sat down at Kathy's table and helped himself to a breadstick.

'But what about you?' he asked. 'Aren't you meant to be back in London?'

'Got my flight details mixed up.'

'Again? Where's . . .'

Henry cast a not-that-surreptitious glance at her hand. His mother and sister must have told him that Kathy had stopped at the house to pick up her engagement ring. Of course Kathy noticed what Henry was looking for.

'The ring made it onto the flight,' she told him. 'With Neil. It might even be back at Tiffany's by now.'

'I see.'

Henry pinched another breadstick. He didn't ask for

a more detailed explanation. Kathy would tell him all about it later.

'So, what are you going to do about this evening's gig?' Kathy asked, playing it cool.

'Dunno. I'll have to find another singer, I suppose. I don't suppose you know anyone who would do a gig at short notice for peanuts and free Prosecco by any chance?'

'Cash in hand?'

'Of course.'

'Split the tips?'

'Definitely.'

'Then I might. I can certainly think of someone who needs to replenish her running-away fund.'

Henry picked up Kathy's drink, took a swig, grimaced, then tipped the half-empty glass towards her as if in a toast.

'Good,' he said. 'Practice starts in half an hour. We'll start with your favourite song.'

'You mean "Yellow"?' Kathy joked.

'I mean *your* favourite song.'

'Can we make it a duet?'

'Of course.'

'Then I'll get changed.'

Henry punched the air with delight.

'I'm so glad you're back, Queen of Sheba. Kathy Brave.'

An hour later, Kathy and Henry were on stage together again. In the warm embrace of an Italian evening, Kathy couldn't remember when she'd last felt so happy or so free. Being on the stage just felt so right.

Kathy and Henry performed together as though

they'd been playing as a duo for years. The audience was enchanted by their easy chemistry. They ended their set, as they had ended it on Sunday night, with 'The Way You Look Tonight'. While the audience applauded, Kathy insisted that Henry got to his feet to take a bow. Leaving his keyboard, he joined her in the centre of the stage. He took her hand and raised it above her head.

Then, with a deeply serious look on his face, Henry wrapped his arms around Kathy and tipped her backwards in a ballroom hold. When he let her come back up again, he kissed her. And this time, it wasn't a nearly kiss.

Acknowledgements

Well, here I am again at the end of another novel. As usual, I wouldn't have got here without the support of a cast of thousands, including. . .

Editorial team Kimberley Atkins and Madeleine Woodfield at Hodder, who worked so hard to turn this book around in a matter of days. Thank you very much. Thank you Louise Swannell for your wonderful PR work. Thank you, copy-editor Hazel Orme for catching all my typos. And thank you Jo Myler, for another lovely new cover look. Thank you also to Laetitia Rutherford and Megan Carroll at Watson Little.

Once again, in what's been another occasionally challenging year, I'm hugely grateful for the love of my friends. Victoria Routledge, Jane Wright and Alex Potter. You're the best friends anyone could wish for.

As always, I'd like to thank my family. Mum, Kate, Lee, Harrison and Lukas for their support and all the good times. And finally darling Mark. Still on tea duty. Thank you for everything.

May 2019

Once in a Lifetime

Do you really only have one shot at love?

Twenty two years ago Dani Parker had grand
plans for her life.

Now, she's a single mother in quaint Newbay working
at the hotel where she got her first ever job. When
she bumps into ex-boyfriend Nat, she wonders if this
might be the start of something not-quite-new. Until
his fiancée walks through the door . . .

Dani's daughter Flossie is sixteen – so of course she
knows best, about everything. And her new boyfriend Jed
is all she could ever want in a man . . . right?

Flossie's widowed grandma Jane firmly believes that
lightning never strikes twice. So when she finds herself
frequenting Bill's pet shop, she refuses to believe that
the L-word has anything to do with it.

In a confusion of cakes, elopements and naughty
puppies, will the three women discover that 'once in a
lifetime' isn't quite as rare as they thought?

Available to buy now!

Bookends

When one book ends, another begins...

Bookends is a vibrant new reading community to help you ensure you're never without a good book.

You'll find exclusive previews of the brilliant new books from your favourite authors as well as exciting debuts and past classics. Read our blog, check out our recommendations for your reading group, enter great competitions and much more!

Visit our website to see which great books we're recommending this month.

Join the Bookends community:
www.welcometobookends.co.uk

 @Team Bookends   @WelcomeToBookends